ELEANOR'S WARS

a novel

Ames Sheldon

BEAVER'S POND
PRESS

ISBN 13: 978-1-59298-861-7

Library of Congress Catalog Number: 2015952348

Printed in the United States of America

First Printing: 2015

19 18 17 16 15   5 4 3 2 1

Cover and interior design by Laura Drew.
Cover photo courtesy of the Library of Congress.

Beaver's Pond Press
7108 Ohms Lane
Edina, MN 55439–2129
952-829-8818
www.beaverspondpress.com

To Benjamin Hazard Stevens—
he inspired this tale and wrote most of the
lyrics attributed to Nat Sutton.

At dawn the ridge emerges massed and dun
In the wild purple of the glow'ring sun,
Smouldering through spouts of drifting smoke that shroud
The menacing scarred slope; and, one by one,
Tanks creep and topple forward to the wire.
The barrage roars and lifts. Then, clumsily bowed
With bombs and guns and shovels and battle-gear,
Men jostle and climb to meet the bristling fire.
Lines of grey, muttering faces, masked with fear,
They leave their trenches, going over the top,
While time ticks blank and busy on their wrists,
And hope, with furtive eyes and grappling fists,
Flounders in mud. O Jesus, make it stop!

—"Attack" by Siegfried "Mad Jack" Sassoon, 1918

Prologue

As soon as Eleanor sees the man standing in the corner of the tent, she realizes she's in trouble. He's busy inspecting the bodies on the ground, but she's so unnerved by his presence that she nearly drops the heavy litter she's helping to carry into the waiting area of the field hospital near Ypres. Silently she admonishes herself to pay attention to the work at hand. She mustn't lose her grip.

"Who is that?" she whispers to the ancient orderly on the other end of the brown stretcher, inclining her head toward the white coat.

"That's the new surgeon, Médicin Henri Boudsocq."

"He seems young," she replies. "He's closer to my age than the other surgeons."

The blanket Eleanor wrapped around the soldier when she first lifted him onto the litter is becoming soaked with blood from the wound to his abdomen. Blood drips onto the filthy floor. Eleanor and the orderly try to keep the stretcher level, but when they lower it, the slight tilt causes the soldier's shattered arm to flop out from under the blanket that was holding it in place. He screams.

Incoming shells from the big guns continue to pound outside, shaking the ground and rippling the canvas walls of the infirmary.

Once they set down their load, Eleanor kneels. "I'm going to move your arm so it gets some support, soldier. I'll be careful."

As she lifts his right wrist, the humerus protrudes farther through the hole in the skin of his upper arm. Carefully she places his mutilated limb back on the stretcher and tucks the blanket in around it.

Rising, she looks toward the surgeon. Their eyes lock. He isn't handsome at all—his nose is too big, his skin is too pale, and his lips are thick—but he exudes so much life-force that Eleanor can't stop staring at him. He smiles slightly. She joins him at the side of the room.

"Mademoiselle."

"Monsieur Boudsocq. My soldier got a lot of shrapnel in his gut, and his right arm has a compound fracture."

"I will look at him next. What is your name?"

"Eleanor Butler. I'm an ambulance driver."

"American?"

She nods.

"What brought you over here?"

"This horrible, horrible war. I came to help where I can."

"*Bien.* We are most grateful, Mademoiselle Butler."

His smile warms her all the way through. For the first time in weeks, Eleanor's stomach, which has been clenched as tightly as a fist, relaxes.

Fall 1942

There'll be bluebirds over
The white cliffs of Dover
Tomorrow
Just you wait and see

—Lyrics from "The White Cliffs of Dover"
by Nat Burton, 1941

One

September

ELEANOR SUTTON RAKES her fingers through her short, curly red hair as she scans the piles of clothing she laid on Nat's bed. She has assembled all the shirts and trousers, jackets and ties, shoes and belts, underwear and handkerchiefs he will need for his first year at Andover. Packing should be a breeze—she's had plenty of practice with her older children. Harriet, better known as Harry, went off to Bennington three years ago, and then Eddie headed to Andover two Septembers ago. Now Nat has to leave too.

She's furious at George for making Nat go. She told him Nat should stay home for at least one more year. He needs more time to mature and gain self-confidence; the boys at Andover will make mincemeat of a child as sensitive as Nat. But George insisted, said Eleanor would "spoil" Nat if he stayed home any longer, whereas Andover would make a man of him.

Ridiculous. Nat isn't ready. And anyway, what does George know about it? He sits in an office all day telling everyone what to do, and then he comes home and tells us what to do. Who put him in charge of everything? She understands her baby better than he does.

And yet Nat is the brightest of her children. He taught himself to read at four and was playing Bach inventions at seven. But he is undisciplined about his studies . . . he is undisciplined about everything except practicing the piano.

Eleanor admits to herself that she isn't ready for him to go. What will she do with herself once her last child is out the door? For more than twenty years, she has completely devoted her life to motherhood. Standing amid Nat's stuff, Eleanor feels dizzy, as though she's looking over the edge of a precipice. She does not want to take the next step.

Her old battered trunk with steel corners and leather straps waits at the side of Nat's bed. She'd brought it down from the far reaches of the attic this morning and suspects it will be musty inside because she hasn't opened it since 1918.

"Mother? Do you want me to . . ." Nat asks, nodding to the trunk. He sits cross-legged on the floor, playing silent octaves on his knees as he watches her. Freckles stand out on his pale narrow face, and new pimples have erupted on his pointed chin.

Eleanor takes a deep breath and exhales audibly before she replies. "No, Nattie. I'll do it myself. It's high time I open up this old thing and air it out."

She squats, her gingham housedress flaring out around her on the floor. She unsnaps the latches, then lifts the lid of the trunk. The stink of moldy leather assails her, and Eleanor is instantly back on the battlefield west of Ypres, moving wounded soldiers into her ambulance. Again she sees that gory arm reaching out of the mud toward her, calling her to rescue the wounded soldier beneath it before he is smothered by muck. She hurries over, but as she gently pulls on the arm, it pops out on its own, severed from its owner, who is nowhere in sight, though she searches the vicinity frantically.

Her hands start to shake. As she leans over the trunk and looks inside, she groans.

"Mummy?"

"It's all right, sweetie."

Eleanor sits back on her heels. She tears open a package wrapped in plain brown paper, revealing her old boots, which have collapsed in on themselves. They are stiff with mud, stained with blood. Henri's blood. She hadn't wanted to lose that last vital trace of him, so she hadn't cleaned it off, though it is much fainter now than it had been when it splashed onto her feet.

Nat must not see any of this. "Please get me a cardboard box I can put this old junk in. There should be empty boxes at the top of the attic stairs."

"Yes, Mother."

While Nat trots down the hall, Eleanor goes to the linen closet for a sheet. Then she removes her muddy boots from the trunk and pulls out her old uniform, the fabric faded to the color of ashes. As she holds up the single-breasted, dark-gray whipcord uniform, she remembers the excitement she felt when she first donned it. It was 1916, and she was so happy because she had a mission: she would be of service to others. Whatever happened to all that unselfish idealism?

She notices a ribbon peeking out of the left breast pocket. Sticking her hand in, she finds a tiny silk bag gathered at the top with a narrow pink ribbon. Inside is a plain gold band she recognizes instantly. She thought she had lost this ring. She places it in her right fist and presses it hard against her heart.

A moment later, she hears Nat humming in the hall. Quickly, she slides the ring back into the bag, drops the bag into the pocket of the tunic, and covers everything with the sheet.

"Here we go," Nat says, setting a tan box down at the end of his bed.

"Thank you, Nat." Eleanor picks up the sheet and the clothing in her arms and dumps everything into the box.

"What's in the trunk?"

"Just some old things from the time I lived in France."

Nat, leaning over the trunk, pulls out a dented aluminum canteen and places it on the floor. "What were you doing in France, Mother?"

"I went there after my first year of college." So many years of hiding the truth about her past! "I wanted to become fluent in French."

Eleanor's eyes are drawn back to the trunk, where she spots a small red cross in the corner. Reaching for the enameled pin, she places it on her palm and extends it to her son. Over the years, she has been careful not to speak of adult matters to any of her children, but now with this war on, her own experiences from the battlefield are starting to prey on her mind. Nat is the child she feels closest to, even though he is her youngest. Nat is the one who depends on her, rather than George, for approval, whereas her other children work to win their father's favor.

"This is from my service as an ambulance driver during the Great War."

"What!" Nat is shocked; clearly this information doesn't match his image of his mother. "You were in the Great War?"

"It was a lifetime ago."

"Why didn't I know about this?"

"Your father doesn't want me to talk about that time."

Immediately Eleanor regrets her confession. Losing control of her mouth like this means she'll have to keep a closer watch on herself from now on. "Please don't mention it to anyone." She closes her hand over the pin and slides it into the pocket of her dress. "Come now, Nathaniel. We have packing to do."

"Can I have your canteen?"

"You *may*." After upending and shaking the trunk to remove the loose dirt, Eleanor sets it back on the floor. As she begins to place piles of Nat's clothing in neat stacks inside, she asks, "How does it feel to be going into ninth grade?"

"Andover doesn't call it ninth grade, Mother." Nat plunks down on the bed. "I'll be a junior, and Eddie's an upper middler." Nat tilts his head to the side. "Thanks for trying to make Father change his mind about sending me away."

"I did what I could."

Over the last five months, Eleanor argued bitterly with George about sending Nat to Phillips Academy Andover, but George wouldn't budge. Nothing she said changed his mind. She's come to understand that George feels it would completely emasculate Nat if he stayed home with her any longer; her husband believes Nat needs the rough-and-tumble so he will learn to get along with other boys and make some friends. Because Nat has to go, she knows she should make the transition as easy for him as she can.

"Actually, Nat, I think you'll find Andover fascinating. You must admit, you were bored at Warden. Andover will be much more challenging intellectually, and that'll be good for you."

"Will Father pay more attention to me once I'm at Andover?"

Eleanor flinches. She can't answer that question. George isn't terribly comfortable with children; it might be years before he'll engage Nat in more than a simple conversation. She has struggled with George over this: her husband simply doesn't know how to talk with a child.

"Now, I want you to promise me you'll change your socks every day—more often when they get wet. If you wear wet socks, you could get trench foot, and then you'd really be in trouble." She is exaggerating, but she wants to impress Nat with the importance of doing as she says. Besides, the smell of his feet when he hasn't changed his socks for a day or two is enough to gag anyone. "You could lose your toes. I saw men die from trench foot."

Oops. She's slipped again. Eleanor quickly moves two dozen pairs of new socks into the trunk.

"Did you see that in France?"

"Yes." Now she wishes she could stuff the genie back into the bottle. "Remember, this is our little secret."

"Can I bring *Swallows and Amazons* with me to Andover?"

"*May I.* Of course you may bring some of your favorite books."

"I'll have to decide what I can't live without."

Feeling as if he just socked her in the solar plexus, Eleanor sits down on his bed. He'll have to learn to live without her. And how will she live without him?

"Promise me you'll write, Nattie."

"Of course, Mummy. Every day." Sitting down next to her, Nat gingerly places his arm around her shoulder and gives her a quick squeeze. "I'm going to miss you so much, Mother."

"I'll miss you too, Nattie—more than I can say." Eleanor knows she'll start to cry if she doesn't move, so she pulls away. "I'd better check on Harry and Eddie now, though they're old hands at this business of packing." As she leaves the room, she glances back at Nat. He's sitting on his bed with her old canteen, his lips tightly compressed.

The drive up from Plainwood, New Jersey, to Andover, Massachusetts, only takes seven hours, but it seems interminable to Eleanor. She wants this ordeal of separating from her youngest to be over as quickly as possible. At the same time, she dreads the moment when she'll have to say goodbye.

Trying to hold off her feelings of anxiety, she chatters about the number of military trucks they pass, the weather, the scenery, but no one responds. In the backseat of the Packard sedan, Eddie tosses a football from one hand to the other. Nat is engrossed in writing something in a notebook. George seems to be staring at the horizon far ahead.

Finally Nat looks up. "Father, you promised I can keep up my piano studies at Andover, didn't you?"

"I said I'd inquire into the possibility. With the war on, the schedule for nonacademic activities may have changed."

"I'll die if I can't play the piano and take lessons with someone really good!"

"I said I would ask, Nathaniel."

Nat says, "Will I have to take sports?"

"You'd better, or everyone will think you're a sissy," Eddie chimes in.

George replies, "Every boy is required to take physical education at Andover. It'll be good for you."

Eddie socks Nat in the arm. "You've got to build up your strength, Nattie. Then you'll be ready to fight whenever anyone attacks you."

"Fight?" Eleanor exclaims, glancing at George.

"Don't worry, Mother," Eddie says. "Nobody fights the juniors. The juniors just have to keep a low profile and do what they're told."

To change the subject, Eleanor says, "What did you think about President Roosevelt's Fireside Chat the other night?"

Nat says, "I hated hearing that Lieutenant Powers's plane was destroyed by the bomb he dropped himself when he released it so close to the target." He shivers.

George says, "I agree with the president. We are not doing enough to play our part in winning the war. I've been thinking about additional roles I might take on."

"What about increasing taxes on individual incomes?" Eddie says. "Didn't the president say that individual incomes should be limited to twenty-five thousand dollars a year? That isn't much money, is it, Father?"

"Roosevelt is right that the nation needs more money than it has to run this war. If his estimate that the war will cost one hundred billion dollars is accurate, the country will certainly need a greater share of our incomes. I'm just not sure taxation is the best approach."

"What would be better?" Eddie asks.

Nat looks back down at his notebook.

"Selling war bonds. Get citizens to invest in the war with their extra dollars, rather than take those dollars away through taxes. It would be much better for morale."

"That makes sense," Eddie says.

Nat shakes his head. Leaning over toward Eddie, he whispers, "You're such a brownnose."

"And you're a wimp. Just don't embarrass me in front on my friends when we get to Andover."

"I'm shaking in my boots, Eddie."

"Don't you dare call me Eddie at school. I'm Edward there."

"Yes, sir!" Nat salutes, then turns back to his book.

Eleanor sighs. She won't miss the brothers' sparring.

As they drive along Main Street in the town of Andover, Nat closes his notebook and starts looking around. After George pulls to a stop outside Eddie's dormitory, Eleanor, Eddie, and Nat, his knapsack in hand, jump out. George sits at the wheel.

"At last!" says Eddie. His dark hair and six-foot frame look much like his father's. "I thought we'd never get here."

"I hoped we never would," Nat mutters, kicking at the dirt in the road.

"Come on, boys," Eleanor says. "Let's get Eddie's stuff unloaded."

The three of them pull Eddie's steamer trunk and a duffel bag out from the back of the car and set them on the grass.

"I'll drive around to Junior House and leave Nathaniel's things there," says George. "Then I'm going to go find the head of school."

Digging into her purse, Eleanor says, "When you're at the head's office, please turn over these ration books for Eddie and Nat." She hands the books to George, who stuffs them into the pocket of his navy-blue blazer. "That's one of the registration requirements this year," she adds.

"Will do," says George. He drives off.

Eleanor asks Eddie, "Do you need help taking your gear to your room?"

"No thanks, Mother. I can handle it."

One of the students coming down the steps calls, "Sutton! You up for some touch football?"

"You bet, Jones," Eddie replies. "As soon as I dump this stuff in my room."

Jones says, "Hurry up. I want you on my side."

Another one of the guys on the steps says, "Isn't it great to be back, Sutton? Summer's such a bore."

Eddie puts his duffel on top of his trunk and picks both up as he replies, "I agree. It is great to be back here."

Eleanor says, "I want you to come see your brother settled in, and you can say goodbye to your parents before you go play football."

Eddie raises his eyebrows at his buddies, then says, "All right, Mother. I'll come find you."

Eleanor and Nat start across the campus. As they walk over the huge quadrangle of grass along Main Street, Eleanor is struck by the lofty elms and the massive red-brick buildings, all columns and wide verandas. The school is as large and formal as an Ivy League college. When she came here before with Eddie and George, the place hadn't seemed quite so *daunting*. Boys with parents stream across the lawn in various directions, but Nat, thin and awkward, plods along a few paces behind Eleanor, his knapsack skimming the ground. Although Eleanor is wearing a tight skirt and high heels, she's moving much faster than he. His reluctance is palpable.

Nat stops in front of a large spherical copper sculpture in the middle of the quad. "Yow, this is creepy," he pronounces. "What's the point of this? An hourglass on the back of turtles, with a man, woman, and parts of a snake and a lion underneath it?"

"I don't know."

Eleanor thinks the sculpture suggests that time destroys everything, but she doesn't want to articulate that. She wants this painful ordeal to be over as quickly as possible: she can't stand to leave him, but at the same time, she can hardly wait to get away. As she looks more closely at the sculpture, she spots the signature.

"This was done by Paul Manship in 1928. He's highly regarded as a sculptor. Didn't we see some Manship sculptures at the Metropolitan Museum of Art?"

Putting his knapsack down, Nat says, "I don't care about that." He looks up at her woefully.

"I know, Nattie, but we have to get a wiggle on."

Nat picks his bag back up. "Mother," he says, "don't forget that Sadie likes to have her belly scratched at least once a day. And if she's really lonely for me, please let her sleep indoors."

Two older boys brush by so closely that Nat has to step sideways to avoid running into them. How can she leave him here?

"She's a dog, Nat. I don't want her to get into the habit of sleeping indoors. She's got to be toughened up."

"But Mother, she's just a puppy. She still misses her mother."

"She's six months old, Nat. She probably doesn't even remember her mother by now." Eleanor glances at her son. His freckles are stark against his pale face.

Nat takes a deep breath. "This isn't so bad," he says, looking around at the buildings and trees. "I thought there'd be a big fence and guard towers, but the campus is wide open."

Eleanor laughs. "Andover isn't a penitentiary, Nat."

"I didn't know it would be so beautiful."

Nat's moods change so quickly these days it is hard

for her to keep up with him. In seconds, he can go from a clingy child to a young man with opinions of his own.

As they continue across the quad, he turns his head from side to side, scanning the scene with an exquisitely expectant look on his face, as though he hopes to see something wonderful around the next corner. Now she feels proud of him—sometimes he can be quite resilient.

"That building with the bell tower is an example of Neo-Georgian architecture," she informs him.

"The blue clock in the middle is gorgeous."

Although she thinks *gorgeous* isn't an apt word for a boy to use, she keeps her mouth shut.

Finally they reach Junior House—an ivy-covered white clapboard structure that had been expanded to accommodate fifty of the youngest boys. They meet Nat's houseparents—Mr. Spaht, a trim gray-haired man in his late forties, and Mrs. Spaht, her ash-colored hair fuzzy from too many home permanents—who greet them enthusiastically.

Shaking Nat's hand, Mr. Spaht says, "We're delighted to have you here in our house, young man. Although your brother did not reside in this house his junior year—he lived in one of the junior dorms—I got to know him well in my mathematics class. He was a hard worker, and I expect good things of you as well."

Nat gulps. "Yes, sir."

They climb the stairs to Nat's room, a spartan space with white walls, white window shades, white bedding, and stained wood floors. Eleanor's spirits sink to see how bleak it looks. And there is her old steamer trunk against the wall. When it was brand new, it sat at the end of her bed in the field hospital. How quickly she learned to move the wounded off the battlefield and into the hands of a surgeon . . .

"Oh good!" she says with forced cheeriness.

Nat shakes his head.

"Your roommate isn't here yet, so you get to choose which bed you prefer. What do you think, Nattie? The one by the window or . . .?"

Nat sits tentatively on each mattress. Eleanor unlatches the trunk. The scent of moldy leather is much fainter now.

"I'll do that, Mother. Don't bother."

The first thing she encounters is her old battered canteen.

"I want to have a reminder of you here at school, Mummy. It's to inspire me to be courageous like you were."

"Oh." Although she doesn't like the idea of Nat's taking her canteen from home without asking, she's touched by his explanation. "Make sure you keep it out of sight." She hands it to him.

Nat stashes the canteen in the top drawer of the closer bureau and shuts it partway.

Turning her attention back to the trunk, Eleanor lifts a stack of undershirts.

"Do you want to see what I wrote in the car?" Nat pulls a piece of notepaper out of his knapsack and starts reading:

Must I go to P.A. ?
Drag myself all that way?
Away from Daddy,
Mom, and May?
And I'm afraid
Once I've gone they'd
Soon forget I'm away.

"I'll never forget you, Nattie. How could you think that?" She'll think of him constantly as she rattles around that big house.

"I just put that part in for the rhyme. Same with May. We haven't had a maid since May went to work in the munitions factory so she could earn a lot more money." His eyebrows rise expectantly. "What do you think?"

"This is what you were working on. Is it a poem?" Eleanor asks, buying time to think of something encouraging to say. He's never written anything like this before, but she's not sure it's any good.

"It's the lyrics to a song—the first stanza. Do you like it?"

"It's very . . . interesting. Do you plan to set it to music?"

"Of course." Nat squeezes his eyes shut. "Oh, Mother, I wish I didn't have to stay here."

He clutches her hand fiercely, and his breathing quickens. He has a look of desperation. Eleanor feels as though someone has put a blood pressure cuff on her heart and is pumping it up. She squeezes Nat's hand hard.

At that moment, George appears, so self-possessed that he seems to fill the room. "Well, good, it looks like you're getting settled," he proclaims.

Eleanor feels Nat grip her hand even tighter. She didn't realize he's become this strong

"I've got it all set up with the headmaster, Nathaniel. As a special favor to me, Randall promised you can start piano lessons with the head of the music department right away."

"Really?"

Eleanor says, "Thank you, George."

"This isn't usual for a first-year student, Nathaniel, so I hope you appreciate the opportunity."

"Thank you, Father. I'm very grateful to you for arranging it."

"Hello?" Eddie saunters into the room, his hands in his pockets. "How'd you get so lucky, Nattie? My first year, I had to share a room this size with two other guys."

"Don't call me Nattie. That's a babyish name!"

"Excuse me!" Eddie responds. "From now on, I'll only call you Nathaniel."

"No, Eddie. Call me Nat."

"Yes, sir." Eddie nods. "And remember, I'm Edward." He heads over to the chest, where the top drawer is partially open. Putting his hand in, he pulls out the aluminum container. "Where'd you get this?"

Nat glances at his mother for an instant. George looks at Eleanor too, his lips forming a thin line. Nat says, "Uncle Drew gave it to me."

Eleanor is relieved, but she's shocked as well. He lied with such finesse.

Eddie says, "This is the real thing: a genuine military canteen. Why would Uncle Drew give this to you instead of me?"

"I don't know," Nat replies.

George strides over to the window and looks out; Eleanor knows he's ready to leave. She says, "It's up to you to show your brother the ropes, Eddie. Introduce him to your friends and help him find his way. Please." As she hugs him, she murmurs, "I'm really counting on you, dear." She kisses his cheek. "Have a good semester, Eddie." Her eyes begin to fill.

George says, "We have a long drive ahead of us, El, and I need to leave for Washington in the morning."

Eleanor has been hoping she and George could stop at that charming inn in Mystic, Connecticut, on their way home, the way they did after they dropped Eddie off for his first year. "Do you really?"

Pulling a wad of bills from his pocket, George gives some to Nat. Then he shakes his hand. "Have a good term, son. Make me proud of you."

"Thank you, Father."

George hands the rest of the bills to Eddie. "Let me know if you need anything. Work hard, Edward."

"Nat," Eleanor says, taking him into her arms. "I'll miss you," she whispers in his ear. Then she pulls away. She knows she can't look at him again without losing control. Turning abruptly, she chokes out, "Goodbye, boys."

"Goodbye!" they chorus as she rushes down the stairs.

She just has to hold on to her tears until she reaches the privacy of their car. George grabs her arm tightly and steers her around the side of the house to the street nearby, where he'd parked the Packard. He opens the passenger door for her. Once she gets inside, she wails.

After a few moments, she feels a tentative hand on her shoulder. "Eleanor?"

She can't answer him. After some shuddering breaths, she says, "Give me a minute."

She is shocked by her own reaction. She hasn't cried like this in decades. What is wrong with her? Finally she lifts her head.

"All right, George. I'm ready to go now."

"Nathaniel will do well, Eleanor. He's tougher than you think."

While George drives south on Route 28 at a steady forty miles per hour, Eleanor starts to consider the good things about Nat's being at school. She'll be free, really free, for the first time in decades. Finally, she'll have George all to herself again. She can focus on revitalizing her marriage—that's something she really wants. It's been ages since they've had fun in bed. The last time she made an overture, George hadn't noticed.

She slides over next to George. "How long has it been since we've been alone together for more than an hour or two?"

"It's been years," he replies.

Eleanor drops her hand to his leg. "Are you sure you have to go to Washington tomorrow? I was thinking we could stop at the Cozy Nook tonight."

Maybe if she unzips his trousers . . . Suddenly she is riding in an ambulance right next to Henri, her hand in his crotch. Immediately Eleanor scoots back to her side of the bench seat.

"I really must go to Washington. Cozy Nook will have to wait."

"You're working too hard, George."

She looks at him more closely. His face is pale, and his cheeks seem thinner than usual. Is he feeling some grief about leaving Nat behind? He certainly hasn't said anything to suggest as much. She really doesn't know what he's thinking these days. When was their last good talk? She can't remember.

Despite her disappointment about Cozy Nook, she tries to keep her tone light. "How are you, George? It's been such a long time since we've had a real conversation."

"Nothing has changed, Eleanor. I'm busy with war work—the factories, new government contracts, the Jewish Refugee Resettlement work." His eyes stay on the road ahead.

"I know you're working day and night, George. I hardly ever see you anymore. Well, with all the children away, I guess I can start spending more time rolling bandages and assembling CARE packages . . ."

George glances quickly at her. "We could stop in Hartford or Waterbury. The Cozy Nook is out of the way, but we could break our journey in Connecticut and make an early start in the morning."

"Wonderful!"

Eleanor repositions the rearview mirror so she can take a look at herself. Her hair is still very curly, but gray strands are beginning to show through. She'll have to try one of those new shampoos that restore the natural red tones. She applies lipstick and then turns the mirror back toward George.

"This will be a special treat," she tells him.

A night by themselves is just what they need to bring some new life back into their marriage.

Two

EDDIE LOOKS HARD at Nat. "Now that the parents are gone, you need to know that I don't want to have to worry about you." He stands, puts his hands in his pockets, and looks down at his brother. His dark-brown hair shows the marks of his comb and is much smoother than Nat's, which is prone to uncouth cowlicks. "I'm going back to my room to organize my stuff, and I suggest you do the same."

"I'm already here in my room."

"Watch it, Nat. If you make smart-alecky remarks like that, you'll get thrashed."

"I'll keep that in mind," Nat says. "When I'm done unpacking, I'll come find you."

"By the way," Eddie says, turning at the door, "tell me if you ever need money. I can help you out. I make at least fifty bucks a month playing cards here."

"Wow! Does Father know about this?"

"No, and you'd better keep it to yourself. Father might not mind so much, but Mother would."

Thrilled by his brother's sharing a secret with him, Nat replies, "Don't worry. I won't tell a soul." He likes his new role as repository of his mother's and now his brother's secrets. They must trust him.

"Excellent." Eddie exits, whistling an indiscernible tune.

Nat digs into the trunk and pulls out a stack of underpants. He places them on top of the canteen in the first drawer of the chest. He proceeds to dump all his undershirts and socks into the same drawer. Then he grabs a pile of trousers, and something small, wrapped in paper, slides out and hits the floor.

Nat bends down to discover one of his mother's special homemade caramels. Mother! Where did she get enough sugar in these days of rationing? Thinking back, he realizes that the family ate nothing but fruit for dessert over the last few weeks. She must have been saving the sugar for him. He pops the candy into his mouth.

He finishes unpacking. Then he looks at his wristwatch: 4:30 p.m. Then he sits on his bed. A moment later, he gets up and looks out the double-hung window between the beds. Golden light is slanting into the room, and a big maple tree fills the view, though he can see a side street through the branches. No one is in sight.

He hopes he'll be able to learn lots more about music here and that he won't humiliate himself too much in any area of school life, especially when it comes to sports. Most of all, he hopes he will find a real friend here.

Have Mother and Father gotten to Boston yet? What is Sadie doing now? Should he go find some boys to talk to? Voices echo down the hall and up from the lawn outside.

A solid-looking boy enters the room. A short man and shorter woman, both wearing brown hats, crowd behind the boy.

Nat is six inches taller than this boy, who must be his roommate, but the roommate is several inches wider. Sticking out his hand, Nat says, "Hi. My name is Nat Sutton."

A lock of wavy brown hair falls across his roommate's broad forehead as he ducks his head and murmurs, "Peter Chase."

"I'm Rusty Chase, and this is my wife, Violet. How do you do, Nat?"

Nat turns to acknowledge the man, whose nose is flat and wide, as though it had been punched in at some point in the past.

"Mr. Chase. Mrs. Chase. I took this bed and the chest of drawers on the right," Nat says. "I hope that's okay with you, Peter."

Mrs. Chase says, "That's fine." Moving forward, she pushes her hand down on the mattress of the other bed. "I'm sure Peter will find this satisfactory. Bring his suitcases in, Rusty."

Between the beds, bureaus, desks, chairs, and people, there is very little floor space left. Nat shoves the trunk next to his bed. "I'll leave so you can have some room to get settled."

Mrs. Chase says, "See, Peter—now there's a considerate boy."

Peter says to Nat, "Please don't go to dinner without me. I don't know a soul here."

"I'll come back to get you," Nat promises.

He wanders down to the living room, which has an upright piano and a phonograph along with three couches and five overstuffed chairs, all upholstered in the same flowered fabric. He sits down on the piano bench, and as he plays a few runs up and down the keyboard, he's happy to find it's in tune. Then he kneels down to inspect the sheet music and discovers some of his favorite classical music there, along with a thick book of Gilbert and Sullivan operettas.

Then he picks up a *Life* magazine on a nearby table. As he sits down, the chair cushion collapses with a whoosh of air. On the second page is a photo of a boy who looks just like Eddie, except he's in uniform, wearing a helmet, poised to throw a grenade. It's an advertisement for the Bell Telephone System, saying how many telephone calls are required to move a million men or to make munitions—it takes twelve thousand calls to make a bomber. "As the war effort speeds up, the load on telephone wires grows. We can't build new lines because copper, nickel, and rubber are shooting, not talking, materials right now." No wonder his parents keep their telephone calls so brief! Even when his mother talks to Grandma, she cuts Grandma off after a couple of minutes.

Flipping through the magazine, Nat stops at an image captioned *Navy Firefighters*. A man carrying a soldier over his shoulders is emerging from a smoky hold. The firefighter is dressed in a white asbestos suit, gloves, cap with visor, and some sort of breathing apparatus on his nose and mouth. This picture gives Nat the creeps. Though he and the boys at his old school boasted about enlisting as soon as they could, Nat is pretty sure he doesn't really want to fight in a war.

He throws the magazine down. As he walks along the hall, he sees that most of the parents are gone now, and in several of the rooms he passes, boys sit on their beds talking. Back in 222, he finds Peter looking out one of the windows.

"Your parents have left?" Nat says.

Peter turns around. "My mother kept messing around with my stuff and giving me advice until I was ready to scream."

Nat nods. He can imagine wanting to scream at Mrs. Chase. He looks at his watch. "I'm going to find my brother."

"You have a brother here? You lucky duck."

Nat wishes his hair were as nice and thick as Peter's.

"I guess I'm lucky. But of course the teachers and coaches will expect me to be just as accomplished as Eddie, and I'm not even close—at least not in sports."

"May I come along? Would you mind?" Peter seems even shyer than Nat.

"Sure." Maybe Peter will turn out to be a real friend.

As they pass by the living room where the Spahts are talking to some adults, Nat waves at the houseparents.

Peter says, "Do we need to ask permission to leave the house?"

Peter must think Nat knows all the rules, which he doesn't, but his looking to Nat makes Nat feel a little protective of his roommate.

Mrs. Spaht waves back. Nat replies, "Apparently not."

This is an aspect of Andover that hasn't occurred to Nat. He can come and go as he pleases, without consulting anyone. This new independence is exciting. At home, he could roam around the farm at will, but he needed his mother's permission to leave the property.

As they cross the quad, Peter stays so close to Nat that their arms brush against each other.

"Do you have brothers, Peter?"

"No, I just have a sister, younger than me."

"Younger than *I*."

Peter blushes. "Right."

"Sorry," Nat says. "It's not up to me to correct you. That just came out of my mouth without thinking."

"Don't apologize. I need to learn to speak properly. Anyway, my sister's name is Charlotte. She's not bad for a girl. I come from Norcross, a small town in New Hampshire with five hundred people—actually there are fewer now with the war on. Lots of guys enlisted after Pearl Harbor, and other people moved away to work in the munitions plant in Manchester. Some of the teachers left too, so they combined grades, and then all the classes were much larger. That's when my parents decided to send me here."

Nat doesn't want to hear Peter's entire history right now. He looks left and right, scanning the names above the front doors of the buildings they pass. There it is— Waverly. It hadn't seemed impressive from the back when they'd dropped Eddie off with his stuff, but from the front, the red-brick building looks massive with three levels of windows and cream-colored stone windowsills spaced evenly across the facade. The entrance is framed in the same stone.

As Nat mounts the broad steps and pushes the large wooden door open, Peter follows close behind. Two huge boys lean against one of the pillars that frame the staircase, talking together. Nat approaches.

"Can you tell me where to find Edward Sutton?"

The boy in the blue shirt and white shorts says, "His room's on the second floor—first one on the left after the bathroom."

Nat looks at the staircase.

"Go on up."

They find the room, but no one is there. Nat spots his brother's football helmet on the bed. The familiar item makes him feel a little less strange. Then Eddie appears in the doorway wearing boxer shorts, a white towel around his shoulders, water dripping from his red face. Nat introduces his brother to his roommate.

"Hi, Pete," Eddie says, throwing his towel on the bed.

"Uh, I prefer Peter," he says softly.

"Okay," Eddie says. "Nothing like a little touch football. Gotta get in shape so I can beat Exeter, just like Father." He pulls a jersey over his head and grabs a long-sleeved shirt from his trunk, which sits open on the floor, full of clothing not yet unpacked.

"Father played football at Andover?"

"Of course. Father caught the winning pass his senior year. How can you not know this?"

"I guess I never asked." Nat feels embarrassed by his ignorance. "When we talked about Andover, Father told me about playing in the mandolin band. He never said anything about football."

"He knew you wouldn't be interested," Eddie answers.

"That's true. I just don't have the wind for sports that involve running." Remembering Peter, who stands near the door jiggling his right leg, Nat asks, "When's dinner?"

"Now," Eddie says.

"May we come with you?" Nat asks.

"All right. You can come with me tonight, but you've got to make your own friends to eat with, Nat. Go on downstairs now. It'll take me a minute to find some trousers."

As Nat and Peter walk through the hall, large upper middlers quickly pass by them as if they were invisible. They wait for Eddie on the front steps.

"You're lucky your older brother is here. He can introduce you to everyone."

"You heard what he said about making friends of my own."

"He's awfully handsome."

Surprised, Nat turns to look at Peter. "Really?"

Peter's neck reddens. "Very," he asserts.

Nat isn't used to a guy praising another's appearance,

and it makes him uneasy, especially because Peter is assessing his brother. He feels relieved when he hears Eddie's distinctive whistling. His brother emerges and moves quickly down the steps. His legs are so long that Nat and Peter have to hustle to keep up with him.

There are many paths crisscrossing the campus, and Nat starts to feel disoriented. He looks around and spots the bell tower to their left, which helps a little, but there are so many tall trees lining the walkways that he can't see very far ahead. After dinner, he'll have to get Eddie to point them in the right direction so they can find their way back to Junior House.

On the east side of the quad, Eddie looks up at an imposing building. "This is the student union," he says. "The Beanery, where we eat, is upstairs."

Once they enter the dining room, Nat stops, astounded by the size and dark elegance of the space. He knows better than to embarrass Eddie by gawking, so he presses his lips together while he looks around at the large rectangles of mahogany wainscoting, framed by vertical and horizontal pieces of paneling, decorated by portraits of old men. He likes the twelve-foot windows, which are curved at the top, and the drapes, which add grace to the room.

"Golly," Peter exclaims. "I've never seen anything like this before."

Nat says, "I can't believe this is named the Beanery. It's more like a club for men. It reminds me of the Union League Club in New York City." He turns to Peter. "That's where Father took me when he told me about coming to Andover this fall."

"It's not bad," Eddie says, threading his way through the first tables. "Seniors sit closest to the entrance," he explains. "The tables for upper middlers are in this section. Have a seat."

Nat and Peter sit, and Eddie introduces them to the three guys already there.

One of them says to Nat, "You don't look as though you play football like your brother here."

"You're right about that," Nat says. "Music's more my line."

The guy says, "What about you, Peter? You could make a good tackle. Or maybe you're a wrestler?"

"I've played a little football."

"Good. We could use some fresh talent."

"I'm not sure how much talent I've got," Peter answers.

Older boys with white cloths around their waists move through the room carrying platters of food.

Eddie says, "Seniors are serving tonight. Every boy at Andover has to take his turn delivering food and clearing the tables for a week each term—it's not just the job of the scholarship students."

This is not good news for Nat, who knows he's terribly clumsy. He can just see himself dumping a tray full of glasses and plates and food onto the floor with a loud, humiliating crash.

A boy with blond hair flopping in his eyes plunks down a platter of sliced meat with a dollop of catsup on each slice.

"Oh no," one of their tablemates groans, "mystery meat already."

Nat leans over the plate. He sees chunks of onion and green pepper. Inhaling the spicy aroma, he says, "I think the meat loaf smells good."

Rolling his eyes, Eddie says, "You would."

The groaner grabs the platter and spears a piece for himself. Taking the bowl of mashed potatoes on the table in front of him, Eddie helps himself and then hands it to Nat. A little melted butter runs down the side of the mound of potatoes. Nat scoops up a spoonful, making sure to catch some, before he passes the plate to Peter.

"Don't take all the butter," Eddie says. "We have plenty at home, thanks to Bessie, but it's rationed here. Don't you know everyone likes butter?"

Nat grimaces. "Sorry."

When a plate of soggy-looking green beans arrives at his elbow, Nat pauses. Then, giving it to Peter, he says, "I just realized something. I don't have to take any of these gross beans if I don't want. Mother's not here to make me."

Eddie says, "You're such a child, Nat."

At the same time, Peter says, "We get to decide things for ourselves now."

Ignoring Eddie, Nat says, "That's something to like about Andover."

Eddie pushes his plate to the side. "Nat, the tables for the lower middlers are over there in the far corner. That's where you and Peter will sit next year."

"How can we tell which tables are which?" Nat says.

"You'll figure it out. If you don't, see the marks along the edge of this table here?" Eddie points to a series of faded scars that look as if they were made with some kind of knife. "There's one mark for each kid who made the mistake of sitting in the wrong place—they were shot."

The older boys laugh. Looking at Eddie, Peter cautiously clears his throat.

"Don't worry, Peter," Nat says. "Eddie's kidding."

Turning his attention to the fellow sitting across from him, Eddie says, "What were you up to this summer, Malcolm?"

✚

Monday

Dear Jessica,

I'm sorry it has taken me so long to reply to your newsy letter of the sixteenth. I was happy to hear that Susan has gotten over her summer cold—especially because she's just as prone to asthma as her cousin Nat. One doesn't expect to get a cold in the summer, but they can be nasty.

The last few weeks have been wild, getting Nat ready to go off to school along with the other two. It was a much bigger production this year. The rationing board (or the Office of Price Administration or whoever is in charge of such things) must have commandeered all the new fabrics for our soldiers because it was nearly impossible, even in the city, to find new, ready-made clothing for Nat and Eddie, who have completely outgrown the jackets and trousers they wore at school last year. When I mentioned this to my mother-in-law, Abigail said she'd have her tailor refit some of George's father's old suits for the boys. She loves to swoop in and do things for my sons, and though I usually resist—George doesn't like his mother interfering, and neither do I—this time I took her up on her offer. Does it surprise you to hear that Abigail had nothing to proffer for Harriet? Fortunately for Harry (from the standpoint of her wardrobe), she hasn't grown taller since she was fifteen.

Now they're all gone, and without any children at home, I can't quite fathom what to do with myself.

I guess I'm a little blue. Every time I walk by Nat's room I start to cry, so now I've learned to keep the door closed. Thank goodness we still have Rosalee—she's wonderful with the canning and cleaning and laundry. Even more important—her matter-of-fact attitude toward life helps keep me steady. And Hamilton is very handy—he takes care of the farm and all the mechanical work. There's just not much for me to do. I can't see asking Rosalee to cook meals just for two, and George is rarely home in time for supper. These days I simply make some soup for myself, and that's it.

Even when George is home, he is so busy with his business and new war duties that he hardly notices me. I should stop complaining, though. My life is much easier than that of most people. It's just that with all this time on my hands, I can get lost in worries and sad memories. Henri has positively haunted my dreams the last few nights, and I have found myself thinking of him during the day as well.

I can almost hear you say that I need to find something to get busy with, something that takes me outside of myself. You're right!

Your loving sister,

Ellie

✦

Ten days after his first meal at Andover, Nat is practically flying along the path from the music building and his piano lesson with Dr. Honiger, glad he finally knows his way around the campus. He's even beginning to get used to the rigid routine—not that he likes it. Fortunately, the older boys haven't bothered him, perhaps because they fear Eddie.

But then a senior wearing a football uniform sticks out his foot as Nat goes by. Nat manages to stay on his feet, which amazes him. Maybe he's becoming more agile as he gets older.

Swinging his helmet menacingly, the senior says, "Why aren't you out on the playing field, kid? It's time for athletics."

"My lesson ran late, but I'm on my way to phys ed now," Nat says.

"I have a small task for you first," the senior says. "We're going to my dorm."

He looks as big as a Neanderthal, so Nat doesn't dare refuse, but he's terrified. What will this guy do to him when they're all alone? Will he beat Nat up or tie him up or . . . His mind shrinks from going further.

The senior leads the way into Croft House and points to a stack of textbooks on a table in the front room. "I want you to carry those books up to my room on the third floor. I'll be right behind you."

Nat picks up the textbooks in his arms and heads for the stairs. When they get to the top, his tormentor says, "Take the books back down to the living room."

Nat trudges back down three flights of stairs. At the bottom, the ape says, "I need those books in my room. Up you go."

When Nat reaches the third floor, the ape says, "My room's at the end of the hall."

At the ape's door, Nat drops the books on the floor and leans over, struggling not to wheeze as he sucks air into his lungs.

"What's wrong with you?" the ape says.

"Asthma," Nat whispers.

The ape shrugs. "In that case, leave the books here. But I need a left-handed screwdriver before suppertime, and if you don't bring it to me, I'll tie your balls in a knot."

"Where can I find a left-handed screwdriver?"

"That's your problem, squirt." The ape turns and thunders down the stairs.

As Nat hurries out of the building, he's relieved the ape didn't do worse to him—at least not yet—but he worries he'll be so late his phys ed teacher will give him a demerit.

Every day at Andover is strictly scheduled from breakfast at 7:00 to geometry to Latin to assembly to ancient history to lunch and then piano and athletics to biology and English and then dinner and study hours and lights out at 10:00. Even the few hours that are supposedly free aren't really. During their "free" Saturday afternoons, he's expected to watch Andover's football team compete against a team from another school and then to attend the Saturday night entertainment, usually a lecture or movie.

He hates having his days so full of requirements because that means he gets very little free time for messing around on the piano. On the other hand, he and Peter are starting to be friends, which he mentioned to his mother in one of his first letters home. He's no longer writing her every day, but her letters keep coming steadily.

Luckily his physical education instructor does not dock him for being late.

Terrified by the possibility of encountering the ape, Nat stays in the middle of the crowd as he moves from class to class to dinner. In the Beanery, he makes his way over to the upper middlers' section and tells Eddie he needs to talk with him.

After Nat describes his tormentor, Eddie says, "Sounds like Rudy Kamisky."

"Where am I going to get a left-handed screwdriver? Is there a maintenance building I could raid, or . . .?"

"Calm down, Nat. Think: What would a left-handed screwdriver look like?"

Nat shakes his head. Then it occurs to him. "There's no such thing, is there?"

"Just stay out of his way. *Always* keep your eyes down when you walk by a senior."

Nat has heard rumors about unspeakable things upperclassmen do to the juniors, but no one will talk openly about it, so he doesn't know what's true.

"Say," Eddie says, "did you see the *New York Times* today? They might lower the age of the draft to eighteen."

Eddie will turn eighteen in a few months. "They wouldn't take you while you're still in school, would they?"

"I don't know. But I wonder whether it means a man could enlist at eighteen."

✦

Thursday

My dear Nat,

Your letter made my day, Nattie! It was so good to hear how you're getting along at school, making friends with your roommate and enjoying piano lessons with Dr. Honiger. I expect you will find much to interest you at Andover.

Things have been very quiet here at home. I'm spending Tuesday mornings rolling bandages for the Red Cross, and Wednesday mornings I assist with blood collection. On Thursdays, I pack CARE packages for the soldiers overseas. You should see us: a group of ten or twelve women, we make a sort of assembly line as each lady goes along, picking up servings of prunes and raisins, canned tuna fish and liver pâté and corned beef, cheese and coffee, dried milk and oleomargarine, biscuits and chocolate bars, cigarettes and soap, dropping them into a box, and then we start all over again. Does this recital make you hungry? You haven't mentioned the food at Andover—I hope you like it well enough.

With your father so busy with his war work, I'm starting to wonder whether there's something significant that we could undertake as a family to help support the war effort. Something beyond the Victory garden we had this past summer. Remember last December when the president said we are all in this war, that "every single man, woman, and child is a partner in the most tremendous undertaking of our American history"? More recently he called on the American people to ramp up production of every kind, from factories to farms. Well, as you very well know, we certainly have a big farm. We could build a big herd of cows to produce lots of milk and butter for the community. Or we could get dozens of chickens and create an egg production operation here next summer. There are all sorts of possibilities to consider.

Meanwhile, it helps so much to know I'll see you in a couple of months. I miss you, Nattie. So does Sadie—she keeps following me around, wondering where you've gone. We're counting the days until Christmas.

Love,

Mother

✚

November 1, 1942

Dear Mummy,

It's been so long since I've seen you. I WISH I could come home for Thanksgiving and sit in front of the fire with Sadie and eat turkey and gravy and stuffing and take a long walk and enjoy some unscheduled time for a change. The pace at Andover is crushing! I really need a break from this, and I think it's cruel of the school to keep running through Thanksgiving, which ought to be a holiday. They say it's to save transportation costs, but I think it's mean! Peter feels the same way.

I never wanted to be here in the first place. I've had enough. Please write the headmaster and tell him you need me to come home. Please!

Your loving son,

Nattie

✚

Monday

Dear Nathaniel,

I'm sorry you aren't allowed to come home for Thanksgiving, but that's the way it is this year. Harry is staying at Bennington until Christmas, and you and Edward must stay at Andover. I truly wish it were otherwise. I miss you more than I can possibly express. But we must all keep our thoughts directed to winning the war, each doing our part to reach that goal. Your part is to study hard and learn all you can.

One of the benefits of getting out and doing war work is that I have found a new friend, a Mrs. Johnson, whom I met rolling bandages at the Red Cross. She's a widow who lost her husband in the Great War, and while she doesn't have children, we have discovered a number of interests we hold in common. Gladys loves moving pictures, and I am happy to go to the movies with her. Last night we saw "Mrs. Miniver." It is a really inspiring tale about the bombing of England and the courage and resolve of the people there. I especially liked the ending, where the minister said this is a war of the people, not only the soldiers, for it's being fought in the streets and factories and homes, not only on the battlefields. That's especially true in England and the Continent and off in the Pacific, but it applies here in this country too. We all have a role to play in this war. Has "Mrs. Miniver" made it to campus yet? If it's shown in the school's Saturday night series, you ought to go see it.

Love,

Mother

Three

December

ELEANOR SITS ON the side of one of the matching blue plush chaise lounges in front of the fireplace in her sitting room. The fire crackles and spits, warming her as she leans toward the oval mahogany coffee table and picks up the plain brown package that lies there. She feels a little anxious about the fact that the item she holds is illegal—it was obtained on the black market—but she hopes it will do the trick.

The night she tried to seduce George at the hotel in Waterbury on their way home from Andover hadn't gone well at all. He said he was tired, and she knew that was true. Maybe she'd been too aggressive. Since then, whenever George turned to her in his sleep, she responded as quietly as she could.

All the silk is going for parachutes these days, but fortunately her hairdresser knows someone. It took weeks before the delivery could be made. Now, glancing up at the portrait of her grandfather, a young Union general formally posed in his blue uniform with brass buttons and pointed hat, Eleanor hopes to borrow some resolve from him. In this negligee, she will *make* George pay attention to her tonight. She imagines stroking George all over, gradually removing his clothing one item at time, rubbing her silky gown against him, and then he will melt and clasp her to him and lift her onto the bed, where he will plunge into her, moaning about how much he loves her. And in the morning, he'll stay and talk with her over breakfast, and they'll discuss the plans for Christmas. Like everyone else in the country, Eleanor is feeling more hopeful since American soldiers landed in North Africa.

She'd turned the radio on a few minutes ago. Now, while the mellow horns of Tommy Dorsey and His Orchestra play "The Last Call for Love," she tears open the package. The negligee Stella's uncle had gotten for her is red; in fact, it's the color of Henri's blood spilling all over Eleanor as she tried to stanch the flow. But she can't think of that now. Closing the package, she takes it into the bathroom, where she starts running water in the tub. She returns to the sitting room to light one candle at her dressing table and another in the adjoining bedroom.

Once she slides into the tub, she tries to relax in the steaming water.

She recalls the first time she met George, a childhood friend of her college roommate. It was right before she left for France. He talked so fast and intelligently that she felt intimidated. On her return from Paris, though, she sought him out. She made sure they encountered each other frequently. She'd been widowed so recently that she still cried herself to sleep, but she was practical too. She needed a husband, and she and George seemed to be well matched.

She would never forget the honeymoon they had taken after Harry was weaned! They had such fun wandering around Scotland together, and in Edinburgh, George bought her a heavy wool kilt. Later in the bathroom of their hotel room, Eleanor removed her step-ins, put the kilt on, and danced into the bedroom, where she performed a vigorous Highland Fling, a dance she'd learned from the nursemaid who helped raise her. As she kicked her legs up higher, George began to chuckle when he caught glimpses of her bare bottom. She continued until he grabbed her. George started calling her his "bonny lass," and from time to time over the years, he asked her to dance like that again. But things changed after the Japanese bombed Pearl Harbor.

It has been a long time since George called her his "bonny lass," and she can't remember the last time she danced for him. It's been so long since they've made love with their eyes open that Eleanor has taken to pleasuring herself. Touching herself gently and subtly, remembering how Henri squeezed her and kissed her and slid himself inside her, she'd reach release but then burst into tears.

Ever since she opened her old trunk from France, Henri has inhabited her thoughts. She keeps remembering the first time she saw Henri in 1917. He wasn't handsome with that big blunt nose dominating his face, but he seemed very masculine to her. The boys she'd known at college were effete by comparison. While Henri struck Eleanor as terribly virile, his touch and his voice were as gentle as a woman's when he leaned over the wounded soldier on the stretcher in the back of her ambulance. An hour later in the operating tent, dressed in his white surgeon's overall, Henri joked with the soldier before he covered his mouth and nose with a pad soaked with chloroform. Henri's face shone with compassion as his fingers delicately opened the soldier's wound. Jessica claims Eleanor is still in love with Henri, but how can that be? He's been dead for nearly twenty-five years.

Eleanor looks at her body under the water and sees how her stomach is pouching and her breasts droop. She isn't as attractive as she used to be, and it's harder to feel alluring. She stretches her arms out. Seeing they're still firm makes her feel a little better. She hopes her sexual life isn't over yet. Nervously, she twists the gold ring with her family crest on the little finger of her right hand. George likes the fact that she came from an old family, and it doesn't hurt that she possesses some money of her own.

The telephone rings. She hears George pick it up downstairs. After his loud hello, his deep voice grows much quieter, and she can't hear what he's saying. This late at night, a telephone call makes her worry that some emergency has arisen.

Eleanor stands and briskly towels herself dry. She calls downstairs, "George. Is everything all right?"

"Fine. I'll be up in a minute."

Taking the stopper off her special perfume from Paris, she daubs Femme Rochas onto her wrists, under her breasts, and behind her ears. She pulls the red negligee over her head and smooths the silk down her thighs. Then, removing the cap from her darkest lipstick, she paints her lips and combs her hair. As the water drains from the tub, Eleanor turns off all the lights.

She arranges herself on the chaise lounge. At first she has both legs sticking straight out, but then she pulls one leg in, thinking that pose will be more appealing. She feels self-conscious to the point of embarrassment.

"George?"

"I'm coming!" He sounds slightly exasperated. He stops in the doorway when he sees her displayed on the chaise. He looks shocked. "What is this?"

"I've been waiting for you. Come here, lover." She hasn't called him "lover" in ages. She pats the chaise next to her.

"Oh, Eleanor, for heaven's sake. Take that thing off."

He sounds so disgusted that her hopes collapse as fast as a punctured balloon.

She surges to her feet, rushes into the bathroom, and slams the door.

Stripping the negligee off, she throws it into the corner and grabs the old terrycloth bathrobe hanging on the back of the door. Wrapping herself up, she sinks onto the toilet and puts her face in her hands. Tears stream down her cheeks. After several minutes, she blows her nose on a piece of toilet paper and wipes her face. Then she opens the door.

George is sitting in a hard-backed chair next to the fireplace with his head in one hand. He looks up at her entrance.

"I'm sorry, Eleanor. I didn't mean to hurt your feelings." His face has the same look of remorse that he wears on the occasional mornings after he's had too much to drink.

"What do I have to do to get you to notice me?" She's on the verge of tears again.

"This war is draining me. I'm sorry, El. Let's just get in bed."

They move into the adjacent room, where their high double bed fills most of the space. Eleanor drops her robe and lifts the covers. George sits to remove his shoes and socks. Then he slowly takes off all his clothing. Once he lies between the sheets, they turn toward each other and hold one another, touching the entire length of their bodies. This is how it usually starts.

Eleanor begins to move slowly. She wishes he'd open his eyes, but they're screwed shut. After a few minutes, she senses George has gone far away, as though his physical body lies here with her while the rest of him is somewhere else entirely. A crushing sense of despair descends on her, and she turns her head to the side.

"I'm sorry," George says after a few minutes.

Eleanor rolls off him, desperately disappointed. "What happened? What are you sorry for?"

"That wasn't any good."

"What is going on? At first you seemed to be with me, but then you disappeared."

"I don't know, Eleanor. My mind started wandering. I'm too tired to concentrate on anything this late at night."

"But—" she starts.

"Let's just go to sleep," he says.

When Eleanor wakes up the next morning, she is shuddering with cold. She dresses warmly and goes down to the kitchen to make breakfast. As she breaks eggs into a pan to scramble, she is still shivering, despite her sweater and woolen slacks. Turning off the burner, she goes upstairs for warmer socks. As she sits on the chaise lounge, she feels her forehead. She doesn't seem to have a fever, but she feels mortally cold. Eleanor remembers how icy her feet were every day and every night in France. Even months after she returned from the front, she couldn't get warm; she thought she'd have cold feet for the rest of her life. Eventually this went away, and she had forgotten about it. Until now. Now the war is bringing it all back.

Eleanor returns to the kitchen to cook the eggs. As she glances out the window, she spots Sadie frolicking in the snow. The children are finally coming home for Christmas—the boys arrive today. Harry will arrive tomorrow. She can hardly wait.

She brings the coffeepot into the dining room, where George sits reading the *New York Times.*

"Good morning," she says.

He looks up from the newspaper. His eyes are rimmed with red, and he doesn't look as if he slept much.

"Are you all right?" she asks.

"Sure." He moves his gaze back to the paper.

Eleanor returns to the kitchen for the scrambled eggs. As she puts a plate in front of George and the other at her own place, she asks, "What happened last night?"

George puts the newspaper down. "Where did you get that atrocious red thing? It looked like silk. There's nothing like that available anymore."

"I have my connections."

George starts eating. "You're talking about the black market. That's treason, Eleanor. You help the enemy when you purchase goods illegally."

She has lost the little appetite she had. Pushing her food aside, she says, "Come on, George. We're not going to lose the war because I bought a lousy piece of silk."

"It's the principle of the thing. If everyone acted like you did, this nation would be in trouble. Our strength lies in everyone's doing his bit."

"I don't believe you really care about contraband silk. That's simply an excuse to get angry at me."

George exhales a sigh. "Maybe you're right." Pulling a cigarette out of the pack in his breast pocket, he lights it and inhales. As the smoke wafts out his nose and mouth, he says, "The negligee isn't really a matter of national security. But it's not the sort of thing *my* wife would ever wear. It's much too gaudy."

Eleanor raises her coffee cup and takes a long swallow. Hearing George refer to her as his wife makes her feel a little bit better. She says, "I'm going to meet the boys' train in the city. Do you want to come along?"

"I have a meeting with the central rationing board in New York, so I'll ride in with you, but I'll need to stay in town all day."

She isn't surprised that it's up to her to fetch their children; George is always too busy for that sort of thing.

The New York Central train from Boston is two hours late arriving at Penn Station. Eleanor is prepared; she brought a book with her. Train schedules are much less reliable now because of the volume of servicemen moving across the country. In fact, she read that while the country has no more trains now than last year, the railroads are carrying 33 percent more freight and 68 percent more passengers.

Finally, the train from Boston is announced. Eleanor puts her book into her satchel, and then, pushing her hands into the pockets of her woolen coat, she moves to the platform. As the train exhales steam and passengers, she stares through the chaotic crowd of soldiers, families, and sweethearts, trying to spot her sons.

"Mother!" Nat cries exuberantly, lurching toward her, his arms weighed down by a suitcase and a knapsack bursting at the seams. He drops everything at her feet and throws his arms around her.

"Nattie!" Eleanor devours the feel of him for long moments, then she pulls away. "Let me look at you." His appearance has changed dramatically. His hair is long and greasy, and his face is covered with angry red acne in the midst of his freckles. She reaches for the safest remark she can make. "You're taller than I am now!"

"Edward!" she calls to her older son, who materializes beside Nat.

As she hugs Eddie, he kisses her cheek. "How are you, Mother?" It is so cold in the train shed that he seems to be exhaling smoke.

"I'm much better now that you're both here," she says, rubbing her hands together briskly. In the background a train hisses.

While Eleanor motions to a porter, Eddie says, "May I stay in town? I really want to walk around and see the Christmas decorations."

"After all these months away?" Eleanor looks at her older son. "I want you home, Edward."

"Please, Mother. John Miner invited me."

Although Eleanor is secretly relieved at the prospect of having Nat to herself, she feels guilty about that. She's used to Eddie's being away from home—and besides, he's much more George's child than hers.

"You may spend the night at the Miners' tonight," Eleanor says, "but I want you to get on a train first thing in the morning—"

"Thanks, Mother!" Eddie dashes off.

While the porter loads the boys' luggage onto a cart, Eleanor hugs Nat again. The sheer sight of her youngest child lifts her spirits, and suddenly she feels buoyant.

"I missed you, Nat. It's been really lonely at home." Leaning her head against Nat's, Eleanor shuts her eyes. A strong scent of sweat assails her. She wrinkles her nose. He smells terribly rank. "When did you last bathe, Nathaniel?"

"Oh . . . hmm . . . I don't know."

"You used to be so clean and sweet smelling."

"I smelled like a girl. That soap you packed in my trunk was scented."

"It was a good smell." He isn't her sweet little boy any longer. She feels annoyed with him for changing, but that's silly; he's supposed to be growing up.

"Never mind, Mother. Tell me about Sadie—did she miss me?"

"Of course she did. Sadie is bigger, as you'll see for yourself. I'll tell you all the news from home when we're on the train."

Once the suitcases are stowed in the trunk of the cab that will take them to Grand Central Station and the porter has been tipped, Eleanor and Nat climb in.

"Peter and I are getting to be really good friends," Nat says. "I don't know if I've ever had a real friend before."

"I'm glad for you, Nat. Is Peter a good student?"

"I have no idea. We don't discuss grades. He studies a lot, though."

"Excellent. I hope you haven't gotten too old now to make Christmas cookies with me the way we usually do. Rosalee and I have been stockpiling sugar for months."

"I love making cookies with you, Mother. Where's Father? I thought he might be here to meet our train."

"He had a meeting."

"Father didn't write me a single letter this fall."

"He's terribly busy with all his war work—that's why he hasn't written to you."

"Mummy . . . my grades are not the best, and I got some demerits. I'm afraid Father will not be pleased."

"Oh no." Eleanor eyes the largest pimple on Nat's nose. "What happened?"

"I don't know." Nat's legs are crossed, and he keeps jiggling the foot on top. "I couldn't get interested in iambic hexameter or '*Veni, vidi, vici*' or the other things I was supposed to be studying."

"What did you do?"

"I read a lot. I listened to music. Oh, and Dr. Honiger started teaching me to play the organ. That's a *lot* of
fun. I just couldn't concentrate. Maybe it's because I keep
thinking about what's going on in Europe and wondering
when the Germans are going to attack here." His tone is
an ambiguous mixture of embarrassment and defiance.
"I'm sorry, Mother. Is Father going to kill me?"

"You can't afford to mess around, Nathaniel—not
these days. We all have to put our noses to the grindstone
and do our jobs."

"You sound just like Father." Nat sighs.

"I'm sure your father will have something to say about
this as well."

"Tell him not to get too mad at me."

"I'm not getting in the middle between you and your
father any longer. You'll have to explain yourself, Nat."

"I promise I'll try harder next term, Mother."

"Tell that to your father."

Harry doesn't arrive home until late Christmas Eve because of the priority given to soldiers on every mode of
transportation, and then the train she finally finds a seat
on is delayed for hours because of the snow. Finally on
Christmas morning they can all gather together. The gifts
are modest and practical this year, but Eleanor believes
what she bought for everyone will be a big hit. She went
to a lot of trouble to make this Christmas as festive as possible, despite all the shortages.

As usual, George passes the presents out.

His mother squints over her reading glasses at the
package she has just unwrapped. "And this is a . . . what?"

Eleanor explains, "It's one of the new ballpoint pens,
Abigail. They're meant to last a long time before you need
to replace the ink."

"I like my fountain pen. Thank you, anyway." She hands the pen back to Eleanor. Eleanor has never managed to find a gift that pleases Abigail.

Harry says, "I'll take it. I could use more than one pen—I have a ton of writing to do these days."

Nat appears to be particularly disappointed by his pen. As Harry and Eddie pick up the wrappings, Eleanor takes him aside. "What's wrong, Nattie?"

"I really hoped you'd buy me the new phonograph records I put on my Christmas list."

"I tried, but the selection at the music store has been completely depleted. The salesman explained that the record companies don't have any more vinyl with which to make recordings—all the vinyl is going to the war effort. I'm sorry, Nat."

"It just doesn't seem much like Christmas this year."

"We've been at war for more than a year now. Life isn't the same as it used to be. But Christmas is about family traditions, Nat—singing carols together and eating special food like oyster stuffing and mince pie. It's mistletoe and holly. It's spending time together as a family. We still have all that."

"I guess," he says doubtfully.

After they eat Christmas dinner and leave the dining room to sit around the living room, slouched in their chairs, groaning about how full they are, Eleanor is happy, content for the first time in months. She rises to get the coffeepot from a side table.

"More coffee, Abigail? It's the last of the real stuff—I saved it especially for today."

Seated next to George in one of the twin wingback chairs, Abigail leans forward to squint into her cup. "I will have a little more." As she looks up, her diamond necklace slides down into one of the folds encircling her neck. "Thank you, Eleanor."

Eleanor thinks Abigail would do better to wear a scarf around her wrinkled neck, though her emerald-colored velvet dress certainly is lovely, even if she has worn it every Christmas for years.

"Mummy, may I have more coffee?" Harry says. "I can't seem to wake up." Harry's face is very pale in contrast to her rosy gown, and the smudges under her eyes almost look like bruises.

Eleanor moves to her side. "Of course." As she pours coffee into Harry's cup, Eleanor scrutinizes her face. "You're exhausted, aren't you, dearie?"

Harry swallows a yawn. "I've been up late every night for a week designing an experiment for my final chemistry project."

Eddie, unbuttoning his top button and loosening his tie a little, says, "Boy, I don't know how you ever got so interested in science. Chemistry is my worst subject."

From one of the window seats, where he is tapping a 3/4 beat against the glass, Nat looks back over his shoulder at his sister. He asks her, "Is this the project you wrote me about?"

"Yes. I've been working on it all semester."

Nat says, "Harry's interested in everything."

"No, not English or history," Harry replies. "But I love chemistry—it's so real."

Abigail says, "No one in our family has ever been good at science, Harriet."

George says, "I beg to differ with you, Mother. I run a chemical company, after all. I studied chemistry in college, and so did Father." He pulls a cigarette out of the pack in his shirt pocket and lights it.

Abigail looks down at her lap.

Eddie says, "Father."

George looks over at Eddie.

"I'm sorry to report that Andover did not beat the Red and Gray this season."

"Exeter?" Abigail puts in.

"How did you play, Edward?" George asks.

"I pulled my hamstring during practice, so I had to sit on the bench and watch Exeter defeat us."

"Too bad," George replies.

"I had a good a son other who."

"Glad to hear it."

The telephone rings. George starts to rise, but Eleanor leaps up. Hurrying down the hall, she wonders who could be calling them on Christmas Day. It wouldn't be her sister or her mother because everyone has been asked not to make any long-distance calls this holiday in order to keep the lines free for war calls. She picks up the receiver and says hello, but there's no answer. After a moment, the connection is broken.

When she returns to the living room, Nat is saying, "We had a very interesting class in biology the other day, talking about genetics and things like hair color."

"I always wondered why I'm the only one in the family with such dark hair," Harry says.

Eleanor replies, "My grandmother had very dark hair when she was young, according to my mother. I only knew Grandma with white hair." She looks around the room.

Eddie says, "Who was on the phone, Mother?"

"I don't know. Whoever it was hung up after I answered. That's been happening a lot."

"Must be a wrong number," says Eddie.

Eleanor says, "Why don't we get a jigsaw puzzle out. Wouldn't that be fun?"

George stands. "I think we should go back to the dining room and bring the map up to date. It's been a couple of days since anyone has paid any attention to it."

Abigail says, "I believe I'll go upstairs to the guest room for a little rest."

As the family moves down the hall toward the dining room, Eleanor puts her hand on George's arm to get him to stop. Quietly she says, "I hope you'll spend some time with Nat before he goes back to school. I've noticed you two haven't had a moment together since he came home. I know you're busy, but I think it's important for you to pay a little attention to him."

"All right. If you think so," George replies, "I will."

Meanwhile, Harry is saying to Nat, "How's it going for you at Andover?"

"It's okay."

"Really?"

Nat shrugs.

"Let's step into the library," Harry says.

Once Harry shuts the door, they stand facing each other. Nat says, "It's not really going well. I don't see how I'll ever fit in. Eddie is so popular, and I don't have any friends except my roommate, Peter. I like him, but he's a little strange. He doesn't have any other friends either."

Harry says, "You should get involved in something—a club or some other activity, maybe something to do with music. That way, you can get to know other boys, and they will get to know you. What about a musical—doesn't Andover put on musicals from time to time?"

"They do, but I don't think first-year students are given any interesting jobs."

"You don't need something big. Just volunteer to help build the sets or . . . anything."

"How about you, Harry? Are you glad it's your last year at Bennington?"

"No. I love chemistry, and I have a wonderful professor. He has encouraged me to go to graduate school, and I would like to, but I'm afraid Mother has other ideas. When she told us she's thinking about turning the farm into a facility for producing eggs on a large scale next summer, I got the feeling she wants me to play a leading role."

"But if you want to go to graduate school, shouldn't you be able to go?"

"I may have to wait until after the war's done."

"That's not fair," says Nat.

"Fair doesn't matter during wartime," Harry replies. "I'll see what Father wants me to do."

When Nat and Harry enter the dining room, they find George, Eleanor, and Eddie perusing the map George mounted on the wall months ago, after President Roosevelt asked the American people to have a world map in front of them during his Fireside Chats, so they can follow while he speaks about the Allies' situations across the globe. Since then, the family's dinner conversations have often revolved around possible strategies for the Allied forces and the geographical impediments they face.

Eleanor, hearing Rosalee in the kitchen, hurries through the swinging door.

"Rosalee, that's enough. I'll finish the dishes later. You should go home to your own Christmas with Hamilton."

The black woman's sleeves are pushed up to her elbows, and soapsuds cling to her arms as she stands before the porcelain sink. Sweat glistens at her hairline. "I don't mind, Mrs. Sutton." She smiles. "I'm nearly done here. Besides, Hamilton is happy to have some time to himself so he can read his newspaper in peace."

"Please, Rosalee. Go home," Eleanor says, shooing her hands at Rosalee.

"All right, ma'am. If you say so."

"And don't come back until Monday."

"Thank you, Mrs. Sutton. That's mighty kind."

"Not at all."

As she rinses and then dries her arms, Rosalee remarks, "The president said we should not stop work for a single day."

"The president was talking about work stoppages by labor unions. In any case, you've earned some rest, Rosalee. I'll see you on Monday."

Back in the dining room, George is saying, "Roosevelt told us this is a new kind of war, waged on all the seas and continents, every island, every air lane encircling the world. We have to fight around the whole world to defend our supply lines and our lines of communication with our allies."

"It's an enormous job," Eddie says.

George asks, "Now what are the most strategic areas the Allies need to control?"

"Do we have to talk about this?" As soon as the words are out of her mouth, Eleanor knows it's a stupid thing to say. But whenever she thinks about the war in Europe, she starts remembering Henri, and she doesn't want that today.

George says, "That's the whole point, Eleanor. Why else would we update the map and the positioning of our troops? We need to stay on top of what's going on with the war all around the world."

Eleanor moves over to rearrange a curtain hanging crookedly.

Harry says, "The Strait of Gibraltar is very important."

"Speaking of Gibraltar," Eddie says, "Father, did you

read the report in *Life* a week or two ago about the first American raid on Italy by the Ninth Air Force?"

George replies, "I don't think I've gotten to that yet."

"It was absolutely thrilling, the way the reporter described the attack. B-24s bombed the fleet at Naples—they got destroyers and cruisers and battleships and submarines. You could see the orange flames go up thousands of feet in the air. They raced away just before the ack-ack guns could reach them."

Eleanor says, "I read that report. It was so well written that you could almost think you were there with the airmen. But never forget, Eddie, the American planes could have been shot down at any moment. War is not a game."

"I know that, Mother," Eddie says sullenly. He turns away from the map and stares out the window.

Eleanor moves over to pat his back.

Eddie shakes her off, and she's not surprised. He's growing up as fast as he can; he rarely allows her to touch him.

She says, "This is enough excitement for me. I'm ready for a nap. Anyone else?"

Nat says, "I've got some practicing to do. Dr. Honiger gave me a very hard piece to learn over vacation."

As he and Eleanor exit the room, George, Harry, and Eddie continue discussing logistics as they stand in front of the map.

1943

CAPT: *I am the Captain of the Pinafore*
And a right good captain, too! . . .
I am never known to quail
At the fury of a gale,
And I'm never, never sick at sea!
ALL: What, never?
CAPT: No, never!
ALL: What, never?
CAPT: Hardly ever!
ALL: He's hardly ever sick at sea!

—Lyrics from "I Am the Captain of the Pinafore"
by Sir William S. Gilbert, 1878

Four

January

ALTHOUGH THE PROSPECT of his second dinner alone with his father at the club in Manhattan ought to be exciting, Nat feels slightly nauseated. The first time they ate at the Union League Club, his father delivered the horrible news that Nat would have to go to Andover. What would it be this time? Probably something about his grades.

Now, trying to escape the cold rain, Nat dashes under the canvas awning in front of the club so quickly that he treads on his father's heel.

"Sorry, Father."

As George turns, tipping his head to the side, rain drips off the brim of his black fedora and falls more than six feet to the ground. Nat likes having such a tall father, a man who is the epitome of elegance with his dark-brown hair, narrow nose, sharp blue eyes, and black coat.

"All arms and legs. Just like I was at fourteen." George smiles.

"I won't be fourteen until later this month. You know that."

"Of course." George reaches for the doorknob.

Nat says, "I can hardly believe you're taking me to the opera tonight. I've never been to the Metropolitan Opera before, and I love music more than anything."

"It's time you experience your first opera," George says, opening the door.

Inside, Nat stares once again at the creamy marble floors, mahogany millwork, and dazzling chandeliers. The lingering scents of whiskey and cigar smoke assail his nostrils.

While George greets the large uniformed black man at the switchboard, Nat looks at the gold-framed mirror on the wall. He wishes his hair were dark like his father's, rather than this reddish-orange color, but at least his tie is straight.

After leaving their coats with the lady with the lopsid-ed smile at the coat check, they take the elevator up to the third floor. At the entrance to the cavernous dining room, Nat pulls his shirt cuffs down from the sleeves of his blazer, then follows George to a small table against the wall. Once they are seated, Nat cannot think of a thing to say. What was on that mental list of conversational gambits he cooked up last night?

"What would you like to eat, Nathaniel?" George asks. "The lobster Newburg is very good here."

"I'll take that. I've never had lobster Newburg before."

"Really? I suppose that's outside Rosalee's repertoire. Your mother's too." He motions to a waiter. "Please bring me a martini. Nathaniel, something to drink? How about a Nehi?"

"That's a kid's drink."

"Pardon me," George says. He looks to be smothering a smile.

"I want a martini too."

George says, "Please bring my son some ginger ale in a martini glass. And we'll start with French onion soup."

Taking a roll from the basket on the table, Nat breaks it open and watches with dismay as crumbs spray across the white linen tablecloth. He puts the roll down on the little plate above his forks and leans forward.

"Father, tell me about Sutton Chemicals. I know you have factories in Newark, but I don't know what you make."

"You don't?" George sounds incredulous. "How can you not know about our business?"

"You don't talk about it at home."

"We manufacture industrial coatings, fabrics, carbon paper, typewriter ribbons—"

Nat interrupts, "Carbon paper? What does that have to do with the war?"

"It would surprise you how much carbon paper the government requires for all their forms in duplicate and triplicate."

"Mother says you don't have to fight because your work at home is essential to the war effort."

George raises his chin. From this angle, his nose looks thin as a knife. He says, "I *am* fighting in my own way." He sounds almost angry. "We work around the clock making chemicals to finish shell casings, bombs, and gas masks, aircraft wiring systems, camouflage cloth and nets, and coated waterproof fabrics. My factories operate three shifts every day of the week, every week of the year."

"I see," Nat replies. His father is too important to fight. Nat feels a frisson of pride.

While the waiter sets their drinks down, George checks his pocket watch. Then, after tasting his martini, he says, "Tell me how you are getting along at Andover."

"Okay."

"Okay?"

"Well, I've made one friend—my roommate, Peter. And I like my piano teacher, Dr. Honiger."

"What about your grades, Nathaniel? Thus far, the reports from Sam Spaht are most disappointing."

"My grades are not so good."

"You must not be applying yourself."

"I'm trying. But this school is much harder than Warden. I'd have to study every hour of the day and night to do well."

"I know you can do the work if you put your mind to it. Bad grades are simply unacceptable."

"But I never wanted to go to Andover."

His father looks through him. "You must do what your father tells you." Then George looks him in the eye. "All the men in our family go to Andover. You know that. I didn't have a choice about where I went away to school. Neither did your brother, and neither do you."

The waiter returns with their soup.

George dips his spoon into the bowl and eases some broth out from under the melted Gruyère and bread.

Cautiously, Nat does the same. Surprised, he says, "This is the best soup I've ever tasted."

"Glad you like it."

For a few minutes, they eat without speaking. Then George puts his spoon down on the tablecloth.

"Nathaniel, you need to understand what the stakes are. Andover is the oldest private school in America, and it's the best too. If you cannot succeed at Andover, we'll have to find some other boarding school for you, and it's not likely to be as pleasant as Andover. If you don't buckle down and start getting some decent grades, I won't pay for any more music lessons. Period."

"You can't do that to me!"

"Oh yes, I can. As your father, it's my job to decide what's best for you."

Dropping his head, Nat stares at his soup. The onions look like transparent snakes. His insides start to seethe. All of a sudden, the sound of dishes clattering and utensils scraping the plates hurts Nat's ears. He finds himself stroking his thumb across his stomach in an attempt to calm himself, and then he stops because his mother has told him not to do this—it makes him look as though he's about to throw up.

Pushing his soup aside, George extracts a cigarette from the pack of Luckies in front of his plate. He tamps the tobacco, then lights up. He inhales deeply and exhales as he removes the cigarette from his mouth, cocking his wrist as he does so. "Andover made a man of me, and it will make a man of you too."

Nat's intestines gurgle. He scans the room for the closest exit in case he has to make a run for the bathroom.

Unobtrusively the waiter slides their soup bowls off the table and places dishes with lobster Newburg in front of them.

"Andover was one of the highlights of my life." George pulls on the cigarette again, then exhales a plume of blue smoke.

Picking up his fork, Nat spears a chunk of lobster meat. Although it is wonderfully sweet and salty at the same time, he can hardly swallow.

"How do you like it?"

Nat nods. He can't speak without screaming or crying or both. He looks around the room as if fascinated by the large portraits of forbidding white-haired men on the walls. Then he tries another bite. And another.

After several minutes of excruciating silence, George puts his fork down on his empty plate and pulls another cigarette out of the pack. Lighting it, he exhales smoke as he surveys the room. He brings his gaze back to Nat.

"When you go back to school next week, I expect you to give it everything you've got."

"Yes, Father."

"Dessert?"

"No. Thanks."

"The club's famous for its meringue glacée. Are you sure? Waiter!" George's eyes gleam.

"I'm sure."

"One meringue glacée."

A thin man in a dark suit approaches their table. "George Sutton," he says, sticking out his hand.

George rises to his feet and shakes the man's hand. Quickly Nat stands as well.

"Nathaniel, this is Mr. Iverson. Mr. Iverson and I are both on the ration board. Frank, this is my son Nathaniel."

"How do you do, young man?"

Nat firmly grasps the bony hand extended to him. He says, "How do you do, sir?"

"This must be a special occasion, dining at the Union League Club with your father. Having a good time?" While Nat wonders whether to lie, Mr. Iverson turns to George. "I was surprised to hear you've gotten involved with that Jewish refugee group."

"What do you mean?"

Mr. Iverson narrows his eyes. "Doesn't seem your sort of thing."

"You think I don't care about the Jews who are desperately attempting to get out of Europe? I care very much.

My best friend at school—the most brilliant guy I know—is Jewish."

Mr. Iverson takes a step back. "That's not what I mean. I'm talking about Mrs. Kaplan."

After quickly glancing at Nat, George moves in closer to Mr. Iverson. "What about Miriam Kaplan?" Nat can see from the pinched look around his father's nose that he's angry.

"Beware of getting involved with her."

George says, "I'm simply serving on her board, Iverson."

"Be careful, Sutton," says Mr. Iverson.

His father leans so close to Mr. Iverson that they nearly touch. "You don't understand. This is the most important thing I've ever done."

Shaking his head, Mr. Iverson retreats. "You can't say I didn't warn you." He turns and walks away.

As Nat and George sit again, Nat thinks there was something nasty about Mr. Iverson's tone. George glances at the dessert that has appeared on the table; then he reaches for his cigarettes. Nat looks down at a stain on the tablecloth where George spilled some of his soup. Momentarily he feels better thinking his father is a slob too, but then he sinks back into wretchedness. He has got to figure out how to do well at Andover, or his life will be over.

"Don't say anything about this to your mother."

Startled, Nat looks at George. The lines on his father's face are more deeply etched than usual. "What?"

"Never mind. It's time to go." George stubs out his cigarette.

Nat wonders what's wrong with his father—he hasn't eaten his dessert.

Out on the street, the sounds of the city assail Nat. Honking horns, squealing brakes, distant sirens, shouts from vendors fill his ears. The sidewalks are slick, but it isn't raining any longer.

A boy in a dirty jacket with big holes at his elbows stands on the corner holding up a newspaper, shouting, "Russians take two key towns!"

George says, "We'll walk. It's just a few blocks to Broadway and Thirty-Ninth."

Nat has to hurry to keep up with his father.

"I thought *Carmen* would be a good choice for your first opera. You'll probably recognize some of the music." After a moment, George adds, "Andover is the place where I learned a new instrument. That's where I started to play the mandolin."

"You told me that before."

"You might enjoy the mandolin. You're a natural musician, so it wouldn't be difficult for you to pick it up."

"I am?" Nat is surprised but pleased by his father's acknowledgment.

At the Metropolitan Opera House, it takes a while for Nat and his father to work their way through all the people decked out in their suits and fancy gowns and furs. Once they reach the second row and sit, George leans over. "Isn't this great? Mother got her hands on these seats decades ago."

"These are Abba's?"

Nat turns around to look at the house. There are three tiers with rows disappearing into the back of each tier, and every single seat seems to be full. The boxes on each level are filled too. Everyone is talking loudly.

Nat turns back to look at his father. "I didn't know Abba was an opera fan."

"Sh."

The conductor has emerged, wearing a black tuxedo, carrying a short white baton. Nat leans forward. Their seats are so close to the orchestra pit that he can see most of the musicians and their instruments, including a harp, a double bass, and cymbals. The maestro takes his place at the music stand in front of the players.

Passing Nat a copy of the score, George opens his own and leans down to examine it. Nat can see the marks a comb made through his father's hair, which glistens with brilliantine.

Nat isn't ready to read the music; he wants to savor the suspense. Gazing at the gigantic stage, his eyes catch on the proscenium arch with its curlicues and the names Gluck, Mozart, Verdi, Wagner, Gounod, and Beethoven.

Then he sinks back into his plush seat and sighs deeply. This is heaven. The golden velvet curtains with long braided fringe remain closed, but they flutter faintly with the activity going on behind them.

George crosses one long limb over the other and cocks his head in his characteristic position for listening. His hair is so thoroughly slicked back that it doesn't move when he leans to the side.

The conductor glances down at the music, runs his fingers through wild brown hair, and then he raises his hands. As the overture begins, Nat watches the conductor, who has a dreamy smile on his face as he wafts his arms toward different sections of the orchestra: he clearly loves what he is doing.

The music *is* familiar. Father must have played this opera on the phonograph recently.

Nat launches into a daydream about performing in public one day. He can see himself on the stage of the Philharmonic, flipping his tails out behind him with an elegant flourish, then sitting down on the bench to play the piano so exquisitely that he gets a standing ovation and lots of bravos.

Slowly the curtains open.

How will Nat ever become a great musician if Father takes away his music lessons? At the thought, his throat tightens; he is on the verge of an asthmatic attack. The theater is very quiet now. Clenching and unclenching his fists, he opens his mouth and sucks air in as deeply and unobtrusively as possible.

George leans over and whispers, "It's all right, Nathaniel." He rubs Nat's leg.

Nat relaxes, and his breathing grows easier. His attention turns to the stage, where glamorously costumed characters dance and sing around each other, and instantly he becomes caught up in the drama. When Carmen sings, "*L'amour! L'amour! Si je t'aime, prends garde à toi*," Nat is amazed by how much emotion she expresses with her voice. Then he wonders, what was Mr. Iverson talking about, anyway?

George gasps. Nat notices he's fidgeting; his father's legs are crossed, right over left, and his right foot bounces up and down. His fingers, long and fluid, strum against his leg. Nat realizes his own fingers, though slightly shorter, look just as thin and flexible as his father's.

Then he glances up at his father's face. George's eyes are closed; his cheeks are wet. Nat has never seen his father cry before. He's noticed tears in his eyes when they sing Christmas carols around the piano, but this is different. Feeling as though he has stumbled upon something very private, Nat turns his eyes back to the stage. Why is Father crying? Nat looks again at his father, whose face writhes with distress. Tears course down his cheeks.

He reaches out to touch his father, but George's eyes are clenched tightly shut and he holds his body so rigidly that Nat withdraws his hand. Nat realizes he's getting a glimpse into his father's soul. He will always remember this moment.

During the intermission, his father seems to have recovered.

"Wow, Father! That Carmen, she's so, so . . . I don't know the word."

George replies, "She's mesmerizing."

✚

Thursday

Dear Jessica,

It's been weeks since I've heard from you. I hope everyone is well and that your Christmas was festive.

We didn't have much of a Christmas as far as presents went, and Nat was especially disappointed, but it was good for us to concentrate on the family aspects of Christmas rather than the mercenary. I know you encountered some difficulty in finding special gifts for Susan and Brooks. How did that turn out? Thanks to the Depression years, I believe we're more accustomed to coping with times of austerity than our children are. I actually enjoy the challenge of seeing how much I can do with less, although I have to admit that I would give a lot for a piece of beef once in a while.

Harry, Eddie, and Nat are back at school now. I loved having them home, but it's exhausting too. I'd almost forgotten how much more complicated life is when they're under our roof, constantly coming and going. Now it's too quiet.

I'm so restless, I can scarcely sit still. I have got to volunteer more hours at the Red Cross and CARE offices. That'll help keep me busy—and doing my part will provide some sense of satisfaction. What I really crave is the escape offered by a good novel. The serials on the radio aren't nearly as effective. Maybe I'll start working my way through Trollope.

How is Mother holding up? In her last letter, it sounded like she finds the rationing rules more than a little overwhelming. Is there anything I can do to help?

Love to you and Drew and the children.

Ellie

✚

Nat remembers Harry's advice. When auditions for Gilbert and Sullivan's *H.M.S. Pinafore* are held on the stage of George Washington Hall in early January, he appears at the appointed time. Because his music teacher is running the audition, Nat doesn't feel quite as nervous as he would if he didn't know the man judging him. He decided not to warn Dr. Honiger that he is coming to the audition because he doesn't want to be told not to bother trying out.

But when he enters the seven hundred–seat auditorium, Nat almost turns back. There are at least one hundred students milling around the front of the hall, and quite a few of them are girls. It never occurred to Nat that girls from Abbot, Andover's sister school, would be auditioning at the same time as the boys. But as he thinks about it, he realizes this makes sense: the directors want to hear how the contenders for the lead parts sound when they sing together.

Scanning the crowd as he approaches the front, Nat sees only a couple of boys he knows by name, though many look familiar. When he spots Eddie on the steps to the stage, he hurries over to him.

Eddie's tie is undone, and his smile is easy. "Hey, Nat."

"What are you doing here? Music is what *I* do, not you. I never thought I'd have to compete with you in this arena."

"Sorry to disappoint you, but I've performed in all the musicals since I came to Andover. This year Dr. Honiger asked me to try out for a big part—Ralph Rackstraw."

"Dr. Honiger?" Nat is jolted by a stab of hurt. He's been thinking of Dr. Honiger as his own special friend and supporter.

"He *is* one of the two directors of this production."

"But Ralph is the most important part. You're only a junior."

"They must have a dearth of tenors in the senior class."

"Dearth? Since when do you use words like that?"

"Since I started making lists of words I don't know in my reading.

"Well, la-di-dah. Aren't you the model student?"

Nat is so frustrated he turns away. "So you're going to upstage me here too," he mumbles to himself as he heads down the right aisle. He takes a seat at the end of the fifth row and slouches down, thinking he'll just watch the auditions for a while before he decides whether he will actually stand up and sing in front of all these people. He has no trouble reading music, but his voice isn't all that great.

At least he knows something significant about their mother that Eddie isn't aware of. For once, Eddie doesn't have everything.

Over the next hour, as Nat listens to the best singers from Andover and Abbot try out for parts, he is struck by how polished they sound. He had no idea there would be so many talented singers here. He has to admit, Eddie's voice is darn good. And where did Eddie acquire all that poise? In the face of such competition, Nat decides not to audition. Instead, he'll ask Dr. Honiger whether there's something he can do on the production side.

After the auditions are over, Nat and Eddie walk back to Junior House together.

Eddie says, "Isn't it a gorgeous night, Nat? Just look at those stars."

"You sound happy," Nat says.

"I am. I received an invitation today to join Andover's best secret society. It's the one Father joined when he was here."

"What?" says Nat. "I've never heard about any secret societies at Andover."

"That's the point, little brother. They're secret."

"What's the name of this secret society that invited you to join?"

"I can't tell you—that's one of the rules."

"Well, what's it like? What do you do? Where do you meet?"

"I don't know yet. All I can tell you is that Andover has secret societies for the gentlemen on campus and so-cieties for the scholars, and then they have the one I'm joining, which is for the men who are both gentlemen and scholars."

"How old do you have to be?"

"Invitations are issued after Christmas break to some of the upper middlers."

"I bet I'll never be invited to join one of those societ-ies," Nat says sadly, though he very much hopes he'll be proven wrong when he's an upper middler.

✛

Nat wishes he could open a window for some fresh air as he watches the second hand inch around the face of the clock on the wall in Latin class. The biggest bully in his form sits next to him and keeps looking over at Nat's desk. The air is so stale and stuffy, filled with motes of chalk from the blackboards and the dry, dusty residue of old radiators . . .

"Mr. Sutton! Translate the first five lines of the third book of the *Aeneid!*" Dr. Blodgett's voice startles him.

Translating on the spot is an enormous challenge. Nat's understanding of conjunctions and adverbs is sketchy, which makes it hard for him to figure out which phrases are dependent and which aren't, much less to decipher the way the entire sentence should hang together. After a long pause, Nat stumbles his way through the translation. Every time he gets a word wrong, Dr. Blodgett interrupts to correct him. By the end of his lines, Nat is sweating profusely.

Dr. Blodgett says, "Your brother never came to class unprepared, Mr. Sutton. See whether you can't do better tomorrow."

"Yes, sir."

To Hank sitting next to Nat, Dr. Blodgett says, "Mr. Clifford, please continue."

Nat is astounded by the ease of the bully's performance. When he glances over, Nat sees that the bully has penciled the meaning of each word above the lines of Latin. Not fair! No wonder the bully translates so smoothly.

When the bully is done, he catches Nat's eye and scowls meaningfully. Nat knows he's supposed to keep his mouth shut.

As the students start to leave their desks at the end of the period, Nat turns to the guy who sits on his other side. "To look at Hank, you wouldn't expect him to be so proficient at Latin, would you?"

"I don't know. What's a Latin scholar supposed to look like?"

Nat tries to come up with a funny response. "Small wire-rimmed glasses? A bow tie?"

The guy looks confused; he's clearly not tickled by Nat's attempt to be witty. Nat still hasn't figured out what sorts of remarks will amuse his classmates, though he very much wants to be seen as amusing.

"Get that paper for me, Sutton."

Nat turns to Fred Hollinshead, reputedly the wealthiest guy in his form. A sheet of Fred's notepaper has fallen onto the floor between them.

"Why should I?" says Nat.

"Because you're a peon."

"I am not. Get it yourself—it's closer to you."

Fred moves toward the paper, and as he picks it up, he tells Nat, "I won't forget this."

Nat isn't happy that he's just acquired another enemy, but on the other hand, what right does Fred have to order Nat around? It's not as though he's Fred's servant.

Later that evening on the way into the library to study, Nat sees the bully standing with his back to him, reading a notice on the bulletin board. For a moment, Nat thinks he can slip by without saying anything. The bully is on the wrestling team, and he has a nasty temper, so Nat has always steered clear of him. But tonight he feels annoyed by the bully's making him look bad in class, and he's still annoyed at Fred as well.

Nat taps the bully on the shoulder. "Hank," he says, "I couldn't help but notice in Latin today that you'd written the English above the lines for our sight translation. You know, that's not really fair. It's actually sort of cheating."

Hank turns around. His frown and the way his brow furrows make him look simian. "Mind your own business, Sutton. If I choose to work ahead, that's up to me."

"Dr. Blodgett might be interested to know why your sight translations seem to roll off your tongue."

As soon as the words are out of his mouth, Nat regrets them. He doesn't mean to sound so prissy, and he has just violated the cardinal rule of life at Andover: never ever snitch on anyone. Eddie impressed that upon him before Nat even got to campus.

Holding his books in his left hand, the bully curls his right hand into a tight fist. "If you know what's good for you, you'll keep your mouth shut."

"It's not fair to the rest of us."

Swiftly, the bully grabs Nat by the shoulder and shoves him up against the wall. "I'm warning you, Sutton . . ."

An upperclassman opens the outside door and comes into the foyer. Nat hopes the guy will rescue him, but he simply glances at Nat and the bully as he continues on his way through.

"You're such a pansy," the bully says.

"What? Why do you call me that? I'm not a pansy."

"You look like one. You act like one." The bully drops his hold on Nat and pushes through the door to the library, muttering, "Fairy."

Nat wonders what he can do to prove he's not a fairy. He likes looking at the naked women in the art books—in fact, that's the real reason he came to the library.

At the front desk, Miss Tome, a portly middle-aged woman with short frizzled hair, sits perched on a high stool, reading.

Nat approaches her. "I'm doing research for a paper on Nathaniel Hawthorne," he says politely, "and I'm wondering if you have a book on nineteenth-century art."

Miss Tome's front is like a ledge that slopes down toward her middle. What must her breasts look like to continue all the way to her waist like that? On the calendar in Eddie's closet at home, Betty Grable's bathing suit breasts are pointy and very separate from each other, not continuous across her front like the librarian's.

"The American art of the nineteenth century could provide an interesting angle to pursue in your research," Miss Tome says. As she smiles, a pale scar running over her bottom lip becomes visible. "Look in section 10 on shelf H." When Miss Tome points in the appropriate direction, Nat sees that her breasts don't move at all. "The books in that section are noncirculating, but you can help yourself here in the library."

"That's fine. I'll study them here. Thank you, Miss Tome."

Nat heads for section 10. After pulling several art books off the shelves, he finds one that has some colored illustrations of nudes. He takes the volume over to a vacant table, sits, and leans down close to the pages so no one can see what he's looking at. In this book, the breasts aren't pointy at all—they're large and round.

Mr. Snake pops up and starts pressing his head against Nat's trousers. Mr. Snake's reaction *proves* he is not a fairy. He has nothing to worry about.

"What are you up to?" Someone grabs the art book and pulls it across the table—it's the bully. "Well, well, you're full of surprises, aren't you, Sutton?"

"Don't say anything to Miss Tome!"

"I won't if you keep your mouth shut around Dr. Blodgett."

"It's a deal."

Back at the dorm, Nat enters the bathroom. No one else is there, so he leans into the mirror to examine his face. He squeezes one of the juiciest pimples on his forehead. Then he looks at his lips. They seem to have gotten bigger. He purses them, wondering what it would feel like to kiss someone straight on, lips to lips. He wouldn't want to do that with a guy. Unless he was just practicing so he'd be ready when the time came to kiss a girl.

✛

Saturday evening

Dear Mother,

I got a job in the production of "H.M.S. Pinafore" that Andover is mounting this winter. It's pretty paltry. All I have to do is turn the lights on and off at the appointed moments—but the rehearsals are great fun. Eddie is playing Ralph Rackstraw, which is a very big deal, and he's supposed to kiss the girl playing Josephine, but I don't know if he really will. He says she has bad breath. She's certainly not as pretty as the girl who plays Buttercup.

Gee, Dr. Honiger is kind! He eased up on my piano assignments because I'm spending much of my measly free time at rehearsals for the musical.

When I read about Sadie sneaking into the house and eating all the butter in the kitchen, I had to laugh. Thank goodness we have lots more where that came from. Or do we? Does Bessie's milk production change in the winter? I never thought of that before.

Well, I'd better get back to studying for tomorrow's math test.

Love,

Nat

✚

After writing to his mother, Nat heads out for a walk. The temperature is surprisingly mild, and for a change, there's hardly any wind. Leaving his coat unbuttoned and his gloves in his pockets, he heads across the street toward the edge of campus. Behind the blackout shades, he can see slits of light in most of the rooms. It seems everyone is still awake. As he rounds Newman House, a figure lurches toward him in the dark, stumbling and then stopping to vomit. Is this an Andover boy or some local drunk who could make trouble?

"Hello?" Nat says.

"Is that you, Nat?"

"Eddie? Are you okay?"

"Oh God," Eddie says. "What a nightmare." He moves over to the steps of Newman and sits gingerly, wiping the back of his hand against his mouth. He spits on the ground a couple of times.

"What happened?"

"They tortured me."

Nat sits next to Eddie. "Who tortured you?"

"I can't tell you. I'm not supposed to say anything."

"Tell me! I'm your brother. I want to know what they did to you."

"I just went through the initiation into ACB, but I can't say anything more."

"I won't tell anyone. I'll keep this secret."

"Promise?"

"I promise."

Eddie spits again. "Several of the seniors in ACB took me down into the basement of the house, by myself, and they made me do a bunch of chin-ups so I'd be breathing hard, and then they made me smoke four cigarettes at the same time—and you know I don't smoke. I had to keep smoking until I threw up into a bucket." He pauses, and Nat can see he's reliving the experience. "Then they made me drink my vomit."

"Oh God, Eddie, that's horrible! It's barbaric!"

"After that, they had me take down my pants, and they jabbed me in the butt with a broom so hard it's excruciating to sit down. It feels like straw is embedded in my ass."

Nat shakes his head. He can't believe Andover boys would be so cruel. "Do you think Father had to go through the same initiation?"

"He must have."

"Is this the sort of thing that's supposed to make a man of you?" Nat asks.

Eddie groans.

"At least I won't be sorry when no one invites me to join a secret society."

Eddie doesn't reply.

"I'm sorry, Eddie. Can I do anything for you?"

"Just stay with me a little while."

"Of course, Brother." Awkwardly, Nat pats his brother's shoulder. He has never been moved to comfort Eddie before, but now he wants to try.

✚

January 30

My Dearest Sister,

Recently I learned about a group of local women who get together to knit every Monday afternoon, and this week I joined them. We knit every kind of woolen clothing a soldier needs. Of course, new skeins of wool are hard to find, so I've started pulling apart sweaters our family hasn't been using. I can reknit that wool into stockings and mittens and hats.

I felt a little awkward walking into a home where I barely knew anyone, even though the hostess assured me I would be welcome. I didn't know anything about these women. Their needles kept moving as they all introduced themselves to me, and then they returned to their discussion about somebody's son who'd been wounded. I didn't know any of the parties being discussed, so I had nothing to contribute. Once they'd finished that topic, one of the ladies asked me if I have sons fighting in the war. I told them I'm grateful my sons are too young to enlist. One young woman sitting near me nodded, though another scowled. Does she think I'm unpatriotic to express a sentiment like that? Perhaps she scowled because all her sons are already in the action and she's worried. I didn't ask, though. I'm going to keep my mouth shut until I know more about my companions. Although some women use "ain't" and sometimes their grammar grates against my ear, these ladies have warm hearts and a firm grip on reality. They are the salt of the earth. I hope they won't find me too high-and-mighty to befriend.

Every topic of conversation turned on the war. No one spoke about anything else. I can't get away from it! The more I think about this war, the more memories of Henri return. I will never forget the look on his face when he vowed to love me "'til death do us part." His brown eyes were so warm with affection—were those tears lurking in the corners? They didn't slide down his cheeks, but I was certain I saw tears in his eyes through the tears in my own. Every time I remember that look—and I keep replaying it—I get a jolt to my gut. What can I do with all this feeling? I'm absolutely obsessed with thoughts of Henri. Memories, sweet and painful. Grief as raw at times as it was when I first lost him. What to do?

Much love,

Ellie

Five

February

LATE SATURDAY NIGHT, Nat sits alone on the steps beneath the bell tower. It's windy and cold on the top of the hill in the center of campus. He covers his ears with his hands as he thinks about the soldiers fighting in Europe and Russia. How do they deal with cold like this? The photographs in *Life* make the war seem real, but most of it is invisible.

Like his mother's war experience. When he tries to imagine what his mother went through in the Great War, all he can see is an old-fashioned truck painted with a red cross. That's it. He tried to get more information from her over Christmas, but she wouldn't tell him anything; she said it was too awful for her to want to think back and remember.

It's getting harder and harder to keep the secret of her role in the last war to himself. He wants to tell Eddie, but that would betray his mother's confidence.

Nat hugs his arms around his midriff.

Will Eddie join up as soon as he turns eighteen? He hasn't said anything more about that since he mentioned they lowered the age for enlisting. Nat is pretty sure he won't enlist himself. He hates fighting of every kind. But he should do something to help win the war. It was an article he read about Bernard Baruch, the financier who donated one million dollars divided among fifteen different war-relief organizations, that sent him up here to think. One of the things that struck Nat was that it cost Baruch only three quarters of a million to make that gift because he used war bonds.

An idea starts to grow. Nat hasn't had much success in making friends other than Peter—for some reason, his jokes always fall flat—but maybe his classmates would be interested if he talked with them about something more serious. What if he organized a drive to sell war bonds at Andover? Certainly that would help the war effort, but maybe it would make him more popular as well. Who would know how he should go about selling war bonds? Mr. Spaht would probably be a good place to start.

Nat heads back to the dorm, where he finds Peter sitting on his bed in plaid green-and-red pajamas Nat has never seen before. For a second, Nat is tempted to tease Peter about the fact that his new sleepwear looks like Christmas, but Peter is riveted on the tablet leaning against his raised knees.

"What are you doing?" Nat asks as he takes off his overcoat.

"I'm just sketching." Peter holds the tablet out to Nat. It's a simple line drawing of a boy wearing a jacket and tie, long pants and shoes, his cap on sideways.

"This is really good, Peter! The kid looks totally disheveled. How did you manage to make his clothing look so sloppy?"

"I made the lines a little loose instead of straight, if you see what I mean. He's an Andover student, but I have no idea what sort of caption to give him. I think I could add a balloon coming out of his mouth and have him say something, but I can't think of anything funny for him to say."

"Will you give him some kind of name that shows he's from Andover?"

"That's an idea," Peter said. "Do you think they'd ever print something like this in the *Phillipian*?"

"They should."

"Well, we'll see. I need to polish him up a little more before I show him to anyone else."

Nat hangs his coat in the closet, and then he sits on Peter's bed. "I want to tell you something . . . Right before I left for Andover last summer, Mother told me a secret that I don't know what to do with. Actually, at first I kind of liked knowing something Eddie doesn't, but now I'm not sure how much longer I can hang on to this."

"I'd be honored to hear your secret, Nat."

"It's really Mother's secret."

"It's also yours now."

"You're right." Nat pauses, then continues, "It turns out that my mother served in the last war, but she never told us anything about it."

"That's fascinating!" Peter says. "What did she do?"

"She was in France driving an ambulance."

"I've never heard of a woman doing that."

"Me neither. She said Father doesn't like her speaking about it."

"What about your father—was he in France too?"

Nat is shocked to realize he has no idea what his father did during the Great War. "I don't know. Maybe he didn't even serve. I'll have to ask him sometime."

Peter says, "Hmm, this is most mysterious. Maybe your father had a very traumatic time in France. Maybe he was wounded in an embarrassing part of his anatomy. Or maybe he was discharged for something that wasn't his fault." "I agree—there must be some kind of mystery here. Thanks for understanding, Peter. I've never had a friend like you."

Peter beams. "Me neither. We're lucky we got each other as roommates."

✚

February 20

Dearest Jess,

You were absolutely right: I need some war work all my own, something I can direct, some project I'm in charge of. At last I have started pursuing my idea of running a large-scale food operation on the farm.

First I thought about cooking large batches of food that we could provide to local hospitals, but that would involve a lot of driving around in order to deliver the casseroles, or whatever they would be, while they were still hot. Producing food seems more crucial.

I considered getting a herd of cows, but the process of making butter and cheese would require expertise and lots of time. Pigs would be messy and smelly, and we don't have enough acreage for beef cattle.

But chickens, whose eggs are easy to collect, chickens will be perfect for me and the children. I see no reason why we can't start this coming summer once Harry, Eddie, and Nat are back home from school.

Meanwhile, I have much to learn about the differences in kinds of chickens and the quality of their eggs, what sort of facilities they need for sleeping and laying eggs, where to acquire the chickens, what to feed them, how to protect them from disease. Then there's the business side of things: what will it cost to raise the chickens, how many eggs will they produce, how would we get the eggs to market, and on and on. I don't know whether one of the state universities has extension classes on these topics, but I will find out. And of course I'll discuss this with Rosalee and Hamilton—they probably know something about chickens.

I hope the man with the big farm stand at the edge of town would be willing to show me around his spread and tell me how he does things. He's always very friendly when I stop to buy eggs and produce from him, but perhaps he would think I'd be competing with him. That makes me think I might do well to find a buyer for our eggs in the city. I bet George will have some ideas about that.

There will be lots to learn. I'm really excited!

You know me so well, Jess. Thanks for helping to set me on this path. I appreciate your encouragement more than I can say.

All my love,

Ellie

Snow is melting on both sides of the path, and the March wind contains a whiff of humus as Eddie and Nat walk back to Junior House after the final performance of *H.M.S. Pinafore.* Nat feels very proud of Eddie for doing such a great job of playing Ralph Rackstraw. Ordinarily, Nat doesn't praise his brother because Eddie already gets accolades from everyone else for practically everything he does. But this time, he can't help himself; he is so impressed by Eddie's performance that he gushes.

"You were remarkable, Eddie. I never knew you could sing and act like that. You were great!"

Eddie replies, "Thank you, Nat. That's nice of you to say. I really enjoyed doing the operetta. Didn't you?"

"I loved it. After all the rehearsals, it was so much fun when the whole thing came together." They continue along the path to Nat's dorm in comfortable silence. Then Nat says, "Did you really kiss Josephine? It seemed like you did, but I couldn't tell for sure from up in my perch."

Eddie says, "I tried to make it look like I kissed her, but actually I put my lips on my own arm. I didn't want any trouble from Alice."

"Who's Alice?"

"She's a girl from Abbot I dance with once in a while."

"Was she there tonight?"

"I don't know. If she was, she didn't come up to me afterward." Eddie starts whistling.

"I think I smell a little spring in the air," Nat says.

"Say, I've got an idea. You should come sit in on our Sunday poker game tomorrow."

"That would be fun," Nat agrees. "Where do you play?"

"We get together in the basement of Commons after dinner." They have arrived at the front door of Junior House. "I'll see you tomorrow, Nat. Good night."

As Nat enters the foyer, the door to the Spahts' apartment opens. "Is that you, Mr. Sutton?" Mr. Spaht pokes his head around the half-opened door.

"Yes, Mr. Spaht."

"I've been looking for you. I spoke with the head of the bank in town today, and he knows the exact steps needed to start a war bonds campaign on campus. I'll tell you all about it tomorrow after dinner if you're free then."

"Yes, sir," Nat agrees. Maybe he can be a little late for poker.

✛

Sunday night

Dear Mother and Father,

You would have been impressed and awfully proud of Eddie if you could have seen him in our production of "H.M.S. Pinafore." He has a very good voice and stage presence. I'm sorry you couldn't be here.

I miss you, and I wish we could come home for a spring vacation. I thought winter would never end, though we are starting to see small signs of spring.

Dr. Honiger is taking a few students—including me!—on the train into Boston next weekend to hear the Boston Symphony Orchestra play Brahms's Third Symphony. I can hardly wait!

It's been a while since I've heard from you, Mother. You must be busy. Please write me all the news when you can.

Your son Nat

✛

When Nat gets to the basement of Commons, he hears a whoop from Eddie. As he steps cautiously into the room, Nat sees Eddie pull a pile of chips toward himself while the other upperclassmen seated at the table groan.

"Not again, Sutton! How do you get such incredible luck?"

"Hey, you just need to know when to raise and when to fold," Eddie says.

Hovering near the door, Nat isn't sure whether he should sit down. Eddie notices him.

"Nat, sit next to me for a few hands 'til you get the hang of this. Then we'll deal you in."

He moves his chair over to make space. Nat pulls an empty chair into the gap and takes a seat. Eddie provides introductions all around.

The guy named Archie shuffles fast. Dealing the cards around the table, he says, "Five-card draw. Ante up, boys."

Eddie picks up his cards, arranges them, and shows Nat his hand. He has a pair of 10s and a pair of 2s. Throwing down the unpaired card, he gets a new one, which is neither a 10 nor a 2. Leaning back, Eddie opens the betting. He wins the hand as well as the next two.

"Get the idea, kid?" Eddie asks.

Archie says, "How do you like rooming with a raging homo, Nat?"

Nat feels his face get red. "Why do you say that?"

"The way Peter Chase walks, the way he talks—anyone can see he's a homo."

"Peter is a good guy," Nat says quietly.

After the game, Nat asks Eddie, "Those guys you play with—are they gentlemen, or are they scholars?"

Eddie answers, "They fall in the category of gentlemen."

"Really? They weren't very nice about Peter."

"They're regular guys, Nat. Guys give each other flak. You've got to learn to take it."

"Are you still thinking about enlisting when you turn eighteen?"

"I'm considering it. We'll see what happens when the time comes."

Should Nat warn his parents that Eddie might enlist? Would that be tattling?

It's an ordinary Monday afternoon in April when Eleanor arrives at Jane Anderson's for the weekly gathering of the knitting circle.

"Come in," Jane welcomes her.

"I'm sorry I'm late," Eleanor says.

"It doesn't matter," Jane says softly.

She leads Eleanor into the living room, where eight women sit with their various efforts to fashion a warm cap or vest or stocking for the fighting men in Europe. Jane takes a wingback chair near the doorway. No one is speaking. Each woman stares at the bit of wool in her lap except for Sally Jones, whose eyes are puffy and red. Sally watches Eleanor cross the room, an imploring look on her face.

"Sally?" Eleanor asks. "What is it?"

"It's Nicky, my Nicky—he's dead."

"Oh no." Eleanor kneels in front of Sally. "What happened?"

"Somehow he got ahead of his fellow soldiers—it was raining, dark—and when he turned back, they thought he was the enemy and shot him dead. They call it 'friendly fire.'"

Eleanor groans.

"I can't see anything the least bit friendly about shooting your own comrade."

Sally's voice rises as she says this, and Eleanor can tell she's on the verge of hysteria. Eleanor takes Sally's hands firmly in her own.

"You're absolutely right, Sally; it's not the least bit friendly to shoot your own. I am so sorry. The accidents that occur when men have guns in their hands are so hard to bear. They're senseless."

Sally swallows hard and closes her eyes. "What a stupid way to die."

Standing, Eleanor says, "*War* is stupid. I've seen way too many soldiers die, and for what? I know we have to stop the Nazis and the Japs now, but how did we get to this pass in the first place? What about negotiation? What about compromise?" She looks around the room at the other women, who are shaking their heads in sad consensus. "There must be a better way to resolve differences."

"I'm with you," Jane says. One of her sons is fighting in Italy, and another is somewhere in the South Pacific.

"Where did you see soldiers die?" Sally asks.

"It was during the first war, in France, near Ypres and then Soissons and Château-Thierry."

"What were you doing there?" Sally seems desperate to hear anything that will distract her from her loss.

"I drove an ambulance, bringing wounded soldiers back to the field hospital. So many died, and they were young men for the most part, many of them younger than I was. I try not to think about it, but sometimes in dreams I'm right back there in the thick of everything." Looking to divert the conversation, Eleanor says, "At least the news from North Africa is encouraging, now that General Patton's troops have joined up with Britain's Eighth Army in Tunisia."

"I hope they destroy every last one of the Axis forces in Africa!" Sally exclaims bitterly.

Eleanor replies, "I'd be happy if they simply surrendered."

Sally picks up her knitting.

Jane says, "Did you see the General Electric ad where they talk about something called television?"

"What in the world is that?" asks Eleanor.

"It seems to be something like a movie projected on the wall of a room in your home."

"Well, I never," Sally replies.

Moving over to a vacant chair, Eleanor says, "I should get to work." As she opens up her satchel, she says, "Somehow knitting doesn't seem like much of an offering toward victory and peace."

Jane says, "We do what we can. And some"—nodding toward Sally—"make the ultimate sacrifice."

Eleanor gets a sick feeling in the pit of her stomach. She remembers being in France, so ill with cholera that she was delirious. Henri materialized in her hazy awareness. He sat gently on her bed, took her wrist to feel her pulse, and looked into her eyes.

"*Ma chérie*," he said, "have no fears. You will return to health. But in order to be strong, you must eat a little." Then he pulled her up into a sitting position and started spooning the most remarkable broth into her mouth. "*Un peu, ma chère, un petit peu.*" The broth was like liquefied chicken and quite salty. After a few spoonfuls, he said, "*Ça suffit.*"

He sat with her and told her how beautiful the sunset was. He stroked her hair away from her face and held her hands awhile before he fed her more broth. This was the first thing she'd been able to stomach in days. She slept deeply that night.

Later she learned he'd taken a day's leave to travel home, where he asked his mother to make her special soup, created by cooking chicken bones and skin and flesh for hours.

Six

June

ALTHOUGH GEORGE HAS said nothing yet about his performance at school, Nat can tell from the cold way his father treats him that a reckoning is imminent. He has been home from Andover for a week now, cringing every time George looks at him. Now his heart booms in his chest as he opens the solid mahogany door to his father's study.

"Shut the door behind you, Nathaniel," George says. "Sit here." He gestures to a leather chair directly across from the mahogany desk, where he presides.

Nat shuffles slowly across the small room. Two walls of the study are lined, floor to ceiling, with books. Windows looking out on the backyard dominate the third wall, and the fourth is taken up with a fireplace and an oil painting of the ocean with two tiny sailboats heeling in the breeze. On winter weekends, a fire burns in the grate, so Nat thinks of the study as a cozy room. But today the grate is empty, and he feels chilled as he sits down to face his father.

"Your report arrived some days ago," George tells him, tapping papers on his desk with his forefinger. "These grades are unacceptable."

Nat does not respond.

"Well, what do you have to say for yourself?"

"Nothing," Nat whispers. He doesn't have an explanation for why it was nearly impossible for him to concentrate on his schoolwork at Andover. He doesn't know why he found himself watching the clock so often in class.

George slams his hand down on the desk. "You have *nothing* to say?"

"What do you want me to tell you?" Nat knows he sounds insolent, but he can't stop himself. "You know I never wanted to go to Andover. I told you that—"

"All the men in our family go to Andover."

"You said that before."

"I didn't have a choice about going to Andover either. My father made that decision, and it was the right one."

"The work at Andover is much harder than it was at Warden."

"Of course it is. One third of the boys at Andover flunk out. But you're eminently capable of doing the work—I never thought you'd struggle with your classes. How did you manage to fail three out of five courses? You must not be trying."

"I don't belong at Andover. I don't fit in. I'm not an athlete or a scholar, and I'm not popular the way Eddie is. I'll never make it at Andover."

"Well, that's about the worst attitude I've ever encountered," George says.

The telephone rings. George grabs it. "Yes." He listens for a few moments. "I'm in the middle of something.

I can't talk now." The skin around his nose turns white, which means he's getting angry. "Listen, I told you not to call me here." He looks up at Nat.

This is odd. Nat has never seen his father behave like this.

"It'll have to wait. I'm busy with my son." After a pause, he says, "Goodbye," and slams the receiver down.

Refocusing on Nat, George says, "Did you study at all?"

"Of course I did! I spent a lot of time studying, but I couldn't figure out what the masters wanted."

"Clearly you did not try hard enough."

"I don't want to go to Andover. I want to study music, Father."

"Music is no kind of profession for a man in our family."

"Music makes life worth living!" Nat cries.

His father smiles slightly.

"I mean it. Listening to recordings of Gilbert and Sullivan was the only thing that got me through the year."

"That stuff isn't serious music, Nathaniel."

"It is so! The lyrics are very clever, and some of the songs are just as beautiful as the arias in an opera," Nat says with passionate conviction. "Dr. Honiger agrees with me. He thinks Gilbert and Sullivan were very good musicians, and he's a Bach scholar."

George stands up. Apparently their meeting is over. "I've spoken with the head. Randall will allow you to return in the fall, but you'll be on probation until your grades improve. Meanwhile, I have engaged a tutor to work with you on Latin, English, and history starting Monday. You will spend two hours with Mr. Murray every morning this summer, and you will spend the rest of the morning studying."

"Bleah, that sounds terrible! I thought I was going to work on the farm with Harry and Eddie."

"You'll spend your afternoons and weekends doing farmwork. You must make some contribution to the war effort."

"I organized a war bond campaign for the whole school, and our dorm came in way ahead of all the other juniors."

"Your mother told me. Good for you."

"That's the only thing you have to say?"

"I said that was good. What more do you want?"

"I don't know." Nat lifts his head and looks George in the eye. "How about something like, 'Good work, Nat. I'm proud of you.'" Then he pushes on, "What's your contribution to the war effort?"

"I've restructured Sutton Chemicals to produce war matériel, and we've added shifts to run round the clock. I'm in charge of our local rationing board, and I raise a lot of money for an organization that's rescuing European Jews from the Nazis. In point of fact, petitioners for Class B and X gas rationing cards will be arriving momentarily. They'll try to explain why they need more gasoline than ordinary citizens. So we are finished here—"

"What about the Great War?"

George's face turns red, and his whole body seems to get bigger. He looks as though he wants to jump over the desk and grab Nat by the throat.

Nat keeps his seat in the leather chair. "You were the right age to sign up, weren't you? You graduated from Andover in 1914."

George eases back down into his chair and leans his arms and hands, palms down, on the desk. He speaks quietly. "I graduated from Andover in 1914, and then I went to Yale. In the summer of 1916, some of my classmates decided to go help the French, though the United States had not declared war on Germany yet. I wanted to join them, but my father wasn't well. He told me my duty was to stay home and take over the company. So I did. I took the helm at Sutton Chemicals. I really wanted to fight the Huns, though, and I've regretted that decision ever since."

"What happened to your father?"

"He rallied after a while, and I returned to finish at Yale."

"Did I ever meet him?"

"No, my father died in 1920. He was forty-nine years old."

"I'm sorry, Father." Nat quickly calculates his father's age, worried by what this might portend about his longevity . . . Father must be around forty-seven now. He'd better not die anytime soon.

"That's ancient history now." George leans back in his chair and clears his throat. "What I'm looking for from you, Nathaniel, is an appetite for work. I want you to learn to enjoy working at school and on the farm. Once you have the habit of applying yourself, you'll find you can accomplish anything you set your mind to. I know you can succeed at Andover." Rising, George comes and pats Nat on the back. "Do not disappoint me."

✙

June 3

Dear Jessica,

   Poor Harriet! When I started planning our egg production operation, I thought it would suit Harry to take charge of that effort after finishing at Ben-

nington this spring. Now it turns out that what she really wants is to go to graduate school in chemistry at the university in Madison, Wisconsin. I had no idea! However, we're too far down the road now to turn back on our egg operation, and we need Harry to direct it. Once the war is won, Harry can go to Madison.

As you know, George didn't attend Harry's graduation—he said he couldn't take time away from work in the middle of the week—and I believe that really hurt her. Yes, it's a long haul to Bennington, Vermont, but he should have been there with me and the boys and you and Susan and Brooks. College graduation is a significant achievement. Thank you so much, dear sister, for augmenting our contingent. I know it meant a lot to Harry that you were there, and it meant a great deal to me as well.

Nat's unhappy too. His grades at Andover were most disappointing, so George decided he should work with a tutor this summer. At least all's well with Eddie. Being a parent doesn't become all that much easier as your children grow up—the problems simply get more complicated. Of course I'm not telling you anything you don't already know.

I was sorry that you and I never found an opportunity for some private conversation when we were together in Vermont, but of course the children were always with us. It's been so long since you and I have had a really good heart-to-heart! I look forward to that time. Meanwhile, we have our letters. I can't tell you

*how grateful I am to have such an understanding
sister, to whom I can say anything and everything. It
has always been that way with us.*

Lots of love,

Ellie

✜

The tutor, Mark Murray, spent the school year teaching
at Warden after graduating from Wesleyan University the
previous spring. He's not that much older than Nat, who
is delighted to find that Mr. Murray is patient and has a
good sense of humor.

Every day after breakfast is cleared away, Mr. Murray
and Nat spread their books out on the dining room table
and go at it. Mr. Murray conducts declensions as though
they are cheers; he speaks each word with dramatic flair:
hic, haec, hoc, huius, huius, huius. Nat can almost see pom-
poms flicking with each word. At first he was tempted to
laugh, but his teacher's earnestness impresses him.

After their first session, Nat asked his mother why Mr.
Murray isn't in the armed services. She said Mr. Murray
tried to enlist, but they wouldn't take him because of his
heart murmur.

After lunch, Nat joins his brother, his sister, and Hamilton to work in the fields. Hamilton has been with the
family for ten years as the mechanic, handyman, and
chauffeur. Now he's responsible for running the farm too,
while Harry serves as second-in-command. Their big task
this week is to bring in the hay crop.

On Wednesday, walking along the edge of one field,
Nat spots Eddie and Harry in the field beyond, raking hay
that has been cut and left to dry on the ground.

"About time you showed up," Eddie says. "We need all the help we can get. You know, this is all your fault. If you had put your nose to the grindstone at school, you wouldn't have needed a tutor, and then Father wouldn't have been in such a foul mood."

Knowing Eddie's right, Nat doesn't reply. He grabs one of the wooden rakes and takes it to the other side of the field, near Harry. He starts pulling the rake against the dead grass, which has dried enough to make this a tough job.

His sister looks up. "Hey, Nat, where's your hat and gloves?"

"Oops. Sorry. I forgot them."

"There are extras in the barn. You'd better get them, or you'll be sorry by the end of the afternoon. Did you take a salt tablet before you came out?"

"Mother made sure of that."

Once Nat dons a hat and gloves, he returns to his job. It feels good to stretch his muscles. He rakes piles of hay together into larger stacks, sinking into the repetitive motion, content not to think for a while. Sweat starts running down his back, and he breathes deeply, evenly.

"Nat, that's enough raking," Harry calls. "Bring your hay over to the truck."

Looking up, Nat is struck by how strong his sister looks. She's really working hard, bending down to insert the pitchfork under a lofted pile of dead hay, then lifting and flinging the stack high onto the loaded truck as though the process were effortless. She's like a goddess of the farm in her skimpy sleeveless shirt, cutoff dungarees, and work boots, moving with smooth, efficient grace. Her limbs are sleek and shine with sweat. Each time she hurls a forkful of hay onto the back of the truck, she rises partway up on her toes, her calves flexing into a taut curve of muscle. As Nat watches her, he admires how her thighs tighten when she reaches up with the hay.

A sudden pressure in his groin is followed by movement inside his trousers. His face flushes with shame. What is wrong with him? He's had reactions like this to beautiful women in movies and magazines Eddie has shown him, but his *sister*?

As soon as he can move without embarrassing himself, Nat heads over to the truck with a forkful of hay. Once he finishes loading the hay he raked up, he ambles over to Eddie, who has amassed a very large pile.

"I have a question for you, Brother." Nat hates to ask, but he's got to know. "Do you ever become sexually excited by the wrong people?"

Eddie stops and leans on his rake. "What do you mean, 'wrong people'?"

"People who are too old for you or maybe too young; people who might be related to you . . ."

"I'm interested in good-looking women between the ages of fifteen and forty who attract me. Why?"

"I don't know." Eddie isn't going to be of much help. "I just wondered."

He could ask Mr. Murray about his body's surprising response to his sister. Mr. Murray's pretty young, but he's more adult than Eddie. In any case, he'd better stay away from Harry for a while. Thank God she can't read his mind!

"Can I help load your hay onto the truck?" he asks Eddie.

"Sure. That'll make it go faster. I'll just keep raking."

"Thanks, Eddie." He sticks close to his brother for the rest of the afternoon.

Eventually Harry calls out, "Let's wrap it up now, boys."

Nat finally dares to look at Harry again. She's back to being his plain old sister.

✚

At the house, Harry, Eddie, and Nat find Eleanor setting the dining room table.

"Whew," she says. "You all look like you could use a cold shower."

"I'll say!" Harry nods vigorously, which makes her short black curls quiver.

"How's the work going out there?"

"It's hot and it's hard," Nat says, "but it's kind of a nice change from studying all the time."

"It's good, Mummy," Harry says. "I like this working outdoors more than I thought I would."

"I never dreamed my children would work as field hands," Eleanor observes. "But of course this is an extraordinary time, calling for extraordinary measures."

"Well, I don't know about the rest of you, but I'm filthy," Eddie says. "First dibs on the shower, Nat."

Nat thinks he'll wait to shower later, when no one's around. Perhaps then he'll be able to relieve the pressure still lurking in his groin.

Over dinner that night, Harry announces that if the weather holds, they should be done haying by the end of the week. George is at a meeting in Manhattan, but the rest of them lounge in the screened porch at the back of the house after their meal, listening to the war news.

"Bombers have finished smashing the ferry connecting Sicily to Italy. Opening up the Strait of Messina was crucial," the announcer reports.

Eleanor sits knitting wool she unraveled from an old muffler to remake into socks.

"Now the Allies have thrown a complete air umbrella over the straits of Italy and thus opened the whole stretch of the Mediterranean, from Gibraltar to the Suez, for Allied shipping of troops and matériel."

Eddie riffles the pages of a magazine.

"Earlier today, Royal Air Force fighters and bombers attacked northern France after a heavy Flying Fortress raid on the Le Mans motor works and the airplane factory there. General Eisenhower said that France is still considered a major invasion possibility."

Nat is daydreaming about taut leg muscles.

"Back at home in Washington, Congress passed a $71.5 billion appropriations bill for the War Department over the next twelve months, which includes the funds to purchase 99,740 new planes."

"That's a lot of planes," Eddie remarks.

"It certainly is," Eleanor says. "Numbers like that make me think the war won't be over anytime soon."

"I hope not," Eddie says. "I'm going to teach those Japs a lesson as soon as I can."

"*No!*" Eleanor cries. "You have no idea what you're talking about, Edward. You must promise me you will not—under any circumstances—sign up with the armed forces. Not until after you graduate from Andover, and not until we have a long discussion. You must promise me!"

Eddie says, "Don't worry. I still have another year at Andover."

Eleanor takes a deep breath. "I do understand your desire to serve your country, Edward, I really do. It's a great impulse, but please, be smart."

"All right, Mother."

"Heavy war demands have caused a critical shortage of pulp," the announcer continues. "Civilians are asked to save all forms of waste paper to help supply paper products for military needs. Waste paper is used to make overseas containers, parts for airplanes, and other weapons of war."

Nat wonders whether Eddie has in fact made a decision about enlisting. Hoping to distract his mother from her worries, he says, "I wonder what parts of an airplane are made from paper?"

Eleanor puts her knitting aside, walks over to the radio, and turns the dial to dance music. "That's enough talk about the war."

"How about some bridge, Mother?" says Harry.

"That would be lovely, dear. Boys, please bring four straight-backed chairs from the living room out here."

Nat leaves the porch with Eddie. Once they are out of earshot, Nat says, "Have you decided to enlist?"

"Yep, the day I turn eighteen."

"That's September 1. So you've definitely decided?"

"All my friends who are old enough are enlisting. We want to make the Japs pay for Pearl Harbor. I've talked to Father about it."

"But what about Mother? Aren't you going to discuss this with her?" Eddie still doesn't know their mother served in the last war.

"Father approves. That's what matters to me."

"You're going to keep this secret until September? That's really not fair to Mother."

"Father promised not to tell Mother until closer to my birthday, and you'd better promise the same!"

"Why aren't they talking to each other?" Nat asks.

Then he remembers what Eleanor told him about George's never wanting to discuss her ambulance-driving days. What else aren't they talking about? If he were to tell Eddie now about their mother's war experience, what would that do to all their relationships with each other?

"Father doesn't talk to Mother about this because she wouldn't understand," Eddie says.

Nat is pretty sure she'd understand quite well, but he won't give her secret away to Eddie. He doesn't dare.

"Are you scared?"

"Nah. It'll be an adventure. I don't understand why Mother is so opposed to my going. It's the right—the patriotic—thing to do."

Nat searches for something to say. "I have an idea that will take Mother's mind off the war. What if we put on *H.M.S. Pinafore* this summer, here at the house, with Harry and the Wymans and the Stevensons and some of our other friends? You could teach the songs, and I could play the piano. It's been ages since we mounted a play for Mother and Father."

"It *would* be fun to play Ralph Rackstraw again."

Back on the porch, Harry is unfolding the card table. Eleanor has playing cards and an official score pad in her hands.

After Nat and Eddie set the chairs around the table, Nat says, "We've decided to mount a production of *H.M.S. Pinafore*. Eddie will be Ralph Rackstraw again, just like he was at Andover this winter, and we'll get our friends to play other parts. What do you think?"

"That's a wonderful idea!" Eleanor replies. "It'll be something to look forward to. Tell me what I can do to help."

"Super!" Harry says. "I can't sing, but I can build sets—that is, if we have any spare wood and paint. I'll see what I can find in the basement. This will be fun for all of us. Great idea, Nat."

For a treat Saturday night, Eleanor and the children are going into the city to see the new hit *Oklahoma!* on Broadway. Nat dons his navy-blue suit, a shirt, his red tie, and brown oxfords, and he heads down the hall to the stairs.

As he passes by Harry's room, he is arrested by the sight of her sitting at her dressing table, carefully easing stockings up her legs.

"Come in, Nat. How do they look? This is my last pair of real silk stockings. After this, it will be rayon hose. How do they feel?" Stretching her leg out, she points her toe at him.

The silk clings very nicely to Harry's shapely limbs. Nat slides his hand along her calf.

"They feel really smooth," he says.

Then he drops his hand and backs away, his face flaming. He flees into the bathroom to dash cold water on his face. He is becoming positively obsessed with sex! He looks into the mirror and sees a gross pimple sprouting on his chin.

Ten minutes later, they all climb into the car. Eleanor takes the wheel, and Eddie joins her in front. Sitting in the backseat with Harry, Nat senses the warmth radiating from his sister's flesh. It feels good.

"You could be sent to jail for ten years," Eddie says.

Nat starts guiltily.

Eddie continues "If you're caught cheating on ra tions."

Nat says, "What are you talking about?"

"We need to make sure we discard our ration points for butter, rather than use them for something else."

Eleanor says, "Don't worry, Eddie. I give them to the hospital."

Leaning forward, Nat asks, "Did you say Father's meeting us at the theater?"

"He'll try to join us, but he doesn't know how late his meeting will run. I wouldn't hold my breath, though." She adds, "It wasn't easy to get tickets to this show." Nat can hear the disappointment in her voice.

Harry says, "Father never does anything with us any-more."

Nat nods agreement.

"He's busy with war work," Eddie answers.

"He's working to save our country and our allies," Eleanor says. "When the war is over, he'll have time for the family again." At least she hopes so.

The car suddenly lurches to one side, and a flapping sound indicates that one of the tires has gone flat. As soon as Eleanor brings the vehicle to a halt, Harry jumps out.

"I'll change the tire, Mother."

Eddie says, "This is a man's job. I'll do it—"

Harry says, "No, I want to. Give me a hand, Nat."

"All right, big sister," Eddie says. "I know you like to show you can do anything a man can do."

"That's enough, Eddie," Eleanor says. "I wish you and Harry would stop competing with each other."

Nat feels touched by Harry's choosing him to help her. He's inexperienced and not very strong, but clearly she believes in him. And he's amazed by how quickly Harry manages to change the tire. It's almost unbelievable, considering she's working in a silk dress with a swishy full skirt, heels, and hose. She has him handle the tires while she jacks the car up, loosens the lug nuts on the flat, and then tightens the nuts on the spare once it's in place. Harry gives such clear instructions that it's easy to help her.

Once they finish and stand to brush off their hands, Nat notices Harry has run one of her silk stockings.

"Harry, look—your stocking. I'm sorry."

Harry shrugs. Nat thinks she's wonderful for not caring too much about her clothing.

"Good job, Harry," Eleanor remarks. "Did Hamilton show you how to change a tire, or did you figure it out for yourself? I know you're awfully good with machines."

✚

Nat settles into his seat at the St. James Theatre as the overture begins. He watches the players in the orchestra until the green curtains draw open. Then Curly leaps over a fence on the stage and starts to sing, "Oh, What a Beautiful Mornin'."

Tears rise immediately into Nat's eyes. Surreptitiously wiping them away during the applause that follows, he turns to Eddie and whispers, "Whoa."

Eddie replies, "Are you crying? Don't let anyone see."

Nat retorts, "It's fine to cry when music moves you. I've seen Father cry at music."

"You're kidding."

"When we went to *Carmen*, I saw tears running down his face."

"I don't believe it," Eddie says.

"It's true."

Eleanor leans over and whispers, "Sh."

As he stands in the foyer during intermission, Nat studies his program. He wants to learn about Richard Rodgers and Oscar Hammerstein. He's heard of them both, but he didn't know they worked together. According to the program, *Oklahoma!* is their first collaboration.

Eddie says, "How about that Laurey? She has nice . . ." He cups his hands in front of his chest.

"I'm a leg man," Nat says, startling himself. "Ado Annie's my favorite. When she was singing 'All er Nuthin',' I was thinking that's the kind of girl I'd like to meet."

"A leg man?" Harry asks. She looks as if she's about to burst into laughter, but then she makes her face serious. "Since when did you become a 'leg man,' Nat?"

"I don't know," Nat replies.

"But you couldn't trust a girl like Ado Annie," says Eddie. "She's dangerous."

"She's exciting," Nat insists.

Harry chuckles.

Eddie says, "Not that you know what you're talking about."

"Children!" Eleanor calls. "It's time to return to our seats."

That night, as Nat is trying to get to sleep, he hears the deep-throated hum of a plane flying low over the house. He can't tell from the sound whether it's a passenger plane or a bomber or a reconnaissance plane or maybe even an enemy Messerschmitt. It gives him the creeps.

A man is shrieking with pain, and she knows she has to reach him, but she's caught in mud so deep and thick and cold that she can only crawl forward an inch at a time. Shells whistle overhead and slam into the earth, shaking the ground as profoundly as an earthquake. Machine guns firing non-stop—flashes of glaring light—thunderous roars of men and beasts—choking smoke from guns and shells. She is surrounded by chaos. Hell. This is hell. But she has to keep moving. Don't look at what must be a foot sticking out of the mud. Ignore the pounding. Keep going. She has to get to him!

Eleanor wakes in a sweat. The windows are dark. The clock on the bedside table tells her it's 3:54.

Seven

July

"AMERICAN PLANES ARE blasting Rome so constantly Pope Pius has canceled his public audiences. Along the Russian front, Russian bombers smashed German airdromes in the vicinity of Orel. In the Far East, the Allies sank thirty Japanese warships and lost ten of their own . . ."

Nat sits at the dining room table listening to the news on the radio about the Axis bombers pummeling Malta as he peruses the map of the world on the wall. He searches for Orel. Eddie has taken the job of moving the pins that represent the German, Japanese, British, and American armies across the map as they advance or retreat. The family also designated special pins for friends and relatives who are stationed abroad; Eleanor usually moves those pins when they get news. Last week, she removed Cousin Stanley's purple pin when they learned his plane was shot down over Italy.

Now as Nat hears the radio announcer talk about the American forces moving swiftly along the southern coast of Sicily, he gets up and repositions a few of the blue pins accordingly; he hopes Eddie won't be mad.

"Coming, Nat?"

Nat jumps at the sound of Harry's voice.

"The chicks get here in forty-eight hours, and we have eight hundred forty-seven hens to inoculate before then. I need all hands on deck."

Nat does not appreciate being told what to do, not even by his sister.

"Now, Nat!"

He's starting to think she's gotten awfully bossy. Being in charge of the chicken operation must have done that to her. She doesn't seem to be having much fun these days. Her tennis partner, Dennis, is somewhere in the South Pacific, and Eddie won't play with her because she always beats him, so she hasn't been playing tennis this summer. She just works all the time.

Annoyed, he pushes himself up from the table and follows Harry outside. He notices that some chicken feathers are stuck to her cutoff dungarees.

"Harry," he says. The silliness of the sight makes him smile. "Turn around. Look what's on your pants."

She stops and twists her neck to see. "What is it?"

Nat grabs one of the feathers and hands it to her. "There are a bunch of these attached to your shorts. They're kind of cute."

Harry grins. "I'll take your word for it. Ready to go?"

"Yep."

"I'll race you to the barn."

Rehearsals for the operetta take place after dinner and much of every Sunday.

Louise Smith, who lives a few houses down from the Suttons, has a lovely soprano voice; she agrees to play Josephine. Eddie is Ralph Rackstraw, and Nat's tutor, Mr. Murray, is enlisted to sing the role of Captain Corcoran, for his voice is superb and he can read music. Eleanor turns to her Wednesday-afternoon knitting circle for help recruiting singers, and she makes calls to other friends and neighbors. Between her efforts and Eddie's and Nat's, they find fifteen other young people to make up the company.

Harry isn't able to find any spare cardboard or wood or paint, so she suggests they use sheets for curtains and forget about sets. That's fine by Nat. As for costumes, Louise's mother, Emily, has an old trunk full of dress-up clothing that she offers. Since Louise's family is relatively new to the neighborhood, Eleanor barely knows Emily, but they enjoy spending several evenings together sewing for the troupe, watching the young people rehearse. Once they complete the costumes, Eleanor continues to sit in on rehearsals by herself, knitting away. Nat doesn't know why the rehearsals would interest her, but with George coming home late, he decides she probably doesn't have anything better to do.

With preparations for *H.M.S. Pinafore* under way, lyrics from the operetta begin to infiltrate everyday life. One night in the bathroom Nat and Eddie share, Eddie starts to sing, "I polished up that handle so carefullee, That now I am the Ruler of the Queen's Navee!" while he brushes his teeth. He sprays spit and toothpaste all over the mirror. Nat thinks this is so funny that Eddie sings the song every night when brushing his teeth. Rosalee wonders about the mess until Eleanor explains.

During the first week of rehearsals, Nat plays the piano while Eddie directs the singers—he is especially particular about making sure they are in tune. Everyone listens to Eddie, even Mr. Murray, who is called Mark now. Once they know their parts, Nat becomes the director, conducting the performers from the piano. He loves the feeling he gets when he raises his hands and everyone watches him intently, waiting for him to signal their entrances.

Whenever Eddie isn't singing, though, he's whispering things to Louise that get her giggling. Louise has long blonde hair and luscious-looking lips. Her legs are skinny and shapeless—but her breasts! Nat has a hard time keeping his eyes off them while she sings, and at night in bed he thinks about touching them. He's glad to find himself attracted to a female who isn't his sister or an image in an art book, but he's furious at Eddie for disrupting the singers.

During the second week of practice, Nat finally loses his temper. "Edward, will you please shut up? Your messing around with Louise makes it very difficult for the rest of us to concentrate."

Eddie gives Nat a mocking salute. "Aye, aye, sir!"

Louise says, "I'm sorry, Nat. Please don't throw me out of the show."

"Don't worry. I know who the troublemaker is. Besides, we need you." Nat blushes. "That is, we need your beautiful voice."

Eddie says, "Can we get this show on the road?"

Nat says, "Mark, take it from the top . . . 'Fair moon . . .'"

Later that night, Nat listens to the family's recording of the operetta on the phonograph again and then practices the tunes on the baby grand in the living room. He jazzes up the timing on one of the songs and improvises from there. It's so much fun! What would a real jazz musician do with this tune? He would give *anything* to hear some real live jazz. All too soon, the grandfather clock in the front hall strikes ten, and his mother comes to find him.

"It's time for bed, Nat."

"I know, Mother. It's just that I'm having such fun, I don't want to stop."

"Six a.m. will be here before you know it, and then you'll have to go feed the chickens. Come on now, Nattie. You need your sleep."

"Give me five more minutes. I promise I'll come upstairs in five minutes."

Nat turns his attention back to the piano as Eleanor walks out to the porch.

On his way down the hall, Nat passes his father's study.

His father must have just gotten home. George is saying, "I cannot believe you don't know the difference between a debit and a credit, Harriet. What did they teach you at that college, anyway?"

Nat cringes at the scorn in his father's voice. Why does he have to be so mean?

"Bennington doesn't have courses in accounting. I'd need to go to a different kind of school for a practical class like that."

Nat is impressed by Harry's calm, rational response. He steps closer to lay his ear against the door.

"It should be intuitively obvious that your expenses must balance your income or your business will get into trouble."

Nat's stomach tightens at George's sarcasm.

"I know that, Father. What I didn't know was that you wanted to make a *profit* on egg production. I thought that only charging ten cents per carton was part of our contribution to the war effort."

Good one, Harry, thinks Nat.

Eddie appears before Nat can move away from the door.

"You're such a snoop," Eddie tells him. "Why are you creeping around listening in on conversations that don't concern you?"

"No one tells me anything." After his mother mentioned driving an ambulance in the last war, Nat started to wonder what else he didn't know. "I have to snoop to find out what's going on around here."

"You better quit while you're ahead, or you might hear something you'd rather not know."

"What are you talking about?"

Eddie walks away, and Nat returns to his post.

Harry is saying, "Why are you so much harder on me?" It sounds as if she's about to cry. "Sometimes when you look at me, it seems like you wonder who I am." Now she *is* crying. "I try so hard to please you, Father, but it's never enough."

By the end of July, the chickens are producing fifty dozen eggs each day. After lunch, Nat and Rosalee, who have the most delicate touch, collect the fresh eggs in baskets. Then they take the eggs into a separate room where empty cartons are stored. They do not bother to candle the eggs, but they pick each one up and examine it for dirt. Then they use sandpaper to gently clean the shell of each before placing it into a carton.

One day Nat says, "I've been thinking: if the war's still on next summer, Eddie could be off getting trained to fight. What would we do without him on the farm?" He's actually wondering what Rosalee knows about Eddie's enlisting. Should he warn his mother about Eddie's intentions so she can change his mind before it's too late?

Rosalee shakes her head. "No sense in borrowing trouble ahead of time, Mr. Nathaniel. Let's hope the war will be over by then."

"Do you ever get mad at having to work so hard?"

"I know what we're doing will help bring the soldiers home. You and Mr. Edward seem to enjoy your preparations for *H.M.S. Pinafore*. You're going to a lot of effort."

"I'm having a great time." How much longer will he have to keep all the secrets he's been entrusted with? The secret about Eddie's enlisting is the worst. If he told their mother, could he save Eddie from going off to fight? "It's a good distraction from worries. I just hope the performance turns out well."

"I'm sure it will." She places her egg in a carton. "I think we're done with this batch. Shall I tell Mr. Edward we're ready to load the truck?" She glances at her wristwatch. "If he hurries, he should be able to get them on the afternoon freight train into the city."

That night, Nat can't sleep. After a while, he hears the sound of gravel crackling under the wheels of a vehicle rolling up the drive. Then a car door slams, and the front door opens and closes. Nat hears his father cough as he climbs the main staircase to the second floor. George coughs some more as he continues down the hall to the master bedroom at the end.

His father is around so little these days. After his mother told him his father doesn't like her talking about her war experiences, and then his father admitted he didn't fight in the Great War, Nat decided his father was jealous of his mother. He sure was making up for that now—with a vengeance.

Moving on in his mind, Nat imagines himself conducting wildly successful musicals on Broadway. Then disastrous performances of *Pinafore*. He pictures the singers forgetting their lines, singing way off-key, mixing up the lyrics. He can see this so vividly that he begins to wonder if he is prescient and the performance next week will flop.

At 6:00 a.m., when his mother appears to rouse him to feed the Leghorns, he feels so desperate for sleep that he sings, "Oh, pity, pity me—" and pulls the pillow over his head.

She chuckles. "You'd better get to bed earlier tonight, Nat."

"But Mother, we still have so much to do. I have to make sure I've memorized the accompaniment to every single song. I can't make any mistakes—piano is our only orchestration."

"I know that, Nattie, and I'm sure you'll do an excellent job. You've already memorized all the songs. Remember, I've been listening to the rehearsals."

After feeding the Leghorns, then sitting down for breakfast and two hours of tutoring, Nat goes into the library to study. He sets his Latin text on the surface in front of him, but within moments, his eyelids drift down. The bobbing of his head jerks him awake.

The next day during tutoring, he's unable to answer Mark's questions.

Mark leans back in his chair. "You were making such good progress, Nat, but now we're wasting time and money."

"We are not," Nat says. "I'm learning a lot—poetry is teaching me about cadence and rhythm and rhyme. I love that because it'll help me with my song lyrics."

"You write songs?" Mark sounds intrigued.

"Yes. And the money doesn't matter. Father has plenty. Just the other day, he said he wished he could buy a new car but there's nothing available anymore unless you're a doctor or a policeman."

In the next room, they hear Eleanor talking on the telephone. "I'm calling to invite you and your family to a performance of *H.M.S. Pinafore* that the children are putting on Saturday night at seven p.m. at our house . . . You needn't bring anything—just yourselves . . . No, Edward is still in school. He will not be enlisting anytime soon!"

Mark says, "Are you aware that you nodded off while I was talking? Am I that boring?" His grin tells Nat that he's teasing. "Are you worried about *Pinafore?*"

"Of course."

"Anything else?"

Mark sounds so sympathetic that Nat feels he can say anything. "I seem to be obsessed with sex, Mark. I think about it a lot. And I'm really confused. I'm even attracted to my sister, Harry."

"That's not so unusual, Nat. Why do you think taboos against incest were created? They wouldn't be necessary if siblings were never drawn to each other."

"Interesting." Nat starts feeling better. Maybe he's not so wicked after all! Emboldened, he goes on. "Then there's my roommate, Peter. I really enjoy him. I like living with him. He's the best friend I've ever had. But some of the guys at school say he's a homosexual. If we're such good friends, does that mean I'm really a homosexual at heart?"

"Not necessarily. Are you attracted to Peter?"

Mark's question makes Nat very uneasy. Raking his fingers through his hair, he answers, "I'm not sure. I really like him."

"Have you asked Peter whether he's attracted to you?"
Now Nat's sorry he brought the subject up. "I'd rather
not know the answer to that question. Let's not talk about
this anymore."

The day of the performance dawns—a beautifully clear
and cool Saturday morning. The house is filled with delicious smells; Rosalee has baked dozens of cookies with
sugar she hoarded over the previous weeks. Eleanor is
squeezing scores of lemons for lemonade.

The operetta will be performed in the formal living
room, where the baby grand piano dominates one corner. The boys and Harry moved the three long couches
into a semicircle around the stage area, and then set up
twenty-five folding chairs around the sides and behind the
couches. They don't know how many people to expect.
The parents and family of the performers will probably
attend, but beyond that? Harry wrote up a few flyers that
she placed in shop windows along Main Street, but there's
no way of knowing whether anyone noticed them.

At 6:00 p.m., while the members of his family are
washing up for dinner, Nat walks through the house, shaking with anticipation. What if they humiliate themselves
tonight? What if nobody comes to see them? What if a
huge crowd of people comes and it's a flop? When Nat
enters the living room, he looks at it as if for the first time:
a long room with three tall bay windows on the side and
two at the end, separated by a massive marble fireplace.
Cushioned window seats are set below the windows, and
sea-blue curtains drape partway down from the center
and loop to the sides of each window. The floor is jammed
with gray folding chairs.

He sits down at the piano. As he starts to play a quiet piece by Brahms, he's alarmed to feel his hands tremble. He continues playing through to the end, though. Someone claps. Startled, Nat looks up. It's his grandmother, standing in the doorway.

"Abba!"

She moves over to sit beside him on the piano bench. Her lime-colored gown covers his leg.

"That was a lovely rendition of the 'Pathétique' piano sonata. Your hands are just like your grandfather's."

"Grandpa Joseph had hands like mine?"

"Yes, he did. He played the piano beautifully. He could reach three notes beyond an octave."

"So can I!" Nat spreads his hands over the keys to prove it.

Why doesn't anyone in his family, aside from Abba, ever talk about the past or who takes after whom? He likes hearing about stuff like that.

The dinner bell rings.

Nat is too excited to eat, but he sits down with everyone at the dining table. They're having chipped beef on toast, and he makes several jokes about "shit on a shingle." His sister and brother groan.

At one point, George says, "A weasel scurried across the road as we were driving in tonight."

"A weasel is the last thing we need with a barnful of chickens," Harry replies.

The telephone rings, and Eleanor jumps up from the table.

Abba says to Nat, "Tell me about the cast. Who will be performing?"

Nat launches into a description of the players, but when Eleanor returns to the table, George interrupts.

"Who was that on the phone?"

"I don't know. They hung up."

When they're done eating, Nat goes to his room and changes his shirt, which is limp with sweat. He forces himself to sit down on his bed and to breathe slowly for a few minutes. The doorbell sounds, and a moment later he hears loud voices in the hall. He glances out the window and sees a stream of people walking up the long drive that snakes through the woods and up to their house.

Nat hurries down the back way to the basement, where he finds the first of the singers assembled in the makeshift greenroom, pulling on costumes and warming up their voices.

"Nat! What was I doing when I agreed to be Josephine? I'm absolutely terrified!" cries Louise when she sees him. "Remind me never to say yes to anything like this again!" Her eyes sparkle.

Somehow Louise's nervousness makes him feel calm. "What, never?"

"No, never!" she replies with the *Pinafore* response.

"What, *never?*" he sings.

Full voice, her arms outstretched, she cries, "Hardly ever!"

"I'm certain you'll set a high standard this evening," he assures her. He's amazed by how smooth he sounds.

After a few minutes, Nat shouts over the cacophony of trills and chatter, "All right, people!" Once the cast quiets down, Nat blows on the pitch pipe and starts them singing thirds up and down the scale.

Then Eleanor appears, wearing a flowered frock. "The place is packed. All the seats are filled, and folks are crowded behind the chairs. There must be a hundred people jammed into the living room. Are you ready?"

"Let's go!" Nat answers.

It is a huge crowd. The sofas and chairs are filled, and people lean against the back and side walls. Eleanor hovers near the door, where she can greet everyone who enters. The telephone rings, and she exits. His grandmother is seated on the middle couch next to his father, whose legs are spread apart, taking up a lot of room. Harry, in a green dress that looks great with her black hair, escorts their father's lawyer and his wife to that couch; Nat didn't expect them. George and Abba move close to make room. Then he spots the family doctor with his wife as well as the head of the local hospital. Even Hamilton and Rosalee are there, standing near the entrance with Eleanor. His mother must have made a lot of telephone calls to get all these people here. The realization makes him feel warm with gratitude. The crowd is comprised of older people and mothers with children—no young men.

The women are wearing light summer dresses, and the men have ties on, though most of them carry their jackets over their arms, for the heat is intense. All the windows are open, but there's no air moving through. Many of the women fan themselves with their hankies.

Although he wasn't planning to say anything to the audience, Nat surprises himself by taking center stage. Standing on quaking legs, he waits for the room to quiet down.

"Welcome. We are happy to see such a large audience." He clears his throat. "Thanks to all the performers in tonight's production. And thanks to all of you for coming. And now, we bring you Gilbert and Sullivan's *H.M.S. Pinafore* or, *The Lass That Loved a Sailor.*"

Wiping his sweaty palms on his trousers, Nat moves to the piano bench and begins to play the overture. Everything goes fine until Nat gets to the notes leading up to Buttercup's first song and Louise's little sister, Gertie, in the role of Buttercup, won't open her mouth. Nat plays through the first verse and then circles back to the beginning. He pauses dramatically and inclines his head to indicate to Gertie that she should start, but she doesn't. The audience begins to move restlessly. Nat plays the first verse of the song again and vigorously shakes his head at Gertie.

She starts to sing, "For I'm called little Buttercup—dear little Buttercup, Though I could never tell why."

She is way off-key. Nat tries not to cringe, then he muffs some notes himself.

After that, things go well for a while. Mark struts across the stage singing "I am the Captain of the *Pinafore*" with such gusto that he draws cheers as soon as he completes his song. A bit later, Nat hears some of the members of the audience singing along with "I polished up that handle so carefullee, That now I am the Ruler of the Queen's Navee."

Then Louise and Eddie come out on the stage. Louise sings, "Refrain, audacious tar," and although her voice is a little quiet, it's clear and true. Eddie sings, "Proud lady, have your way," and he sounds good too. They launch into their duet, where both of their songs intertwine and their voices blend beautifully.

Then Eddie gestures broadly, moving his arm around to touch his heart, but in the process he catches one of the sheets, which drops down from the ceiling and lands on top of him, so that he appears to be a ghost.

The children in the audience burst into laughter. Someone—is it his mother?—says, "Oh God!" Adults shush the children while Eddie continues singing. He acts as though the sheet isn't even there until the song is over. Then, turning toward Nat, he lifts the sheet and grimaces his apology. After he pulls the sheet all the way off, Eddie turns toward the audience and picks up Louise's hand. They bow together. The audience claps wildly. Nat can't believe they applauded such a fiasco. He is furious at Eddie.

The next disaster occurs when Louise forgets the words to the song about the quaking of her guilty heart. She sings "la" to the first line of notes. Thankfully, Abba starts singing the proper words in her thin, quavering voice, and then others in the audience join in, so by the refrain "Oh god of love, and god of reason, say," many of the adults in the room are singing along. People clap fervently after that song as well. Louise looks at Abba and curtsies to her in thanks.

By the end, while he bows with the cast, Nat senses that the audience has actually enjoyed the performance, despite all the terrible mistakes, for he can hear that their applause is not perfunctory. Harry and a few others are standing up and shouting, "Bravo!" Everyone is getting to their feet as the applause continues.

Then Harry shouts, "Director! Take another bow, Nat."

And then the applause grows even louder. They are honoring him. Nat bows deeply, again and again. This is fabulous. Finally he moves to the side.

He notices that George is frowning. Then his father swipes his eyes with his handkerchief. Does music always make his father cry? Nat was shocked the first time he noticed his father's tears during *Carmen* last winter.

After a few minutes, the clapping subsides, and the singers disperse into the crowd. Nat goes to stand next to the piano so he has something to lean against; he feels completely spent now. On his left, a vaguely familiar lady says to her neighbor, "Such a pleasant change! I don't believe I thought of the war once in ninety minutes!"

Someone else says to his mother, "What a comfortable home you have, Mrs. Sutton. It's lovely."

Rosalee starts circulating through the crowd with a large tray of the cookies she made plus brownies from Abba's cook. Hamilton is stationed at a table nearby pouring glasses of lemonade.

Eddie approaches Nat. "I'm sorry, Nat. I got a little carried away."

"I know you love the spotlight." Nat tries to make his statement sound like a joke, but it comes out sounding like he means what he says.

Their grandmother moves toward them. "Bravo!" she exclaims. "I'm glad to see the musical talent in our family lives on." Abigail's eyes sparkle as brightly as the diamonds around her neck. "You made an old lady weep. Of course, everyone in our family cries at good music."

"Really? No one ever said that to me before," Nat responds. "See, Eddie, I told you."

"So you did," Eddie replies.

Louise appears with a cookie in her hand. "Nat, forget what I said earlier about never doing anything like this again. It was great!"

"You sang beautifully, Louise," Nat responds.

She grins. "Thanks!" She turns toward Eddie.

"You certainly did," Eddie says. "Let me get you some lemonade."

Behind Nat, Eleanor says to someone, "Please let's not talk about the war for one night!"

Mark comes and stands so close to Nat that he can smell his tutor's breath. "That was fantastic, Nat! I had such fun."

Mark's brown eyes on him are so warm that Nat's heart expands.

"I've been thinking . . . how would you like to go into the city with me to hear some jazz? On Fifty-Second Street, there are several clubs in one block. I go there every weekend. Want to come along?"

"Are you kidding? Would I!"

"That sounds swell," says Harry, joining them. "Any chance you'd have room for a third wheel?" Her voice has a flirty tone to it.

Nat likes the idea. "What do you think, Mark?"

Mark stares at Nat. His silence is eloquent.

Harry says, "Never mind. I can tell when I'm not wanted."

"It's just—" Mark starts to say.

"Forget it," Harry tells him. Turning her back to Mark, she says, "Great job, Nat. I'm proud of you." She moves away, swishing her skirt as she goes.

"Is your sister furious with me?" Mark asks anxiously. "It's not that I don't like her, Nat, but I imagined it would be just you and me. Is that all right with you?"

"It's fine. But wait a minute—will they even let me into the club? Am I old enough?"

"That won't be a problem. Don't worry."

Eventually, all the guests take their leave. After they bid good night to the last straggler, George turns to Nat and says, "Good job, Nathaniel! I was skeptical about whether you could pull this off, but I'm proud of what you accomplished."

Nat has never felt so happy. He goes up to his room to listen to his favorite radio show, "Your Saturday Date with the Duke," while he undresses and gets into bed.

"One million Nazis have been destroyed in the weeks since they began their abortive offensive in Russia on July 5. In Sicily, the American casualties were estimated at seven thousand four hundred men. In New Guinea, thirty-three Japanese planes were shot out of the sky . . ."

A knock on his door is followed immediately by his mother, who comes and sits on his bed. "Simply super show, Nattie," she says, slurring the *s*'s. She shuts her eyes momentarily, then lifts her glass and takes another drink.

He hates it when his mother has been drinking, and it seems to him that she's had too much more times than usual this summer.

"I'm exhausted, Mother." In case she doesn't get the hint, he yawns widely.

He's terribly disappointed because he'd like to thank her for her help and share some of the highlights and low-lights of the evening with her, but he can't trust anything she would say to him now, and he knows she wouldn't remember their conversation tomorrow anyway. He's learned that the hard way.

"Good night."

"Night-night, honey." His mother rises and sways before she leans over to kiss his cheek. "Sleep tight."

This was his night of triumph, but now she has spoiled it.

He turns the dial on his radio and clings to the piece of piano music that's playing. Is it Chopin or Schumann or . . . he wonders as he drifts into sleep.

Eleanor sits alone at the piano in the empty living room after everyone else has gone to bed. She holds another glass of Canadian Club in her hand, though she knows she's already had more than she should. She sets the glass down. All evening a feeling of dread has risen in her. She sees the summer drawing to a close, Eddie's final year of school looming, and then—off to war? Gingerly she touches one key on the piano and then another, hoping the simple notes will dissipate her fear.

Suddenly it's as if bombs were exploding all around her while men who've been hit scream in agony. Who should she go to first? Everything is *so loud*. She can't think. She sticks her fingers in her ears, but that doesn't help. Maybe one more drink will drown out the roaring in her brain.

The following morning, Nat does not want to wake up. After coming into his room and pulling up the shades, his mother calls "Rise and shine!" in a cheery voice. Nat groans. He's glad his real mother is back, sober now, but his body feels like lead. When he arrives at the table, his mother, sister, and brother are eating scrambled eggs and toast.

Sitting down, Nat asks, "Where's Father?"

"I've already taken him to the train. He had to get to his office early this morning," Eleanor says.

"On Sunday?" Nat questions.

Harry and Eddie exchange glances.

Nat realizes he has an advantage now: he'll more likely gain his mother's assent if he mentions Mark's invitation when his father is absent. Taking the plate filled with food that his mother hands him, he says, "Mother, would it be all right if I go to the city with Mark next weekend? He invited me to hear some jazz with him."

"I don't see why not," his mother replies.

Harry says, "I think Mark is a fairy. There's something very limp about him."

"What do you know about fairies, Harry? I'm dismayed you've even heard the term," Eleanor says.

Eddie shakes his head. "Nat's too young. People will be drinking. Nat isn't eighteen yet."

"Mark is a perfectly respectable young man," Eleanor states. "He's a teacher at Warden, and I'm sure he'll look after Nat."

"So, I can go?"

"As long as you get home before midnight," she answers.

Nat stands and picks up his plate, silverware, and glass. Eddie follows him out to the kitchen. Rosalee isn't there yet.

Eddie says, "I agree with Harry—Mark's a faggot. What if he makes a pass at you, or something worse, once he gets you all alone in the big city? You have no idea what could happen." He steps closer and sticks his nose one inch from Nat's. "Are *you* a faggot, Nat? Is that why you spend so much time with your roommate, who's definitely queer? Is that why you want to go off with Mark?"

"No! I want to hear live jazz! That's all there is to it."

"Well, you should know that the guys at school think you're a faggot because you're always seen around campus with Peter. I don't like it. Make some other friends."

"Stop telling me what to do!" Nat cries.

In the dining room, Harriet and Eleanor sit drinking their ersatz coffee. After a moment, Eleanor observes, "Before long, it'll just be us women holding down the fort here at home."

"Don't forget Hamilton, Mummy. Sometimes you act as if he's invisible."

Eleanor grimaces. Harry's been awfully prickly this summer. "I'm sorry, Harry. I didn't mean to overlook Hamilton." She sighs. "Thank you for going easy on Nat—I know he hasn't really done his share of the farmwork these past few weeks."

"It's wonderful to see him so excited," Harry replies. "I thought he did a super job on *Pinafore*, didn't you?"

"Yes, I did. What are those boys arguing about now?"

"Sounds like Nat doesn't want Eddie to boss him around. Well, we'd better get to work," Harry concludes. "The hay won't mow itself."

Hoping for a more personal exchange, Eleanor says, "Do you have a tough day ahead of you?"

"Nothing we can't handle."

Eight

August

ON SATURDAY NIGHT after supper, Nat and Mark, dressed in sport coats and ties, board the Pennsylvania Railroad train for New York City. It's packed with people, mostly soldiers carrying duffel bags, but there are mothers with adolescent children and older couples as well. The car is loud with the chatter of folks anticipating an evening out. Nat and Mark move along the crowded aisle until they find a spot at the rear where they can stand against the wall.

Nat turns toward Mark and grins. "I'm so excited. I've never heard live jazz before!" The train starts to move. Nat widens his stance so he can keep his balance. "I listen to jazz on the radio almost every night."

"Who's your favorite jazz musician?"

"Duke Ellington."

Mark says, "The jazz you hear tonight will be very different from the Duke. It isn't like anything you've ever heard before. The new jazz, the kind Dizzy Gillespie and Charlie Parker are playing, hasn't been recorded yet." Mark smooths back his wavy brown hair. "The only people familiar with this music go to the clubs."

Nat loves the fact that he'll be part of a select few who are in the know. The train lurches around a bend. Mark quickly throws his arm around Nat's shoulders to hold him so he doesn't fall. It almost seems as though he might kiss Nat.

Is Harry right about Mark? Nat ducks out from under Mark's arm and forces a laugh. "Sorry about that," he says, taking hold of the nearest seat to steady himself. He does not want Mark touching him. "So! What club are we going to?"

Mark draws back as though he's received a blow. "We'll start at the Three Deuces. And then perhaps we'll go on to the Spotlite. We'll see."

"Tell me about Dizzy Gillespie and Charlie Parker."

"They got together earlier this year in the Earl Hines big band. Though they haven't been playing together very long, it seems they were born to make music together."

"Why do you say that?" Nat asks.

"They're so smooth, the way they improvise together, and yet they're playing at top speed. Their music sounds frenetic—it's not at all calm. It's much more reflective of the times we're living in than swing music."

"What instruments do they play?"

Mark replies, "Dizzie plays trumpet, Charlie alto saxophone. I read that Dizzie's from Philadelphia; Parker's from Kansas City. And they're young men—they're just in their twenties—but they're creating a whole new kind of jazz."

"New in what way?"

"Well, as I said, it certainly is different from swing, which seems kind of sweet and tame in comparison. Besides the frantic tempo, they use new harmonies, flatted fifths—that sort of thing."

"Flatted fifths? I know what that is, but why would they do that? Flatted fifths sound so strange."

"Their music is kind of unsettling, but I find it very exciting."

"I can't wait," Nat replies, drumming his fingers on his legs.

Finally they arrive at Penn Station. The hiss of the steam is very loud as they descend the stairs of the train and proceed along the platform, jostled by soldiers moving even more quickly than they are.

They reach the huge waiting room and stop to get their bearings. Nat looks up at the ceiling fifteen stories high. The space seems like a gigantic greenhouse with its domed ceiling created by thousands of panes of glass supported by pieces of curved steel. People rush by, hurrying in every direction, lugging large suitcases. The place reverberates with the sounds of high heels clicking along the marble floor, people calling to each other, vendors shouting their wares. This is the first time Nat has traveled with anyone but a member of his family. The realization makes him feel grown up.

They walk toward the sign for the IRT line. They pass shops emanating the greasy smell of dough fried in cheap oil and newsstands displaying newspapers and magazines, cigarettes, and chewing gum. Nat suddenly has the sensation that this experience is almost like a date.

When they arrive at the ticket booth for the subway, Mark says, "I'll buy our tokens."

Nat follows Mark through the turnstile and down another set of stairs.

Mark asks, "Have you traveled on the subway much?"

"No. When I come into town, we usually take a cab."
He walks to the edge of the platform and looks over.

Mark joins him at the edge. They see a light in the tunnel, and then the subway train pulls to a stop, grinding metal wheels on metal tracks. Mark and Nat wait until passengers disembark, and then they rush in to take two empty seats next to each other. As the train jolts into motion, Mark's leg presses against Nat's. Nat pretends not to notice. He plies Mark with questions until they reach their stop.

They climb the stairs to the street, where the sidewalk is jammed with people. At one-quarter their usual power, the streetlights are dim. All the neon lights have been shut down since German submarines were spotted offshore. But light and music spill out from several doorways. Mark points across the street to a painted sign that advertises the Three Deuces. Several sailors are standing in the doorway.

Mark leads the way inside, saying "Excuse me" as they brush by the sailors. He asks a muscular man standing inside, "What's the cover charge tonight?"

"Three bucks," the guy responds. He leans forward to see his newest customers better.

Nat's guts clutch. Is he too young to get in?

Mark hands over a ten-dollar bill, saying, "Keep the change."

Stepping aside to let them pass, the man says, "Enjoy the music."

Inside the club, the music is so loud Nat can't hear anyone speaking. The blare of a horn and the ferocious speed of the drumming remind him of the traffic outside. The room contains twenty tables pushed close together, and most of them have at least four people sitting around

them, some leaning forward, others tilting back. The tables are illuminated by candles stuck in wine bottles, and
there are spotlights on the stage, which is raised two feet
above the floor. It's small enough that the pianist with his
upright, the stand-up bass player, the drummer, and the
saxophonist completely fill the space. The audience is
mixed, but all four musicians are black.

They find a small table in the back corner, and Nat is
glad to sit down. "The way everybody's drinking—"

"What?" says Mark. "I can't hear you."

Nat shouts, "The way everybody's drinking and talking
and eating, it's like there's no tomorrow."

Leaning across the table so they're just inches apart,
Mark says loudly, "With the war on, there might not be a
tomorrow for some of these guys."

"Of course." *That was a stupid remark!* Trying to re-
deem himself, he says nonchalantly, "Let's have a beer."

"Are you sure you want one?"

"What did you expect—that I'd want a Nehi orange?"

Mark motions a waiter over, then says in his ear, "Two
beers, please."

Nat has never had a beer before, though he isn't going to tell Mark that. He starts to tap his foot, but he can't
keep up with the music. He flutters his fingers on the table along with the beat. He listens closely, trying to hear
a melody or theme or something he can recognize as a
variation on what he has already heard.

"How do you like it?"

"What?"

"The music! How do you like it?" Mark shouts.

It's so complex and intense that it's almost intoxicat-
ing. It's certainly disorienting. "This isn't anything like
swing!" Nat cries.

Mark laughs and leans back in his chair.

Nat's glad it's too loud to talk, so he can really concentrate on the music.

When the beers arrive, Nat takes a little sip. He hopes it'll help him relax.

Putting his elbows on the table, he becomes engrossed in watching the pianist. His cigarette hangs from his mouth as he rocks backward and forward over the keyboard, while his long black fingers fly across the keys with such smoothness and grace that it seems he has no bones or joints. Nat can't believe he can play like that with his eyes closed. The keyboard must be tattooed on the back of his eyelids.

"I want to be as good as that man," Nat tells Mark.

"What did you say?"

Nat yells, "*I want to play as well as that man!*"

A woman at the nearest table turns around and looks at Nat.

Mark says loudly, "That's Art Tatum. He's the best pianist on the street today."

"He's remarkable."

Art Tatum opens his eyes briefly and then closes them partway, squinting at the smoke from his cigarette, leaning into the keyboard, expressing powerful emotions.

Nat turns to Mark. "Do you ever smoke?"

"I've tried. It makes me sick."

A tall man in an elegant dark suit stumbles against their table, knocking Nat's beer to the floor.

Mark stands abruptly. "Watch where you're going!"

The man, swaying on his feet, looks helplessly at the mess on the floor. "Too bad. Can't be helped." He straightens the striped silk tie that hangs down in front of his snowy white shirt and steps sideways.

"Wait a minute. You can't walk away. Either clean up the mess you made or find someone who will." Mark isn't tall, but as he flexes his hands, he seems menacing.

Nat is afraid Mark will take a swing at the guy. He gets up quickly and puts his hand on Mark's arm.

Mark says, "The least you can do is to buy my friend another beer."

The man sticks his hand into his pocket and pulls out a bill. Throwing it on their table, he lurches away.

"Why are you so angry?" Nat asks. "It was an accident."

"I hate arrogant guys like that. He reminds me of some of my students' fathers. They treat me as if I were beneath their notice. I can't stand it."

"He *was* kind of arrogant."

"The worst thing about rich people is they think they're better than anyone else. But they're not better." He sounds bitter. "They're just luckier."

Leaning forward, Nat speaks quietly. "I know what you mean."

Mark says, "I see it at Warden all the time. Rich people believe they're in a special class by themselves, and they have no respect for anyone else. They view the rest of us as peons who are either too stupid or lazy to achieve their kind of success. I hate that attitude."

Nat says, "I don't think my family is like that. Mother says we're not rich; we're just comfortable. We don't act like that, do we? Except maybe my father."

"Don't worry, Nat. We wouldn't be here if you were like that."

"I can't imagine anything better than listening to Art Tatum with you." After the words are out of his mouth, Nat worries he might be giving Mark the wrong impression.

"You see why I come every week," Mark says, his voice warmer now. "Maybe we can get back here again next weekend."

Nat isn't ready to commit to spending another evening with Mark so soon. "I'll have to see what my parents say."

Mark says, "Speaking of parents, we'll have to head back to the station pretty soon, so we should move on to the Spotlite now."

"Would it be all right if we stay here? I'd like to keep watching Art Tatum."

"Whatever you want, Nat. Did you know Tatum is nearly blind?"

Over the next thirty minutes, Nat feels he's starting to live his real life, and this is how he wants to spend it: listening to music, making music.

Then a man and woman moving through the crowd catch his eye. The man is as tall as his father, and he's wearing a hat and a coat like his. He has his hand on the elbow of a woman who is much shorter than he, guiding her toward an empty table. As they remove their coats and hats, Nat sees it *is* his father with a woman he doesn't recognize. She has short, very dark hair, and she wears crimson lipstick.

Mark says, "Say, isn't that your father over there?"

Nat feels he might get sick. What should he do? Go over and greet him before his father spots him? What would he say? Nat has been careful not to mention this outing to his father, which hasn't been hard, given how infrequently he's home.

"Don't say anything," Nat tells Mark, sliding down in his chair.

He's terrified his father will see him. He would have to explain what he's doing there . . . and his father would have to explain his own presence as well. What is his father doing at a jazz club on a Saturday night with some woman? Nat has a very bad feeling about the whole thing.

"Let's go," Nat whispers.

Mark stands up immediately and pulls some money out of his pocket, which he leaves on the table.

Nat sidles toward the door, hugging the wall as he tries to keep Mark between himself and his father.

They get outside without George's noticing them.

While they retrace their route to Penn Station, Nat refuses to think about what has just happened. But once he and Mark are settled next to each other in the train, he faces the suspicions growing in his mind. Who *is* that woman with his father, and what are they doing in a place like that on a Saturday night, when his father should be home with his mother? Should Nat tell his mother what he's seen? Or would it be better for him *not* to say anything to Eleanor? Considering the feeling in his gut, he thinks it would be safest to pretend he hasn't seen anything at all.

"I can't imagine what Father was doing there," he says out loud.

"Do you want to talk about it?" Mark asks.

"No. Let's try another subject."

"Okay. Tell me what's different about the music you heard tonight."

Glad for the distraction, Nat thinks a moment. Finally he says, "Instead of playing one tune and then repeating it through each verse, over and over, this music is like a journey. The musicians take off down the road, and they go on and on, with side trips. But they never repeat themselves until the very end, when they return to the original tune. And then they wrap it all up into a neat package."

"That's very well put," Mark replies.

Nat's chest expands with pride. "I'd like do this again sometime."

"I agree." Mark stretches his arm out along the back of the seat behind Nat. "You'll ask about next weekend?"

✚

Only one light is on inside the house when Nat's cab drops him off near the front door. He gets into his nightclothes, brushes his teeth, and shuts the door of his bedroom tight so Sadie has to stay in. Then he turns the radio on low and climbs into bed. His thoughts about the woman with his father make him thrash for a long time. She looked gorgeous. Who is she, and what is she doing with his father? She must be someone who works at Sutton Chemicals. What is going on?

The next morning, Nat wakes early and gets dressed. He goes to feed the chickens. Then at breakfast, he finds himself telling his sister and brother all about the new jazz.

At the end of his monologue, George walks into the room while Nat is saying, "It's so much more interesting and complex than swing music."

"Swing is great music for dancing," Harry says.

"But it's bland and boring compared to the new jazz."

George interrupts, "How would you know about the new jazz, Nathaniel?"

Nat realizes he's caught himself in a trap. He tries to extricate himself. Glancing at Eleanor, he says, "I heard some last night when I went to the Three Deuces with Mark."

George blanches. "When were you there?"

His father is definitely guilty of something. Otherwise he would laugh and admit he'd been at the club last night too. Nat feels sick. He looks at Eleanor—he can't look at George.

"Actually," he lies, "we didn't stay at the Three Deuces for long. Mark wanted to see the group playing at the Spotlite."

George puffs on his cigarette and exhales noisily. "It's raucous music, isn't it—the new jazz?"

"Maybe I can come along when I get leave . . ." Eddie muses.

"*Raucous* is a good word for it," Nat quickly agrees, relieved the danger with his father has passed. But what is Eddie talking about?

George interjects, "But I don't like the idea of your going to clubs with Mark—not one bit."

"Why not?"

"He's your tutor, he's older, he's . . . I just don't like it. Not again."

"But—"

"You're too young, Nathaniel."

Furious, Nat explodes out of his chair, knocking his milk over in the process. How can his father do this to him? How can he do this to his mother? He runs out of the room.

"Nathaniel!" George shouts. "Get back here and clean up your mess!"

A few minutes later, Nat returns to the dining room. Eleanor is the only one left at the table, though the room still seems to reverberate with Nat's explosion.

Eleanor says, "Don't worry about your father. He'll calm down before long."

"I'm sorry, Mother. I'll clean up the milk right away."

"The rags are under the sink."

Once he's mopped up the milk, Nat says, "May I clear the table?"

"Thank you, Nat." Standing, she picks up her plate and silverware. "My knitting ladies are coming this morning, so I should get a wiggle on."

"Is there anything else I can do to help?"

"Once you're done clearing, you could wipe the table with a damp cloth."

"Will do. You sure look nice this morning, Mummy. Your hair is all soft and curly."

"Well, thank you, Nat. It's the humidity." She heads into the pantry.

"Let me know if there's anything else," Nat calls after her as he carefully picks up the lazy susan, with its salt and pepper shakers and sugar bowl, and moves it over to the sideboard.

Eleanor steps back into the room. "No more jazz clubs this summer. Maybe next summer when you're a little older."

Later that night before bed, while Nat is messing around on the piano trying to re-create some of the tunes Art Tatum played at the Three Deuces, he decides he wants to take up smoking. Tiptoeing into his father's study, he steals a cigarette from the open pack of Luckies left out on the desk, and then he sneaks outdoors with it. Although it makes him very dizzy, he loves the image of himself as a sophisticated young man with a cigarette drooping from his lips.

He's so stimulated by the nicotine that he doesn't know what to do with himself. Then he thinks of writing a song. He finds some staff paper in the piano bench. What was that song he started last fall about not wanting to go to Andover? How did it start? "Do I have to go to P.A.?" Is that it?

Don't even think about the dark-haired woman with Father.

No, it was more like . . . "Must I go to P.A.?" That's right.

Forget the sight of Harry's thighs pumping as she runs.

"Drag myself all that way." That's it. What about a tune? Nat hums a few notes. He turns to the piano and lets his fingers roam.

Her lipstick was as dark as blood.

Stop it, Nat! Now try the words with some notes. "Must I go to P.A.?" Try a different key. "Must I go to P.A.?" That's better. Now, the notes should descend but then rise again at the end. "Must I go to P.A.?"

Nine

September

GOLDEN LATE-SUMMER SUNLIGHT shines through the windows, glancing off the chandelier. Eleanor looks over the large mahogany dining table, decked out with a damask tablecloth and linen napkins in silver rings, candles, crystal goblets for water or milk, silver cutlery, and her favorite Limoges wedding china. She has outdone herself; even her mother-in-law seems impressed. A lovely centerpiece of flowers from the cutting garden graces the middle of the table.

This is the last time her family will all be together for a long time. Tomorrow Eddie and Nat return to school for the fall term.

Straightening her favorite green silk blouse, Eleanor raises her glass of sherry and realizes it's empty. George is engrossed in discussion with his mother, so Eleanor rises and goes over to the sideboard to make herself an old-fashioned. Usually it's George who mixes their drinks; he's already done so for his mother and himself.

Eleanor asked her children to dress up for dinner tonight, and she feels proud of how spiffy they look. Harry is wearing a raspberry-colored linen shift and a little lipstick for a change. It occurs to Eleanor that this is as pretty as Harry gets; it won't be easy for her to attract a man. Eddie and Nat wear navy-blue jackets and white pants, and all of them look healthy from their work outdoors over the summer. George, on the other hand, appears pale, his lack of color intensified by the stark white of his suit and light-blue shirt. His face is terribly worn.

The talk swirls around Eleanor as she raises her glass again. She gazes up at the oil painting on the wall beyond George, a view of the ocean and shoreline from the porch of their house at the beach. Her mother painted it years ago, and ordinarily it makes Eleanor feel peaceful. Not tonight.

Apparently George has been encouraging Eddie to enlist after he graduates from high school next June. George hasn't told her, though—neither of them has. She pieced it together after a comment Eddie let slip. She's furious with George, but she'll allow no scenes tonight. Returning to the table, she takes a big swig of her drink.

She reads the newspapers thoroughly every day . . . there's no assurance the war will end before next summer. She has imagined cutting off some of Eddie's toes so he couldn't pass the physical. Of course that's insane.

"Mummy." Harry's voice breaks through Eleanor's thoughts. "These candles are a nice touch. It's been ages since we've had candles."

Rosalee bustles in, wearing a white apron over her dress and carrying a tray of soups, which she sets on the sideboard. She places brown jellied consommé in front of Abigail and then Eleanor.

Once everyone is served, they hover over their bowls, waiting for Eleanor to pick up her spoon so they can start. Although the family has no tradition of saying grace, Eleanor feels this occasion calls for some sort of recognition.

"It'll be a long time before we'll be able to gather again, so I'd like to give thanks that we can all be here together tonight." Her voice wobbles a little.

Dipping her spoon in the consommé, she says, "Let's enjoy our soup."

George looks around the table at his offspring. "You've all worked very hard this summer." Lifting his old-fashioned, he says, "Harry has led you extraordinarily well."

Eddie cries, "To Harry!"

They all raise their glasses. "To Harry!"

Harry's blush is as red as her dress. "Why, thank you, Father! Thank you all."

Abigail leans over to whisper something to George. He laughs uproariously and then whispers something back to her. Eleanor hates how her husband behaves with his mother, teasing and flirting in ways he never does with her anymore. *What are they talking about?*

Abigail says, "Tell me about your map."

She lifts her arm to point at the wall. The soft flesh wobbles underneath her arm, and Eleanor thinks that if Abigail knew how that looks, she would never wear a sleeveless dress again, no matter how elegant.

"I assume the colored pins have significance," Abigail continues.

An unexpected vision of herself in Abigail's shoes, a solitary widow eating at the table of one of her children twenty-five years from now, rises in Eleanor's mind. She pushes her foot on the button under the table to call Rosalee.

Rosalee hurries in to clear the bowls, two at a time.

Eddie jumps up and begins to explain that the colored pins represent the British, French, Russian, and American armies, while the black pins are for the Axis. The arrows show the movement of the armies across the globe. Everyone is listening to Eddie, but Eleanor is suddenly back at Château-Thierry, where Henri died. Explosions are crashing outside the walls, making the ground shake.

Rosalee enters carrying a silver platter with a large roasted capon, which she sets in front of George. The room fills with the smell of chicken. George starts carving while Rosalee brings in dishes of vegetables, a bowl of hot buttermilk biscuits, two plates of butter, and finally the gravy boat.

George asks, "White meat or dark, Mother? What's your pleasure?"

"White, please," Abigail replies.

After placing a piece of white meat on Abigail's plate, George passes it to Harry, who adds a large spoonful of mashed potatoes.

"Not so much, Harriet!" Abigail interjects.

"Eleanor?" George says.

"Just a little piece of dark meat, please. And no potatoes, Harry."

Once everyone has their plate, Eddie starts the corn on the cob around, while Nat takes the platter of thickly sliced tomatoes. Eleanor passes the homemade mayonnaise to go with the tomatoes, and Harry takes the dish of green beans.

"Please pass the butter," Nat says.

Abigail uses the ladle to drizzle gravy over her meat and potatoes before handing the gravy boat to Nat, who pours gravy onto his plate.

"That's too much, Nat," Eleanor says.

"Everything looks very tasty," Abigail says. She stabs a piece of meat, the gravy dripping off it, with her fork. "Who made the gravy?"

Eleanor replies, "Rosalee."

George says, "Eleanor, you don't have enough to feed a fly. Take a biscuit and an ear of corn."

"This is plenty." Eleanor looks down, feeling she might cry. "I'm not very hungry."

She puts her fork and knife down as the telephone rings in the hall. Harry rises to go get it.

"Who wants more meat?" George asks. "Speak now—there's not much left. Before the war, we would have had at least two birds on the platter."

Eddie says, "I do."

Abigail turns to Eleanor. "Harriet looks a little heavy. Don't you agree?"

"Not at all," Eleanor replies as Harry returns, shaking her head.

"Who was on the phone, dear?" Eleanor asks.

"Whoever it was hung up after I answered."

Eleanor's stomach lurches. "That's happening a lot lately," she says.

George pushes his plate aside and lights a cigarette. Then he begins coughing.

"Are you all right, George?" Abigail asks.

In an effort to lighten the mood, Eleanor adds, "I hope it's not robbers checking to see whether anyone's home before they come make a heist."

"A 'heist,' Mother?" Eddie says. "It sounds like you've been listening to too many cops-and-robbers shows on the radio."

"You have no idea how I spend my time, Edward." Eleanor is shocked by how sharp she sounds. "You're always off with your friends."

"I'm sorry, Mother."

Abigail looks extremely uncomfortable. She directs her attention to George, who's drinking from his water glass. "Tell me more about this refugee group you keep asking me to support." She turns toward Eleanor. "I've written at least three checks at George's urging, and I don't know anything about what they're doing."

George says, "It's the Jewish Refugee Resettlement Organization. You'll have to attend the dinner we're holding at the Plaza Hotel next month to raise money. I'll make sure you get an invitation. The executive director will speak about the work they're doing, and I hope we'll have a couple of refugees there to talk about their struggles."

Harry asks, "Can you tell us a little about what the organization does?" Her eagerness to please her father is painfully clear to Eleanor.

"We raise money and work behind the scenes to get as many Jewish refugees out of Europe as we possibly can. I serve as a liaison between people in Washington, the shipping lines, employers with jobs for the refugees once they arrive here, and social service agencies that find housing for them."

"Do we care that much about the Jews?" Abigail asks.

George's eyebrows slant into wings as the space between them narrows. "Mother, that's bigotry!"

Abigail places her hands in her lap and stares straight ahead. Eleanor notices her mother-in-law's lower lip quiver.

George continues, "It's important to help bring talented people into the States, where they can find jobs that make use of their abilities. In the long run, this will benefit us all."

Nat turns to his father. "I saw a lady at the jazz club the other night who caught my attention, and it just occurred to me she might be Jewish."

George gazes steadily at Nat as he takes a drink from his glass. "When were you at a jazz club?"

"A week ago Saturday. I told you before—Mark and I went to the Three Deuces the weekend before last."

"What time were you there?"

"I don't know what time it was, but I definitely noticed her. She was short, she had very dark hair, and she caught my attention."

George scrutinizes Nat a bit longer. Then he shakes his head a little. "You can't tell who is Jewish by looking at them, Nathaniel. Anyway, you shouldn't categorize people by their religion."

"But you did when you talked about the refugees," Nat argues, furious.

"I was merely being descriptive," George says coldly.

Eleanor doesn't understand why George and Nat suddenly seem so angry with each other.

George glances at his watch and then rises from the table. He moves over to the large RCA console. The scratchy sound of tuning the radio fills the room as he says, "It's time for President Roosevelt's Fireside Chat." George hones the receiver in on the station, and then the president's voice comes through.

"My Fellow Americans," Roosevelt begins. "A few years ago, there was a city in our Middle West which was threatened by a destructive flood in the great river."

Eddie says, "Please pass the biscuits."

No one looks up.

"Every man, woman, and child in that city was called upon to fill sandbags in order to defend their homes against the rising waters. For many days and nights, destruction and death stared them in the face."

"Harry, would you please?"

"Oh. Sorry." Harry takes the bowl of biscuits near her father and hands it to her brother.

"As a result of the grim, determined community effort," FDR continues, "that city still stands."

George says, "Roosevelt is going to announce the new war bond campaign. We've been gearing up for it over the last month."

"Today," the president continues, "in the same kind of community effort, only very much larger, the United Nations and their peoples have kept the levees of civilization high enough to prevent the floods of aggression and barbarism and wholesale murder from engulfing us all. The flood has been raging for four years. At last we are beginning to gain on it—"

Harry interrupts, "Does this mean the tide of the war has turned, Father?"

"There are encouraging signs. Listen."

"But the waters have not yet receded enough for us to relax our sweating work with the sandbags. In this war bond campaign—"

"The president sounds really tired," Eleanor says, putting her napkin down on the table.

"Sh!" Eddie hisses.

Harry picks up her fork and stabs the last green bean remaining on her plate.

"Only a united and determined America could possibly produce on a voluntary basis so huge a sum of money as fifteen billion dollars. . . ."

At the other end of the table, Abigail's knife and fork clatter as they drop onto her plate. "That can't be right. Fifteen billion dollars? That's an enormous sum of money."

George replies, "I can assure you, we'll reach our goal for the Third War Loan drive. When a little is deducted from each paycheck every week, the numbers add up fast. The Second War Loan drive last April brought in more than eighteen million dollars in three weeks. Where else could we find the money? We just came out of the Depression, so we know all about debt and foreclosures and banks failing. Besides, there aren't any countries we could borrow the money from. It's actually a brilliant strategy."

Abigail asks, "Brilliant in what way?"

"Americans working on the home front are earning very good wages these days, but there isn't much available for them to buy right now. Investing in war bonds yields a guaranteed return, and it gives everyone a way to contribute to the national defense. That's good for morale."

Harry says, "Could you explain war bonds to me, Father? I don't think I understand."

George replies, "They're quite simple. You can purchase bonds in denominations of twenty-five dollars, fifty dollars, one hundred dollars, and so on up to ten thousand dollars—as many of them as you like. A bond with a face value of twenty-five dollars costs seventy-five percent of that amount. In ten years, when the bond matures, you will receive twenty-five dollars for the bond you paid eighteen dollars and seventy-five cents to purchase."

The president is concluding. "The harder we fight now, the more might and power we direct at the enemy now, the shorter the war will be and the smaller the sum total of sacrifice. . . . Every dollar that you invest in the Third War Loan is your personal message of defiance to our common enemies—to the ruthless militarists of Germany and Japan—and it is your personal message of faith and good cheer to our Allies and to all the men at the front. God bless them!"

"You know," George says, "it was Nat who inspired me to get involved with war bonds."

"Really?" Nat's fork stops in midair as he looks uncertainly at his father.

"Absolutely. When you told me about your success organizing the war bond contest in Junior House, I thought I could help in that arena too."

It almost seems to Eleanor as though her husband is trying to placate their youngest child.

"All right," she says. "Time for dessert. I could use some coffee. Would you like some, Abigail?" Eleanor presses her foot on the buzzer to summon Rosalee.

The door between the dining room and kitchen swings open as Rosalee enters. She starts clearing the table.

Leaning forward, Harry says, "What are the encouraging signs that the tide is turning, Father?"

"Allied troops have landed in southern Italy. This is the first time the Allies have set foot on European soil since the Dieppe Raid in August '42. Who can show us where Dieppe is?" George scans the children's faces.

Eddie moves over to the map, where he points to a pin on the northern coast of France.

The tide is turning. The last time Eleanor thought the tide had turned, when the Germans were pushed back over the Marne and the French retook Soissons, it appeared that the Allies were finally starting to win some battles after three and a half years of horrific losses. Eleanor and the other ambulance drivers and Red Cross workers had been ecstatic about the new momentum; they expected the war would come to an end any day.

But then the fighting grew even more savage. The horrors multiplied. That was when Henri was delivered to her in the field hospital in Château-Thierry, his leg gone, a hole in his side that she could fit her fist into. She didn't understand what he was doing there. Doctors weren't supposed to get wounded like soldiers—they *cared* for the wounded.

The orderlies moved Henri onto the table. He kept murmuring, "*Je regret, mon amour. Je regret.*" Eleanor put her hand inside him, trying to hold his life within his body, saying, "Please, Henri—stay with me. Don't go," over and over. But he died in minutes. Later she learned he'd been out on the battlefield applying tourniquets and sewing up wounds when a shell landed. He shouldn't have been on the battlefield!

Eleanor drains her old-fashioned. She rises and moves over to the sideboard. A bottle of bourbon stands there, along with a silver pitcher of water, an ice bucket, a small jar of Angostura bitters, and a bowl of sugar cubes. Deciding to forgo the water, she picks one cube up with the tongs, drops it into her glass, and then pours three fingers of whiskey before she adds a couple of drops of bitters. As she stirs the concoction, she turns around and sees her children watching her. She salutes them with her glass and sits back down.

George is saying, "The Russian army has cut the Bryansk-Kiev railroad line one hundred and fifty miles from Kiev. And in Berlin, the streetcar and subway system has been paralyzed by the RAF."

"That does sound hopeful," Harry says.

"And we're finally making progress in the Pacific now," George says. "General MacArthur announced that the headquarters for the Japanese army, fuel, and ammunition stores in the Madang, New Guinea, sector have all been blown up."

Eddie points to Madang on the map.

Harry said, "Eddie, are you really serious about enlisting once you graduate? You're too young to go to war."

Eleanor feels sick to her stomach. "Please, let's not go into this tonight."

Eddie resumes his seat at the table as he says, "I've been planning to enlist for a long time."

Abigail's face appears pale against the deep purple of her silk dress. "In my day, all the men we knew finished college and went into a profession. They felt no need to hurl themselves into combat. They were bent on making a mark in business or law."

For once, Eleanor is on her mother-in-law's side.

Abigail goes on. "At least if you feel you must go, Edward, make sure you sign on to be an officer."

"Stop! This conversation must not continue," Eleanor proclaims.

"Actually, Abba, I enlisted in the regular army, thinking that will stand me in good stead when I go into politics."

"*What?*" Eleanor stands so abruptly her chair crashes to the floor behind her.

Eddie smiles proudly. "I enlisted on Friday, Mother. Next year might be too late." He glances at George.

"You promised me, Edward!" cries Eleanor.

"I talked to Father. He encouraged me."

Nat is frightened to think of Eddie going off to war so soon, but at least his mother doesn't realize this news is not a surprise to him.

"That's not the same as talking to me," Eleanor shouts. "You can't go!"

Grabbing the crystal glass that holds her old-fashioned, she hurls the vessel across the room at her husband. Drops of alcohol spray the table while George ducks; the glass lands behind him with a thud.

"I won't let you go," Eleanor cries. "You're just a boy, Edward. You don't know what you're getting into. You have no idea! You think war is all about medals and glory. It's nothing like that! War is blood and gore and mud and waste. You'll die if you go. Just like Henri." Tears stream down her face, but she doesn't care.

Her children and Abigail have frozen, but George gets up from his chair. "Eleanor, take control of yourself. You should be proud of Edward for signing up to help end the war. That's the act of a real man."

"Oh, please!" Eleanor shrieks. "You're going to sacrifice your son because you never saw any action yourself? That's despicable!"

Icily, George responds, "For twenty-five years, Eleanor, you've condescended to me for not serving on the battlefield. I had to stay home. I had a duty to my father."

Eleanor glares at her husband. "You have no idea what war is like, George. None of you do." One at a time, she looks each of them in the eye as she continues. "I'm the only one in this room who has spent days and nights on the battlefield, dragging wounded soldiers back from the front so they can be loaded like cords of wood into ambulances. Have you ever had to hold a man down while his leg was being amputated?"

"This is appalling!" Abigail says. "How dare you speak like this at the dinner table. What's wrong with you, Eleanor?"

"Do you know what gangrene smells like? Have you ever seen what the inside of a head looks like when the nose and one of the eyes have been blown away? How about driving over muddy ruts and shell holes with an ambulance full of men who groan and cry at every bump? There is absolutely nothing glorious about war."

The color drains from Eddie's face. Nat starts to shake. George roars, "*That is enough!*"

"You never told us you served," Eddie whispers.

"I hoped I'd never have to! I can't bear to think about it."

Softly Harry asks, "Mummy, who's Henri?"

"He was my husband!"

Eleanor sees she has shocked them all. Eddie looks more stunned than anyone.

"Oh, damn." She grabs her spinning head with her hands. "Damn it to hell!"

George says, "Your mother doesn't like to remember that time. Like many other women, she lost her husband in the war. But unlike most, Eleanor was right there with him when he died. You can understand why she wouldn't want to dwell on it."

Eleanor says, "I have to go to bed." Leaning her hands on the table, she pushes herself to her feet. "I'm sorry for the mess," she murmurs, looking down. "It won't happen again."

Fall 1943

If I should die, think only this of me:
That there's some corner of a foreign field
That is for ever England. There shall be
In that rich earth a richer dust concealed;
A dust whom England bore, shaped, made aware,
Gave, once, her flowers to love, her ways to roam,
A body of England's, breathing English air,
Washed by the rivers, blest by suns of home.

And think, this heart, all evil shed away,
A pulse in the eternal mind, no less
Gives somewhere back the thoughts by England given;
Her sights and sounds; dreams happy as her day;
And laughter, learnt of friends; and gentleness,
In hearts at peace, under an English heaven.

—"The Soldier" by Rupert Brooke, 1915

Ten

TEN DAYS LATER, Eleanor and Eddie walk briskly though the Pennsylvania Railroad station in Rahway, New Jersey. Nat is back at school, and George and Harry had work they couldn't get out of today, so it's just Eleanor and Eddie, which suits her fine. She has some things she wants to say to Eddie.

They pass clots of families surrounding uniformed boys and couples frantically kissing goodbye. Eddie looks handsome in his new custom-fitted khaki uniform and sturdy boots, carrying a large duffel bag in his arms. But Eleanor's heart is constricted with dread. She reaches out to straighten his cap, which is cocked at a perilous angle.

Eddie jerks his head away from her.

"Your cap looks like it'll fall off any minute," she explains.

"It's fine. I still think bringing twelve pairs of woolen socks is excessive."

"You must remember: make sure to take your boots off and dry your feet whenever you can. Change socks if they are the least bit damp, and make sure you grease your toes."

"You're joking."

"This is no joke. I saw almost as many men die from trench foot as from enemy fire. Trench foot is nasty stuff. Your feet swell, they get red and blood blistered, they hurt terribly, and then they get numb. Basically, they start to rot. When I tried to take socks off men with trench foot, huge chunks of skin would tear away with the fabric. Smell your feet every day. Your nose will tell you the difference between dirty feet and rotting feet."

She grips his upper arm. "That reminds me—I bought some fancy cologne for you to put on your handkerchief. The smells you'll encounter will be unimaginable, and once you're out in the field, they'll be inescapable unless you can bury your nose in a scented handkerchief."

Eddie lifts his chin a little as he says, "I'm sorry I kept my plans a secret from you, Mother, but I knew you wouldn't approve."

"You were right about that," she replies wryly. "I don't approve." Then she smiles sadly. "And I'm sorry I kept my war experience a secret from you. Perhaps if we could have talked about the realities of war, we wouldn't be where we are today." This is the regret she can't escape.

"I wish I'd known," Eddie says. "But that's all water over the dam now. I've enjoyed our time together these last few days, especially the talking we did while we worked on that damned jigsaw puzzle."

Eleanor says, "At least I understand a little more about your reasons for going off to fight."

Eddie starts whistling as they descend a set of stairs leading to the platform where the train that will take him to basic training at Fort Dix awaits. The engine and cars remind Eleanor of a huge beast that's been running and is now steaming with the effort it takes to catch its breath before racing off again.

No longer whistling, Eddie puts his duffel bag down on the concrete floor. Eleanor hands him the bottle of eau de cologne, which he tucks into a pocket in his trousers. She moves in so close to him that her sleeve brushes the arm of his jacket. As she glances toward the train and sees soldiers starting to board, Eleanor's stomach tightens. She puts her arm around Eddie's waist and holds him close.

"The night of the blowup, what did you say about going into politics?"

"I want to get into politics eventually, which probably means I should obtain a law degree after college at Yale And of course I'll need to finish up at Andover first."

The fact that Eddie can see a future for himself gives Eleanor a shot of hope.

She turns her face into his neck so she can smell his hair. She remembers how easy his birth had been and what a happy baby he was. *This is really the end of Eddie's boyhood; when he returns, he'll be a man.*

In a quiet voice, Eddie says, "Father came to my room in the middle of the night last night. He didn't say anything. He just pulled a chair over next to my bed and picked up my hand. He held it for a long time."

That news touches something deep in Eleanor. She nods her acknowledgment of Eddie's statement, but she can't trust herself to speak.

A voice calls, "All aboard."

Taking hold of herself, Eleanor says, "I'm sorry I behaved so badly the other night. I didn't mean to frighten you. I guess I just went a little crazy thinking about you in the war." While Eleanor was horribly ashamed of herself for losing control, she's also fishing now; she hopes to hear that Eddie doesn't hate her for exploding like that.

Eddie grabs the lapels of Eleanor's coat. "It's those old-fashioneds, Mother. You shouldn't drink so much."

Does he think she's an alcoholic? She certainly doesn't want him to be distracted by worrying about her. "I'll stick to sherry, Edward." She squeezes her son as hard as she can.

He backs away. "I've got to go, Mother."

"When will I see you again?" Suddenly she feels as desperate as a girl bidding her first beau good night.

"Basic training lasts six weeks. I think I get leave at that point."

"You'd better."

Eleanor takes Eddie's arm and kisses his shaven cheek. He leans down to pick up his duffel bag and moves over to the bottom step leading into the train, while Eleanor stands watching him. He begins to wrestle his bags up the stairs.

She says, "I'll miss you. Be careful."

At the top of the steps, Eddie puts his bag down and lifts his cap. "Goodbye, Mother."

"Goodbye, Edward."

Eleanor waves and keeps waving as Edward's train begins to back out of the station. Tears spill down her cheeks. *Don't worry,* she tells herself. *He's not Henri. He will survive . . .*

He must.

It's noon when Eleanor arrives back at the farm. Rosalee has made egg salad sandwiches. Eleanor sits down across from Harriet.

"I am so tired of eggs, I can hardly stand it! I'm tempted to skip lunch today, but I'd better not." She picks up one of the sandwiches.

Harry pours milk into her glass. "I'm sorry I couldn't go to the station with you this morning, but that was the only time the vet could make it over here. Did Eddie get off all right?"

"His train was crammed full of servicemen. He managed to squeeze in, though, and away they went. I could hardly bear to say goodbye to him."

"Mother, I've wanted to talk with you, but I haven't been able to catch you by yourself. I have some questions."

Eleanor has been avoiding her daughter because she hasn't figured out how much to say to her.

"Henri." Harry places her hands on the table. "How did you meet him?"

"Oh, Harry," Eleanor says, "this is hard." Her voice breaks.

Harry tilts her head to the side. "What was he like, Mummy?"

It strikes Eleanor that Harry is now older than she was when she went off to France in 1916. Harry can probably handle the truth now.

"His name was Henri Boudsocq. He was a Frenchman—obviously. He was a surgeon, attached to the field hospital I got assigned to. He was a passionate man, a very intelligent and intense man who cared greatly about every patient he encountered."

Eleanor pauses, noticing how good it feels to be able to tell Harry about Henri after all this time. "I don't understand how he could allow himself to care so deeply about people without being overwhelmed by the slaughter. He treated everyone with respect and consideration. And he was so attractive! Anyway, we fell madly in love. We'd known each other for two months when we went to Paris and got married. I'll never forget how happy we were during that leave, our honeymoon. The time we had together was much too short, but it could not have been sweeter."

"When did he die?"

"About six weeks later."

"I had no idea."

"Your father, of course, is aware that I was married briefly to a Frenchman, but we don't discuss it much."

"I can hardly believe this. I assumed you were an ordinary mother like anyone else."

"That was my intention, Harry. I work hard to be a good wife and mother, and I think I've done pretty well. It's this war that made me come unglued."

Shaking her head from side to side, Harry says, "This is a lot to take in, Mummy. Why haven't you ever told us about your past?"

"I've tried to forget it. I taught myself never to think about what happened in France. It's much too painful. When I do remember, my nightmare comes back." Eleanor finishes chewing the bit of sandwich in her mouth and swallows forcefully.

"Nightmare?" Harry asks.

"It's the same dream, over and over. I'm so scared and helpless and so desperate—it never changes." She shakes her head, dismissing the subject. She takes a long drink from her glass of water. "But while I was driving home from the train station just now, it occurred to me that I could go back into nursing. The Red Cross is calling for more nurses' aides. Apparently, the local hospitals are desperate for help, and so are the new military hospitals opening up. I'd need some training, but I'm sure my experience would come in handy now."

Harry says, "Whoa."

"I'll have to talk this over with your father, but I can't imagine he would object so long as the farmwork gets done."

"Don't worry about the farm. Hamilton and I can take care of everything."

"What did the vet have to say?"

"Bessie has an infection in her teats. We need to give her medicine and stop milking her until she's better. I was so glad I got to watch the vet—it was fascinating! Maybe I'll become a vet after the war's won."

"I could see that, Harry, with your interest in science. You know, your father was saying the other day that you've really come into your own this summer, managing the farm." Eleanor reaches across to pat her daughter's arm "He's very proud of you, Harry."

Eleanor thinks that if she gets a job directly tied to the war, she and George will have more to talk about. The other night, he started to say something. She thought he was going to utter her name, but what came out was "M—." Then he addressed her as "my dear," which he never did before.

Has George fallen in love with someone else?

The idea drops into her mind like a bomb, and suddenly all sorts of things she hasn't allowed herself to think about make sense. Is it true? Who could her rival be? Is she beautiful? Does George really love this woman? The world that Eleanor has spent decades creating has just been completely obliterated. How could he? She's never been unfaithful. She's never loved anyone since she and George married.

But what about Henri? You never stopped loving Henri.

That's not the same.

A week later, after dinner, Eleanor and Harry sit on either side of a small coffee table in the parlor. Eleanor occupies her usual high-backed burgundy armchair while Harry has taken George's, which is just like Eleanor's, though its seat cushion is much flatter. The windows, open to let in the air, look onto the tennis court and the orchard and the woods beyond.

Eleanor fidgets with her hair, and then she lifts her glass of Canadian Club on the rocks. She feels so edgy she almost wishes she smoked. Nat sent her a long letter asking a multitude of questions about which battles she'd been involved with and what sorts of weapons the French army used and how exactly her husband died. She doesn't want to think about any of that.

She tried to concentrate on cooking this week instead of brooding about George and what he might be up to. *Might* be. She and Rosalee canned quarts of beans and tomatoes along with jars of tomato catsup. Then they turned to making applesauce—cutting the apples into quarters, cooking them to mush, and running the mess through a Foley food mill to catch the skin, seeds, and occasional worms. The work has worn her out physically but not mentally.

The only really significant thing she accomplished was to arrange a meeting with someone in the New York office of the American Red Cross next Wednesday.

With a sigh, Eleanor opens the book she's in the midst of, *The Valley of Decision*, an engrossing saga about a family in Pittsburgh over three generations.

Harry pages through the latest issue of *Life* magazine, her legs crossed, her top foot rocking nervously. "Look at this, Mother."

Harry hands the magazine across to Eleanor. On the cover, a young woman with the Women's Land Army is shown in a cornfield, her arms filled with ears of corn. She is identified as "Harvester."

"This could be a picture of you," Eleanor replies.

"I guess it could. But you know, I've had enough of the farm for today—I've got to get out of here."

Harry heads out of the room, and Eleanor hears her pick up the telephone on the table in the front hall. After a murmured conversation, she races up the stairs.

Eleanor still holds *Life* in her hand. As she starts paging through the magazine, she notices that every single ad displays a product in service to the war. Here is an ad about the Stratford pen for soldiers writing letters home. Every day she watches for the mail; thus far there's been only one letter from Eddie. Basic training sounds pretty tough. Then there's the ad for Veedol Motor Oil, which reminds the reader that "Oil Is Ammunition—Use It Wisely."

Even the ad for Campbell's Soup shows soldiers standing next to a jeep with cans of US Army Field Ration C Meat and Vegetable Stew in their hands. The headline says, "How to Pull a Hot Dinner Out of a Jeep."

Eleanor can hardly imagine.

According to the ad, "Many a soldier on field duty tucks his can of army rations under the motor hood of his jeep. When mealtime rolls around, there is his chow, warm and ready for roadside eating. Campbell Soup Company, making foods for victory."

Harry returns to the parlor wearing a skirt, blouse, and flat shoes. "I'm off to the movies with Jane and Missy. Are my lines straight?" She turns around so Eleanor can see the back of her legs, where she has painted makeup to replicate the seams of silk stockings.

"Not bad."

"Gotta go. Night, Mummy." Harry dashes out.

The telephone rings. It's George, announcing he will be on the 9:40 train from New York. The 9:40 is one of the last trains of the night. What is George really doing so late? She takes a swig of her drink and picks up *Life* again.

Turning the page, another ad catches her eye: it shows a woman trying on a new dress with help from a saleswoman.

"Why, Nancy!" the shopper says. "Whatever are you doing here in a department store with your mouth full of pins?"

Nancy replies, "Working, my dear. How could I sit at home with the Government urging women to get out and take jobs?"

"How about Charley—did he mind? You know how stuffy some men are."

Nancy says her husband is delighted.

The ad goes on: "Every woman who takes a job helps speed the day when our men will return victorious. All kinds of essential jobs are waiting to be filled. . . ."

The tagline concludes, "The More Women at Work— the Sooner We'll Win."

George had better be glad she wants to volunteer with the Red Cross.

At the station, Eleanor sits at the wheel while George climbs into the farm truck. His suit is disheveled, his face drawn and white.

"You look terrible," Eleanor says.

Yawning, he says, "It's been a long day." He leans his head back against the seat.

"Next time you come home this late, take a cab. I'm tired too, you know. I'd rather be in bed than driving you around in the middle of the night."

"As you wish," he says coolly.

He seems so distant and uncaring that Eleanor suddenly feels furious. "I'm finished with my job on the farm," she says defiantly.

"What are you talking about, Eleanor? You're doing essential war work on our farm."

"It's the end of the season, George. Harry can manage without me."

"Farming involves a lot of repetitive tasks. You should know that by now."

"Don't condescend to me! I want to do something that really makes a difference."

"Like what?"

"Like taking care of soldiers.

"Oh no you don't. Don't bring the old war back."

"It's already here. Come on, George," she pleads. "You must understand. I want to use my nursing experience to help fill the shortage caused by all the doctors and nurses who've gone abroad with the military."

"What about the cooking and washing and whatnot?"

"Rosalee can handle that. And Harry said she and Hamilton can manage the farm without me."

"You've already discussed this with Harry?"

"George, I need to do something, or I'll go crazy wor rying about Edward." *And wondering about you.* "If I go to work as a nurse's aide, perhaps it'll help bring Edward safely home to us."

"That makes no sense."

"Maybe it's not logical, but it feels right to me." She pulls the truck to a stop in front of the house.

George opens his door and gets out of the car. "I don't like this, Eleanor. I do not want my wife taking a job outside our home." He slams the door.

Eleanor sits, clenching and unclenching her hands on the steering wheel.

Eleven

October

LAST YEAR, ELEANOR hadn't even been aware of the Jewish Refugee Resettlement Organization gala because George hadn't mentioned it, but this year she knew it was coming. When it became clear that he planned to attend yet seemed reluctant about her joining him, she reminded him that it's been two years since she's been to a formal party. He attends special events so frequently that he keeps his evening clothes at his mother's apartment in the city. It isn't fair to leave her at home every time. Now she's riding the train into town alone because he left earlier to help prepare for the event.

Eleanor enjoys dressing up in a flattering gown and high heels, circulating through a crowd. Before the war, she and George attended several fund raisers each year, so she has a closet full of old dresses from which to choose for this evening. She decided on a burgundy satin.

As Eleanor hurries through Penn Station, a few men smile at her and one acknowledges her with a nod of the head. She remembers that when she was much younger, most men seemed to notice her. Back then she found their attention annoying—now she appreciates it. Tonight she knows she looks her best.

Up on the street, she waits in line for a taxicab. It's very noisy because so many people are walking by, talking, laughing, and shouting to each other. And it's hard to see because the lights in the buildings and shops are blacked out or completely extinguished. Fortunately, the dim headlights on cars, buses, and cabs provide a little illumination.

When it's Eleanor's turn, she tells the driver—a woman!—that she wants to go to the Plaza Hotel. After climbing in and arranging her skirt on the seat, she extends her arm to admire the diamond bracelet George gave her after Eddie was born; fire flickers from the facets. In addition to the bracelet, she's wearing the diamond-and-opal brooch she received after Nat's birth. She's wearing her diamonds to make up for the fact that her dress is out-of-date, but maybe she's overdone it? Feeling a little less sure of herself, Eleanor pulls out her compact and pats powder onto her shiny nose. Then she inspects her lipstick—it still looks fresh.

When the taxicab arrives at the Plaza Hotel, Eleanor is struck by how somber it appears with its windows covered by blackout curtains. This is the first time she's been to the Plaza since the start of the war. Because she associates the hotel with gaiety and light, its present reality shocks her a little.

Inside, however, she finds the same old Plaza with lights blazing from sconces along the walls and chandeliers on the ceiling, while vases of fresh chrysanthemums and other fall flowers grace the larger tables she passes on her way to the main ballroom. A sailor arm in arm with a giggling girl brushes by as Eleanor approaches a crush of people crowded together, talking loudly, holding glasses that tinkle with ice cubes. She doesn't see anyone she knows. She worms her way through the crowd, murmuring "Pardon me," toward the ballroom, where finally she spots George, welcoming people at the entrance.

He looks handsome in his evening clothes, though they seem to hang on him. How much weight has he lost in the past year? His hair glistens with brilliantine, and his face is flushed. His mother, Abigail, wearing a long silver satin gown, hovers just behind George.

Before they see her, Eleanor ducks into the ladies' room to check her appearance in a full-length mirror. Her hair, once a vivid red, looks pale and washed out in the strong lights above the mirror. She leans in to examine the hair at her temples, which is definitely turning white. It's high time she uses a rinse on her hair. At least her figure still looks attractively slim. Inspecting her face, she pinches her cheeks to put some color there, and then she goes out to join her husband and mother-in-law.

"Eleanor, here you are." George appears terribly tense.

She kisses his cheek, which is so smooth she realizes he must have shaved at Abigail's.

"I'm on duty tonight," George says, "so would you see that Mother is taken care of while I welcome our guests?" His eyes are moving around the room.

"George! You haven't said anything about how I look."

George brings his attention back to Eleanor. "You're fine."

Eleanor does not feel complimented.

Abigail steps forward. "I'm ready for a cocktail. How about an old-fashioned, Eleanor?"

Eleanor was hoping her mother-in-law would stay with George so she could circulate, but dutifully she asks, "Would you like to come with me?"

"Yes, I'll join you."

As they plunge into the crowd of beautiful women in long dresses and jewels, girls in short frocks, and many older men in black, George calls behind them, "We're seated at the head table."

Once they find the bar, Eleanor says to the handsome man standing next to her, "How are you associated with the Jewish Refugee Resettlement group?"

He glances at her and then, picking up the two drinks he ordered, he murmurs "Excuse me" and walks away.

Eleanor turns to Abigail, standing next to her. "That was rude."

"Quite," Abigail agrees. "It's bizarre that there's no one we know here. Usually with events at the Plaza, I recognize practically everyone."

"I guess this is a different crowd tonight."

After getting their drinks, Eleanor and Abigail move back from the bar, old-fashioneds in their hands, as people press around them.

Eleanor says, "George seems to be spending a lot of nights at your apartment."

"Oh?"

Looking confused, Abigail pauses for several moments. Eleanor can almost watch her mother-in-law's brain skitter around searching for a response.

Finally she says, "Well, I always feel safer when George is there." Abigail takes a sip of her drink. "What do you hear from Edward?"

"He's been given latrine duty, and he hates that, but he hasn't complained about much else."

"The training is probably good for him."

"I agree, Abigail. It's what comes afterward that scares me."

Abigail replies, "Indeed." She takes another sip before speaking. "I must say, I'm impressed by that Miriam Kaplan. She has raised an enormous amount of money for her group."

Eleanor asks, "Who's Miriam Kaplan?"

"Oh, George was singing her praises the whole way over here. And then I met the lady herself."

Eleanor can feel her lips purse. She knows that the less she says, the less Abigail will have to pounce on, so she keeps quiet, drinking and looking around the room. Then she hears Tommy Dorsey and His Orchestra strike up "Opus One" in the ballroom.

Relieved that now she has an excuse for terminating their tête-à-tête, Eleanor says, "Let's go in."

Abigail nods assent.

The crowd begins to move into the huge space. The orchestra plays on one side of the stage, behind the dance floor. Most of the room is filled with round tables set with flowers, candles, crystal, flatware, and white linen.

As people take their places, Eleanor and Abigail head to the front. George and two women hover near the steps to the stage, where four black-and-white photographs of faces, larger than life, are displayed on stands. Several people sit at the table closest to the stairs. One of them, a dapper man with dark hair and a pencil-thin mustache, stands as Eleanor and her mother-in-law approach. He is short, perhaps five foot seven, and wears an exquisitely cut black suit.

"How do you do?" he says, shaking hands first with Abigail and then with Eleanor. "I'm Jacob Kaplan. Miriam, my wife"—he gestures toward the dais—"is the founder of the Jewish Refugee Resettlement Organization."

"I'm glad to meet you," Eleanor says. "I'm Eleanor Sutton, George Sutton's wife, and this is his mother, Abigail."

"Charmed," Abigail says.

"Please, sit down," Jacob invites them.

Eleanor takes the chair to Jacob's left so she can see the stage. Abigail sits on Jacob's right.

After everyone around the table introduces themselves, Eleanor leans toward Jacob. She says, "I'm looking forward to learning about the Resettlement Organization."

And at the same time, Abigail comments, "You have a lovely wife."

"Thank you, Mrs. Sutton. I think she's lovely too." Then Jacob turns to Eleanor. "I've heard a great deal about your husband. Miriam is very grateful for all the help he is giving her."

"And you—what do *you* do while your wife is busy with the Jewish Refugee Resettlement Organization?" She emphasizes the second *you* with a playful lilt in her voice.

"I work with Broadway producers."

Eleanor says, "That must be *fascinating*, Jacob. Are you a director?"

Abigail addresses the older man on her right as Jacob says, "I'm an attorney. I help with their contracts and litigation and whatever other legal assistance they might need."

"I've never met a musical lawyer before. Are you musical?" Now she's teasing him a little.

Jacob's eyes crinkle as he laughs. "Not at all, but I enjoy music."

"I do too. You must see a lot of musicals."

Eleanor can tell Jacob has heard this comment before because his eyes wander a moment, and then he winks in the direction of the stage. Eleanor looks up. The younger woman with George, wearing a bright red dress, smiles at Jacob. That must be Miriam. Her dress is short enough to show off her shapely calves, and the styling makes Eleanor think it must be brand new. Where did she get a dress like that during wartime?

Suddenly Eleanor feels that keeping Jacob's attention is the most important thing in the world.

"It must be wonderful to be able to attend any musical you wish. Did you get to *Oklahoma!*, by chance?"

"I certainly did. It was pleasant—light but perfectly pleasant. I watch most of my clients' productions, but actually I prefer opera."

"My youngest son is very interested in music. In fact, he organized the production of a Gilbert and Sullivan musical at our home this summer. Maybe he could talk with you sometime about the musical theater business."

"I don't know whether I can help, but I'd be glad to talk with your son." Jacob smiles warmly at her.

Then the band stops playing and people quiet down. Eleanor directs her attention to the stage. George sits on a folding chair between two women. On his right, Miriam rises and steps over to the podium. She is short, so she adjusts the microphone downward. She seems larger than her actual size, though, for she oozes energy, and the red of her gown amplifies the intensity of her presence. Her red lips match her dress, and her eyes are as dark as her short, curled hair. Eleanor feels colorless by comparison.

"Welcome, everyone. We are very pleased you all came to participate in this benefit event. My name is Miriam Kaplan. I have the privilege of serving as the executive director of the Jewish Refugee Resettlement Organization. On stage with me are George Sutton, the chairman of our board, and Rachel Goldstein, the head of our department of placements. Please feel free to start eating while we make a few remarks."

Jacob passes the rolls to Eleanor, who takes one and passes them on. She picks up her salad fork.

Miriam's voice is so low that it's soothing to listen to. Eleanor glances at George. He's making notes on the papers in his lap. Miriam doesn't seem to use notes at all. Eleanor studies Miriam as she proceeds.

"Most of you know the purpose of our organization. We're working to rescue Jewish refugees who have managed to escape from Germany, Poland, Rumania, Austria, and Russia. These people have lost everything"—Miriam gestures with her arms and hands wide open—"except for what they can carry on their backs. They have nowhere to go. We find transportation to help get them to this country and then housing and employment once they arrive here. What you may not know"—Miriam pauses dramatically, bringing her arms back to her sides—"is that we have managed to help one thousand families this year alone." Hitting her fist on the podium, she says, "That's nearly five thousand people!"

The audience claps enthusiastically.

"The people we serve are desperate, but many of them are very talented as well. They are some of the most accomplished in their fields; they discerned the growing threat and made plans to leave their homelands. Unfortunately, Hitler and his army moved faster than anyone anticipated. That's why so many of our people are now in such dire straits. That's why we need your help."

Again Miriam pauses. Eleanor admires Miriam's aplomb, for she could never stand on a platform and speak to a crowd like this.

"I encourage you all to come up at some point in the evening to take a look at these photographs of some of the refugees we have saved." Miriam gestures to the right and left. Her voice softens, but it is no less intense. "You can see in their eyes the hardship they've endured but also the hope they cling to. They will move you to tears and—I hope—toward your pocketbooks. We must ensure that their hopes are not in vain." Miriam pauses. "And now, George Sutton."

She bows her head in acknowledgment of the applause, then returns to her seat. George moves to stand behind the podium. From Eleanor's perspective, he looks tall and commanding. Eleanor feels proud of how imposing he appears, but she'll never tell him so; good looks are not something to compliment a person on. As her mother always says, "Handsome is as handsome does." On the other hand, when someone (especially her children) makes an effort to look nice, Eleanor tries to acknowledge the fact.

After adjusting the microphone, George says, "I would like to express my personal gratitude for this overwhelming turnout. Thanks to each and every one of you for your generous support."

Aside from his voice, the only sound is the clicking of silverware against plates.

"The Jewish Refugee Resettlement Organization is one of the most effective groups of its kind, and I am proud to serve on its board. During the last war, for personal reasons, I was kept from serving our country—I was unable to defend the freedoms we all hold so dear." As George's voice wobbles a bit, Eleanor is touched by his unusual display of emotion.

"But now," he goes on, "I can make a real difference to the men and women fleeing for their lives from Hitler's obscene machinations. We can all make a difference. As President Roosevelt said, the war is about the Four Freedoms: freedom of expression, freedom of religion, freedom from want, and freedom from fear. So too is the work of the Jewish Refugee Resettlement Organization. Moreover, bringing Jewish refugees to the United States will help us build a stronger, smarter nation here in the years to come." George looks directly at Eleanor for a moment. He continues, "I'm happy to report that seven hundred and sixty people paid fifty dollars per plate for tonight's dinner, and others who could not attend made contributions as well. The food was donated, and the Plaza waived its usual rental charge. Thus, this gala will net"—George raises his notes—"well over forty-five thousand dollars for the coffers to support the efforts of the Jewish Refugee Resettlement Organization."

The audience claps loudly. Eleanor notices George's hand is shaking. Usually George seems comfortable in public situations.

While he keeps speaking, Eleanor watches Miriam. She sits very still, gazing intently at George.

As George takes his seat, dinner plates loaded with stuffed chicken breasts and limp vegetables are whisked onto the tables. Rachel Goldstein, an older woman with a robust figure in a tight satin gown, gets up and talks about the activities of her department. Eleanor can't concentrate on what Rachel says; she's too busy watching George and Miriam.

Finally the speeches are over. As the speakers leave the stage, George stands back so Miriam can precede him down the steps. Eleanor notices he extends his hand, ready to catch Miriam should she falter, but he does not touch her. At the bottom, he offers his arm to Rachel and escorts her to the table. Then he holds a chair out for Miriam, but she scoots around the table to greet them.

"You must be George's mother." Miriam offers her hand to Abigail. "Thank you for coming tonight." She continues around the table to Eleanor and shakes her hand. "And you must be Eleanor. Welcome. I'm glad to meet you after all this time. That's a beautiful diamond pin."

"Thank you." Up close, Eleanor can see tiny lines radiating from Miriam's eyes and a small scar above one eyebrow. "I have to say, Miriam, you ensured that everyone in the room would feel good about the work of the Jewish Refugee Resettlement Organization and their own role in supporting such an important group."

"Thank you. We need everyone to know what a big difference each contribution makes. We must do everything we can to enlist help—the needs are absolutely unimaginable."

As Miriam turns away, Eleanor looks at her smooth neck and flat stomach. George again holds out Miriam's chair as she approaches.

Once they are seated, Eleanor picks up her utensils. She stabs the chicken breast with her fork and saws through the tough meat with her knife. Her eyes return to Miriam. A number of people have gathered around her, and she stands to speak with them. Her hands flutter as she talks, and the red of her nail polish catches Eleanor's eye. *Miriam would be the sort of woman who paints her nails.* Eleanor looks at George, inserting a chunk of carrot into his mouth. After he chews and swallows, he picks up the cigarette burning in a nearby ashtray. Eating and smoking at the same time is one of his most annoying habits.

The orchestra starts to play again, and the serious tone of the evening dissipates as men and women get up to dance. Waiters stop by, taking orders for fresh cocktails.

Eleanor listens to Jacob telling Abigail about his recent trip to Hollywood.

"That explains your tan," Eleanor interrupts.

Jacob nods to Eleanor, then resumes speaking to Abigail. Eleanor looks over at her husband, sitting directly across the large round table, right next to Miriam. George is talking to his neighbor, and apparently he's making a reference to Miriam. But instead of turning her way, he simply inclines his head in Miriam's direction. As she watches, Eleanor observes that George is very careful not to look at Miriam, but she perceives an electric sense of awareness between them that gives the lie to George's avoidance.

Something *is* going on between George and Miriam. She isn't crazy.

All the breath seems to leave Eleanor's body. Miriam is vivid and gorgeous, like a flower in full bloom, whereas Eleanor knows she's past that. There is no way she can win against Miriam.

Miriam touches George's arm to get his attention. He flinches but keeps talking to his neighbor. Eventually George turns toward Miriam and addresses her shoulder. *He thinks if he doesn't look at her, he won't reveal his feelings.*

Putting her fork down, Eleanor picks up her drink and drains it. How could he betray her like this? She's given him everything: her body, mind, and heart, her attention and thoughtfulness, wonderful children, a comfortable home. She's entertained his colleagues and put up with his mother.

As her realization sinks in deeper, she begins to feel desperate. Looking wildly around the table, Eleanor wonders who else knows. She looks over at Abigail. Is her mother-in-law aware of her son's perfidy? Is this affair a secret, or is Eleanor a laughingstock?

Eleanor glances at Jacob, whose eyes are on his dessert plate. She pokes his arm. "To get back to my son . . . Do you know Rodgers or Hammerstein or anyone else of that ilk whom Nathaniel could talk to?"

"I know Oscar Hammerstein. Tell me about Nathaniel."

"Nathaniel is a talented musician. As I mentioned, this summer he organized a production of *H.M.S. Pinafore*. And he's writing songs with lyrics and music."

What am I doing seeking a favor from the husband of the woman my husband has fallen in love with?

Blindly, she rises. "Would you excuse me?" She flees for the ladies' room.

Everything she's drunk and eaten over the last twenty-four hours comes out in the toilet. She has nothing left.

As they ride the train home after the gala, George seems totally spent, sitting with his head against the seat, his eyes closed.

Fishing for a sense of George's feelings for Miriam, Eleanor says, "Miriam is so intense—it must be exhausting to work with her."

George opens his eyes. "Actually, I find it exhilarating to work with someone who has such passion and so many ideas."

"Well, she certainly is much more vibrant than I am. I know I must seem very dull compared to Miriam." Eleanor can hear that she sounds angry.

George doesn't reply.

She lifts the window shade to look out. Glimpses of the moon appear between the passing clouds. When Eleanor drops the shade, she sees that George's eyes are closed again.

She *is* angry. But she's scared too. The ground she's stood on is no longer solid.

She closes her eyes. Henri is there, leaning over the body of a boy on a stretcher to listen to his heart. He lifts his eyelids, pulls his shirt aside to examine the hole in his shoulder. He tells the soldier not to fear—his wound is not terribly deep. Then Henri looks up and greets her with a quirky raising of his eyebrows. She loved him so.

When Eleanor returned from the war, she was desperate. She didn't know what she would do, how she would live. George saved her. In all the years since then, she's counted on him. Would George leave her for Miriam? Should she confront him, or would that force him to do something stupid? Maybe if she doesn't say anything, the affair can blow over without destroying their marriage.

How can George do this to her? Did she lay the groundwork for this affair long ago? Does he love Miriam with the same sort of passion she'd felt for Henri?

The next week, Eleanor accepts a job with the Red Cross. She takes the required forty hours of nurse's aide classes and completes forty hours of supervised practice. Eleanor knows she's completely capable—it's simply a matter of showing them.

George makes it clear he isn't pleased, but after saying as much, he refuses to discuss the matter any further.

Twelve

November

AT 7:00 A.M. Monday morning, Harry drops Eleanor and George off at the Rahway train station. They stand near each other on the platform, waiting but not speaking. George reads the *New York Times* until his train pulls to a stop, then he heads toward it without a word.

"George," she calls. "Will you be home for supper?"

Turning around, he appears startled to see her. "I don't know. I'll telephone."

"See if you can figure it out by noon and let Rosalee or Harry know. I won't be home before six." Her tone is curt.

A few minutes later, she boards her own train, and once it starts to move down the tracks, she feels better. She might not know what to do about her husband, but she knows how to take care of soldiers, and she's finally on the way to her first day as a nurse's aide at Halloran General Hospital. Eleanor stretches her legs out in front of her. Her new white shoes look pristine, and her white rayon hose are smooth. She thinks her thighs still appear firm and attractive from all the work on the farm, but she wonders what the soldiers will think of her. She might be faded compared to Miriam, but the men in the ward will probably appreciate her.

When Eleanor contacted the Red Cross to volunteer her services on a full-time basis, the volunteer coordinator was thrilled. Her experience in the Great War was especially valuable; most medical personnel who'd seen action were working abroad.

Some things have changed since she'd served: giving injections of morphine and other tasks she performed years ago now require a nursing license. Eleanor doesn't want to go to school for six months, so she enrolled in the nurse's aide classes instead. Her title doesn't matter to her—if she takes really good care of the soldiers on her ward, maybe she'll earn enough credit with God to keep Eddie safe. Not that Eleanor believes in God, exactly, but working as a nurse's aide can't hurt.

The train slows to a stop at the Linden junction. Eleanor walks down the steps and out onto another platform to wait for her next train. When it arrives, she climbs aboard and takes an empty seat near the back next to a large woman whose khaki uniform shows below the buttoned front of her coat.

Will the soldiers on her ward be as rambunctious as the ones she cared for last time? Will she be able to handle their teasing, the smells of their wounds, their pain?

"Hospital station next. Get off here for Halloran Hospital," the conductor calls.

Eleanor descends from the train along with twenty other passengers, all of whom wear uniforms of one sort or another. She follows them toward a huge compound of large brick buildings, some eight stories high. She knows

Halloran is the medical hospital receiving casualties from the battlegrounds in Europe, and she expected it to be big, but she didn't imagine anything like this series of tall buildings linked by smaller ones. The size of the facility stuns her. They must treat thousands of soldiers here.

Once she finds the front desk, Eleanor asks for directions to her floor. She feels proud as she walks along the crowded hallway wearing her gray Red Cross uniform with its white collar and sleeves, three stripes on one arm for her service from '16 to '18, her Red Cross pins, and a white cap with a Red Cross emblem embroidered on the front. The smell of disinfectant and the white-coated physicians hurrying by feel very familiar. She belongs here.

At the nurses' station on the third floor, she asks for Nurse Downey. While she waits for her supervisor to appear, nurses in white uniforms and nurse's aides wearing Red Cross uniforms brush past her. An orderly pushes a man on a gurney with a bandaged head and gaunt face.

A pair of doors swings open, revealing a young woman in white with short auburn hair that curls around her cap. Moving briskly toward Eleanor, the woman says, "Mrs. Sutton?"

She is slightly plump, and freckles lightly sprinkle her pale skin. Her eyes are hazel. She looks about twenty— young enough to be Eleanor's daughter.

Putting out her hand, the nurse says, "Welcome. I'm Nurse Downey. We're glad you could come help us." Nurse Downey has a sweet smile that reveals a gap between her front teeth. "I'll show you around."

Eleanor and the nurse walk abreast down the hall. "You'll see we need all the help we can get. We have lots of amputees and paraplegics with spinal cord injuries, who require a good deal of assistance and frequent turning. That takes a fair amount of strength." Nurse Downey glances at Eleanor. "Think you can turn a man on your own?"

"Do I look that old? Of course I can turn a man. I know that paraplegic patients need to be turned every hour or two or they'll get serious bedsores."

"I don't mean to offend, Mrs. Sutton. I have trouble with the larger men myself. We wouldn't want anyone to throw her back out."

"I'm sorry, I—"

"Not to worry." Nurse Downey stops at the entrance to one of the wards, "Here they are."

Eleanor looks through the window into the long room with a wide aisle dividing two lines of sixteen beds pushed up against white walls. The cots rest on white metal frames that stand almost three feet above the brown linoleum floor. Many are occupied by men who sit up against pillows, smoking. Other men lie flat under covers sleeping, and a few appear to be reading. The room is very bright, with fluorescent lighting along the brown ceiling above each row of beds, extending the full length of the room. Eleanor is startled to see how young the patients are. Somehow she expected the patients to be her own age, as they were the last time she took care of soldiers. She's aged, but these guys aren't much older than Eddie.

As they turn away from the ward and proceed down the hall to the supply area, Eleanor says, "They look so docile. When I served before, I worked on the battlefield or very near it. I guess I came to associate nursing with lots of noise and blood."

"Makes sense," Nurse Downey replies. "Here, you won't get a lot of noise from the men until their morphine wears off. Some are better than others when it comes to handling pain." At the end of the hall, she opens a door. "This is where you'll find fresh sheets and blankets and towels. The mops and buckets are over in the corner there."

"What about dressings and salves?"

"The bandages and rubbing alcohol and everything else we need to treat the wounds are on the ward. We keep the medications up at the nurses' station."

"The quiet strikes me as gloomy."

"Saturday afternoons my cousin comes in and plays Irish jigs on his fiddle. The men seem to enjoy it. They hoot and holler after each tune."

Eleanor sees something merry in Nurse Downey's eyes, and she warms to her.

"That sounds like fun. Is there a radio we can turn on?"

"We don't have one."

"Would it be all right if I brought one in?" As soon as the words are out, Eleanor starts to worry whether she's being too pushy.

"We can try. Getting the men to agree on a station may not be easy, but we'll see how it goes." The nurse steps into the small supply room. Eleanor follows right behind. "We need to bathe the men. Please grab a stack of those towels over on that shelf. I'll bring the basin and soap and washcloths."

As she follows Nurse Downey back to the ward, Eleanor becomes aware of a feeling of fullness in her chest. It's as though her heart has expanded. Nurse Downey marches through the swinging door. When Eleanor enters, her nostrils are assailed by an odor she remembers all too well. The smell is as putrid as rotting meat, and it makes her feel sick because she knows this means gangrene is present. Automatically, she begins to breathe through her mouth.

When they get halfway down the aisle, a man in the bed to the right says, "Hey, Red, who's your pal?"

Nurse Downey stops at the foot of the bed and turns to face the man. He has no hair on his head, but he looks too youthful to be bald from natural causes.

"This is Mrs. Sutton, our new aide. Be nice to her, Sergeant Jones."

"Where'd you get those bars, Mrs. Sutton?"

"I served in France with the Red Cross during the Great War, Sergeant."

"You go on your way, Red—take care of the guys in your other wards. We're obviously in good hands here with Mrs. Sutton."

"Sergeant Jones," Nurse Downey says sternly. "As you very well know, it takes more than one person to take care of you guys. Now stop teasing. We have to get on with our work."

"Yes, ma'am, Nurse Downey!" Sergeant Jones gives her a mocking salute.

They continue to the large sink on the far wall. Nurse Downey shows Eleanor where to put the towels while she runs water into the basin. Eleanor pushes her sleeves up above her elbows.

"Watch out for Sergeant Jones," the nurse whispers. "He's a troublemaker."

Sergeant Jones reminds Eleanor of the soldiers from her past. She says, "He just wants to get a rise out of you."

"Right you are." Nurse Downey hands the basin to Eleanor and turns back to the room full of men. "We'll start here."

She moves to the bed on the left side at the front of the ward. The young man in the bed isn't very tall. As he struggles to pull himself into a sitting position, he grins at Eleanor.

"Welcome."

"I'm glad to be here. What's your name, young man?" He looks as if he isn't even twenty-one yet.

"I'm Horace Peabody—Private Horace Peabody. You have a nice smile, ma'am."

"Thank you. May I call you Horace?"

"Please do."

Nurse Downey stands behind Horace. "Unbutton your hospital gown, Private. Mrs. Sutton, you'll want to dampen and soap up one of those cloths."

While Nurse Downey supports Horace's torso, Eleanor is about to start washing his chest when she realizes she doesn't know all the places he's been wounded. "Are you okay from your waist up?"

"I'm fine everywhere except this one leg."

"All right, then," Eleanor says. Folding her washcloth into a sort of mitt, she proceeds to rub his chest and back. "I hope you don't mind my asking, but where did you get a name like Horace? I like it very much, but it's an unusual one."

"My father is a classics professor at Yale." Horace's dark-blue eyes shine with amusement.

"*That* explains it."

Horace laughs, but then he grimaces.

Eleanor says, "Pain?"

"A little."

Eleanor feels self-conscious as Nurse Downey and Horace both watch her finish cleaning and drying Horace's torso. She's never bathed a grown man before. In the Great War, she worked in the midst of the action. Everyone was filthy all the time.

"How often do you bathe the soldiers, Nurse?"

"Every day."

"Oh." Then she and Nurse Downey slide Horace down and roll him over so they can clean his butt. Once they have rolled him back, Nurse Downey says, "You take the groin; I'll take his legs."

As Eleanor gets her washrag warm and soapy, she thinks it's kind of Nurse Downey to refer to Horace's leg and stump as "legs." She washes his stomach and hips. Is Nurse Downey testing her, to see if she can handle cleaning his penis and testicles?

"Tell me what happened to you," she says, reaching for his genitalia, pretending she is washing some less sensitive part of his anatomy.

"A twenty-millimeter shell exploded a few yards away from me. That was six months ago. At first I lost my foot, but the surgeons had to cut more away because of gangrene."

She hopes this never happens to Eddie.

"I'm sorry, Horace." She rinses out her rag and wipes him off, looking this time to make sure she got all the soap.

Then Nurse Downey says, "Please lift this leg so I can change the bandage."

Eleanor moves to hold Horace's stump a few inches up from the bed while the nurse swiftly removes the bandage. The smell of gangrene intensifies.

"Don't you worry, Mrs. Sutton. Once I'm better and they fit me with a prosthetic leg, I'll be ready to go dancing." He sucks in his breath as Nurse Downey swabs his stump with a cloth dipped in alcohol.

"You like to dance?" Eleanor prompts cheerfully, though her heart breaks a little, considering his loss.

While Nurse Downey rewraps what is left of Horace's leg in a clean bandage, Horace says, "My girl and I love to dance."

Once she is done, the nurse looks up. Eleanor gently places Horace's stump back on the bed and dries his pelvis area and the rest of his leg. She pulls his covers up so they lie smoothly over his body. Horace's eyelids descend.

Eleanor dumps the dirty water from the metal basin and fills it with fresh warm water. Then she and the nurse continue down the line. By the third sponge bath, Eleanor no longer feels embarrassed by the intimacies she's foisting upon these young men.

The fourth man sits up in bed with his head bandaged so completely that she can't see his hair. His eyes are the color of melted chocolate.

"You can call me Guido, but I won't take a bath unless you join me. You got a tub in the back room for the both of us?"

Eleanor laughs. This is more like the treatment she used to receive from soldiers. The patients she cared for in the Great War were always touching her bottom or her breasts.

"Sorry, Guido. That's against the rules."

"You'd be fun to bathe with."

Nurse Downey raises her eyebrows.

"How old are you?" Eleanor asks flirtatiously.

"I'm thirty-five."

"You're old enough to know better."

"Can't blame me for trying."

Guido unbuttons his gown and leans forward. A wide bandage runs around his middle, stained with green pus. She doesn't like the smell or the look of it, but she's careful to keep her face from showing anything. Nurse Downey produces a pair of scissors from her pocket.

"Wait," Eleanor says. "Do you have any Vaseline? Vaseline will loosen that bandage so it doesn't hurt the skin when you remove it."

"I've never heard of that," says Nurse Downey.

"We did this all the time in the Great War."

"Removing the bandage with Vaseline won't pull on the flesh?"

Eleanor shakes her head.

"Let's try, then. I'll go get some."

Eleanor says, "Now, Guido, tell me what you did to incur the wrath of the Nazis."

"I made it off the ship onto the beach near Salerno. Our warships were firing at the German positions in the hill overlooking the beach, and our planes dropped bombs on them, but we were sitting ducks as we scrambled across the sand. Nazi shells chewed up the beach and any man nearby. I never saw the guy who lobbed the shell that got me. Suddenly I felt like I'd been hit in the gut with a battering ram, and at the same moment I heard a loud report and everything went dark."

Nurse Downey hands a jar of Vaseline to Eleanor. She scoops some out, places it on the palm of her hand, and folds her fingers over to add heat.

"It's important to warm it up," she explains.

After thirty seconds, she smears the Vaseline on the edges of the bandage where it is stuck to Guido's skin. Then she gently smooths the Vaseline into the gauze bandage, adding a bit more heat with the friction she applies. Then, very slowly, she raises the end of the bandage up, and it comes cleanly away.

"That's remarkable," Nurse Downey says.

Eleanor continues to pull off the bandage. She's amazed that Nurse Downey didn't know about using Vaseline on bandages. Wasn't anything learned from the last war? Then when she sees how deep and putrid the wound is, she moves behind Guido to hold him still.

"What do you think, Nurse? Am I going to die? I don't want to die." Guido's voice sounds conversational. Then he whispers, "Please don't let me die!"

"Don't be daft, man. You're getting the best medical care in the world." Nurse Downey places a thick pad of cotton on Guido's abdomen to soak up the fetid liquid. "We'll have you up and running around in no time."

She pulls a fat syringe out of her pocket; it looks something like a turkey baster. The nurse inserts the syringe into Guido and sucks out the pus.

"Mrs. Sutton, please get some saline solution so we can wash out the wound."

When Eleanor returns with the saline in her hand, blood spills from Guido's gut, and she is back in France. Guido's blood is darker than Henri's was when she threw herself across his body, trying to staunch the bright liquid shooting from the severed artery. It hadn't helped. Frantically, she'd peeled off her shirt and knotted its arms around him for a tourniquet, but that didn't help either. Then she pulled off her skirt, wadded it into her hand, and pushed down with all her strength. Then she saw the hole in his side. Nothing she did saved him. Bile rises in Eleanor's throat.

Nurse Downey says firmly, "Mrs. Sutton. We need fresh water. Please go get some. *Now.*"

After finishing up with Guido, they move on to the next man, who looks closer to Eleanor's age. Sitting against the back of his bed, his legs straight out in front of him, he puts down the thin volume he's been reading. His lined face is dominated by his long nose, which bends over like a beak. She doesn't consider him good-looking, but he strikes her as very masculine. Like Henri. She pushes her hair behind her ears. Nurse Downey leaves with the basin of dirty water.

"I'm Major John Peterson. And who are you, lovely lady?" He sticks out his hand, and as he smiles, his full lips curve beneath his well-trimmed mustache.

"Eleanor Sutton, Major Peterson."

While they shake hands, Eleanor is surprised by how wonderfully soft and warm his hands feel. She's reminded of Henri again, though Major Peterson's mouth looks wider and his lips are thinner than Henri's. She had loved Henri's lips—they'd been so plush and kissable. Dropping the major's hand, she stares at the wooden floor, trying to regain her equilibrium. Then she wonders why a commissioned officer would stay in a ward with enlisted men and noncommissioned officers. Would it be rude to ask?

Returning from the sink with fresh water, Nurse Downey says, "It takes only one person to help Major Peterson bathe, so I'll leave you to it."

"I can use my arms and hands to roll over and sit up," he explains. "I can't move my legs, but otherwise I'm absolutely fine."

"Are you paralyzed from the waist down, then?"

"No. My injury involved nerve damage. The doctors don't know whether I'll be able to walk again or not." He unbuttons his hospital gown and pulls it over his head.

"Let's hope you will."

"May I?" He reaches for the washrag. As he starts to scrub his chest, he says, "First day at Halloran?"

Eleanor moves the basin of water closer. "Yes. First day back in uniform. It feels strange yet very familiar."

"I would imagine so." He inclines his head at the stripes on her sleeve. "Looks like you've seen action before. Where did you serve, Eleanor?" He rinses the rag in the basin.

She finds his use of her first name presumptuous. "I was at the battle of Aisne-Marne in July '18. I served at Ypres and other battlegrounds before that. Where did you serve, Major Peterson?"

"Please, call me John. I fought in France in '17 and '18. If I lean forward, would you wash my back?"

"Of course." She soaps up the wet washrag, sets the basin on the floor, and leans around to his back. It is just as warm as his hands were. "Such a terrible war. What got you into it a second time?"

"I volunteered, and they took me, despite my age, because of my experience leading men."

"I see." Eleanor rinses the washrag. As she wipes his back clean, she says, "Do you want to talk about what happened?"

"A bullet from a machine gun caught me down near my tailbone. I'm lucky. If it had struck my spine, I wouldn't be alive."

"You've got a good attitude, John."

"I've managed to dodge bullets for many years, Eleanor. It was inevitable that one would get me eventually."

"Tell me about it—that is, if it doesn't make you uncomfortable." She likes the tone of his voice, devoid of the impatience and bitterness George's holds these days.

"Three months ago, we parachuted into Sicily with the Eighty-Second Airborne. It was a night drop to attack the German rear positions. Our equipment consisted only of rifles with fixed bayonets, knives, and grenades. It was so dark we couldn't tell where we'd landed, but it seemed to be a large, fairly flat plain. We advanced, and then suddenly the Germans started firing mortars at us."

"That must have been terrifying." Eleanor grabs the towel to dry his back.

"A bunch of white phosphorous shells went up. There we were, all lit up like a football field."

"What's phosphorous like?"

"When the shells explode, chunks of phosphorus fly through the air. If they land on you, they'll burn right down to the bone, so you have to pick the pieces out immediately."

"I remember the way sulfur mustard ate through clothing in the First World War."

"It's diabolical stuff."

John's back is flaky with dead skin. Eleanor says, "Hang on a minute. I'm going to get some cream."

Eleanor returns and spreads it all over his back.

John goes on. "There was a hedgerow growing visible as the sun started to rise. We made a rush for it. Then we crouched down behind the hedgerow, and I was talking with one of my men when suddenly I felt as though someone had swung a baseball bat . . . and hit me as hard as he could in my lower back."

"You don't have to say any more. It's upsetting to relive it all over again."

"It's good for me to talk." His smile is crooked now. "Sort of like lancing a boil."

"Go on, then."

"It seemed like I rose a few inches in the air, and then I crumpled onto the ground. When I came to, there was no feeling in my legs. I couldn't move them. A medic came by and pulled me into a ditch with another guy, who must have been shot in the chest—the poor kid was gurgling and crying out for his mother. I could tell he was a goner, sounding like that. Eventually I didn't hear anything more from him."

"How long ago was this?"

"About six weeks. Many of my men were seriously wounded in that battle. We had to be stabilized before they could evacuate us stateside."

Standing beside John's bed holding the basin, Eleanor says, "This water has gotten cold. Let me fetch some warm water. I'll be right back."

Eddie's been in the army for more than six weeks now, though he hasn't been sent abroad yet.

When she returns to his side, John has his hospital gown on and the blanket covering his limbs is pushed aside.

"I can wash my own legs."

"What did they do to stabilize you?"

"First it was blood transfusions and treatment for shock. Some of the guys had surgery. And then most of us needed sulfa drugs and intravenous fluids for nutrition. Several of my men are here in this ward."

"Is that why you're here instead of one of the officers' wards?"

"I believe I'm here because this is primarily a rehabilitation ward, but we also seem to get some overflow when other wards are too crowded." After John finishes bathing his legs, he says, "I can't quite reach my feet. Would you mind?"

"I'd be happy to wash your feet, John."

Eleanor pulls a chair over so she can sit at the bottom of John's bed. Taking one of his feet in her hands, she massages it briskly before she grabs the warm washrag.

"Tell me how blood transfusions are handled these days. In the last war, we had to hook nurses or aides or doctors up to the wounded so the blood could flow directly from the donor to the patient. It was always tough if the wounded soldier had a rare blood type."

When she looks up from his foot, she sees a sort of desperate hunger on John's face as he gazes at her. Her heart flips.

John clears his throat. "It's different now. They have dried human plasma the nurses reconstitute on the spot. They have every blood type, even Negroes'."

Eleanor thinks about explaining that Negroes don't have different blood types, but she doesn't want to seem critical. Instead, she concentrates on finishing with his feet. They are perfectly formed and warm but so pale they seem especially vulnerable.

"Please roll over now so I can finish the backs of your legs." He does so. "What are you reading?" She inclines her head toward the slim volume he put aside on the table.

"Rupert Brooke. It hurts my heart to read his poems, but I feel uplifted too. Do you know what *squamous* means?"

"I think it means 'scaly,' something like that." She finishes drying his legs. "Done now. You can roll back over."

Once he is on his back, John says, "I was decorated in the Great War."

She wonders why he needs to boast. Is he trying to get her to stay a little longer?

"I got a Distinguished Service Cross."

"That's nice." Eleanor feels unsettled. "Well, John, it's been a pleasure talking with you, but I need to move on to the next patient. I'll see you later."

By the end of the day, Eleanor is tired, but she feels she's been useful. When she stretches her legs out as she rides the train home, she sees that her new shoes are spattered with blood and iodine and something yellowish green.

She thinks about Nurse Downey, who thanked her for her hard work. She thinks about John too. She likes the fact that he asked her about herself and that he was confident enough to inquire what *squamous* means. George would never put a question to her that betrayed ignorance about anything.

Harry is waiting at the train station. Eleanor climbs into the truck on the passenger side.

"How was your first day at the hospital?" Harry asks. "Was it different from what you did in France?"

"Very different. In France, I worked with soldiers who'd just been wounded; the patients at Halloran were wounded weeks, even months, ago. They're fighting against infection and gangrene, blood loss, malnutrition."

Harry glances over. "Well, you can sit back and relax now."

"It's frightening to see bed after bed of men without legs or arms and to think about what their lives will be like if they do recover."

Her eyes on the road ahead, Harry says, "They have a tough row to hoe. I see more and more service banners like ours with the blue star in the front windows around town. It seems like every family has someone who's gone off to war."

"I wish the soldiers could all come home now. I'm so scared for Eddie."

"I know, Mother. Me too." Leaning over to turn up the radio, Harry says, "News time."

The announcer is saying, "The Red Army has pushed through to a point only eight miles from the Germans' last escape railway from the Crimea, trapping tens of thousands of German soldiers. The Nazis are rushing troop reinforcements to the Russian front from Italy and Norway. Allied heavy bombers smashed industries on the Italian Riviera and at Genoa. In the Pacific, Yanks invaded Bougainville Isle, the last big Jap base in the Solomon Islands."

"You know, Harry, life is never the same after war. I had nightmares for years . . . I still have one about trying to drag wounded men out of harm's way while I'm stuck in mud over my knees. I'm sinking, and then I wake up in a sweat."

"In Washington, President Roosevelt, faced with another general coal strike, seized the coal mines and ordered the miners back to work on Monday. 'Coal must be mined,' the president asserted. 'The enemy does not wait.' It is now 6:03 p.m. Eastern War Time."

"Mummy? When exactly did Henri die?"

Eleanor looks at her daughter. Her stomach seizes. She has been dreading this moment for years.

Harry says, "I'm a little confused about the timing of things. When did you come home from France? When did you marry Daddy?"

Stalling, Eleanor says, "Do you really want to get into this now, Harriet?"

"Who's my real father? Tell me the truth, Mother. I really want to know."

Eleanor stares ahead, her arms held rigidly against her sides. "George is your father."

"That's what it says on my birth certificate. But is that really true?"

Eleanor sighs, suddenly feeling sad and defeated. She turns toward Harry. "Henri was your father, but he died before you were born. I returned from France in August '18. I was a new widow, pregnant with you."

"*How could you?*" Harry cries.

Eleanor is horribly afraid that Harry is judging her a wanton woman for marrying Henri in such haste. Does Harry think her mother was thoughtless? Selfish?

"How could I what? He was the love of my life!"

"No, why didn't you ever tell me?" Harry shakes her head sadly. "Why didn't you trust me with the truth about my own father?"

"George is your father in every way that matters. He's given you everything he gave your brothers. To all intents and purposes, he *is* your father."

"Mother, do I look like Henri?"

"Your eyes are the same warm brown, and you have the same build."

Harry's eyes fill with tears.

"You're a scientist too, so you take after him in that way."

Harry pulls the truck over to the side of the road and shifts into neutral. Placing her hands over her face, she starts to cry. After a few minutes, she raises her eyes to her mother.

"This explains a lot," she says. "No wonder Father is so much harder on me than he is on the boys."

"Is he really?"

"No question," Harry asserts.

"I didn't know what to do when I found out I was pregnant with you. Your father was dead. How could I take care of us both? George came to our rescue."

Harry reaches over, takes Eleanor's hand, and gives it a squeeze.

"Your brothers do not need to know about this."

"It'll be our secret."

The two women sit in silence a moment, looking at each other. Then Harry slides over the bench seat and hugs Eleanor hard.

"You're a good mother," she says.

"I try," Eleanor replies. Now her eyes fill as she sees she should have confided in Harry years ago. "I try really hard!"

"I know you do, Mummy."

✚

Thursday night

Dear Jessica,

Harry knows now. She asked directly who her father really was, and I felt I owed her the truth. I worried so much about her before she was born, and then it was a very tough birth. As you'll remember, Harriet only weighed six pounds. I fed her constantly those first few months, waking every couple of hours round the clock. I suppose that's when I grew to feel so close to her. I'd sit and study her features, looking for traces of Henri. Eventually George told me I was doting on her too much; he said she'd be spoiled if I kept paying that much attention to her. Then Eddie came along and then Nat. I didn't want them to feel left out. I turned my attention away from my girl. I probably love Harry more deeply than anyone living, but I don't show that, and I don't believe she knows how much I love her. I wonder whether I've overcorrected too far. You've seen us together, Jessica. What do you think?

No new news from Eddie. He's still at basic training with a very tough drill instructor. I suppose they need that so they learn to obey without a moment's hesitation.

*Thank you for letting me know about Mother.
Pneumonia is no joke. I'm so glad you're nearby to
help her out when she needs something.*

*And Drew, how is he holding up? It must be
tough running a newspaper with half his staff gone
off to fight.*

Love,

Ellie

Thirteen

THE FIRE IS warm and crackly. With her feet up on an ottoman not far from the blaze, Eleanor is physically spent and quite content. It is her third week working at the hospital, and she and Harry sit drinking coffee in the library after dinner.

"What does Nat have to say, dearie?"

Picking up the letter that came for her today, Harry replies, "He writes that he can't get used to being at Andover without Eddie there. He keeps expecting to see him every time he rounds a corner."

"He didn't say that in his letter to me," Eleanor remarks.

"He doesn't want you worrying, Mummy."

"What else does he say?"

"He claims the food isn't nearly as good as it was last year."

"Maybe they lost their cook," Eleanor says.

She picks up her knitting. Since she told Harry the truth about Henri, she and her daughter have enjoyed some pleasant evenings together chatting by the fire. But she knows it's not necessarily good for a young woman Harry's age to spend so much time with her mother.

"This isn't a very fun time to grow up, is it?" Eleanor says. "I wish you could meet Horace Peabody. He's one of my patients."

She tries to visualize Horace with Harry, though it's hard to imagine, especially since Horace often speaks of his "girl."

"I wish you had some young men around to show you a good time. I don't want you to miss out on a happy life."

"Don't worry, Mummy. After the war, everything will be different."

"You could go to the movies with friends again some night. Please don't feel like you have to stay home and keep your old mother company."

"I like spending time with you. But you're right. I should go out more."

They hear the front door open and close. George calls out, "I'm home."

Eleanor says, "We're in the library."

George walks into the library, looking as if he slept in his navy-blue pinstripe suit and white shirt.

"Did you manage to get yourself fed?" Eleanor asks.

"I had dinner at the club." He sits at his desk, picking up the day's mail.

Harry stands. "Well, I'm off to bed."

During their recent evenings together, Harry told her mother that she doesn't like being around when her mother and father speak unpleasantly to each other. Eleanor is sorry, but she can't seem to temper her impatience with George these days.

Eleanor says, "Would you like a drink?"

"Yes, the usual bourbon and water. No ice."

Eleanor goes into the pantry to make his drink. Back

in the library, she finds George standing at his desk with a piece of paper drooping from his fingers. She hands him the glass.

"Thanks," he says.

She sees he's holding a letter with a Phillips Academy Andover seal at the top. George says, "This is Nathaniel's midterm report. He has been taken off academic probation."

"Good," Eleanor replies. "The tutoring must have helped."

"But his housemaster writes that he's developed a disrespectful attitude toward his teachers. He rolls his eyes and makes rude sounds."

"Nattie has such an expressive face—you can always see exactly what he's feeling."

"According to his housemaster, Nathaniel will do just about anything to get a laugh from his classmates. He's turning into a clown."

"He must feel more comfortable at Andover now."

"I'm not paying for him to become a clown. Nathaniel must behave seriously if he wants to be treated seriously. He's got to straighten up and fly right."

"What do you want me to say, George? Nat didn't want to go to Andover in the first place. Now that he's doing better academically and actually getting into the swing of things, you're still not happy."

"You're completely irrational when it comes to Nathaniel."

Eleanor doesn't think that's accurate. "Why are you so tough on him? You don't have to be this hard, George."

"Fathers need to hold their children to high standards so they'll aim high." He takes another swallow of his drink. "I don't know how else to be."

"You can encourage him. High standards are good, but encouragement is too. You need to show Nat you believe in him. That will build his confidence."

"Expectations were all I got from my father, and I didn't turn out too shabbily."

While George is certainly successful professionally, Eleanor thinks his father made him too cold and critical for his children to love him as they might.

"A little compassion for Nat would go a long way, George."

He turns and walks over to sit at his desk.

On Sunday, Eleanor makes one apple pie for her family and two for her patients at Halloran. As she enters the ward Monday morning, the first thing she sees are John's dark-blue eyes, watching for her. He winks. Blushing, she looks down at the old hatbox in her hands as she walks to Horace's bed.

Horace appears particularly pale against the white pillow. His condition is the most critical of all the patients in the ward. That's why he occupies the cot closest to the door; if necessary, he can quickly be transferred onto a gurney and moved to the operating room. She wonders if he knows this.

Placing the large hatbox next to him, she says, "Open it, Horace. I've brought you a treat."

"Really? Something for me?"

She sees a hectic, glittering look in his eyes, which concerns her greatly. "Yes, for you."

Opening the lid, he bends down and inhales. "Apple pie! How did you know? Apple's my absolute favorite." He raises his head and grins.

"What's that, Nurse Sutton?" Sergeant Jones calls from across the wide aisle that separates the two rows of beds.

"I brought in some pies. Enough for everyone to have a slice."

"This is terribly kind of you, Nurse Sutton," Horace says.

Eleanor heads toward the rear of the room. "I'll get plates and silverware." She'll also get a thermometer so she can take Horace's temperature.

As she passes John, he says, "Have they stopped rationing sugar, Eleanor?"

"No, not at all."

"How did you manage to make pies for your patients? Black market?" His tone tells her he's teasing.

"Oh no. My sons aren't at home, and the rest of us don't eat sweets." She finds herself avoiding any mention of her husband. "Anyway, I used maple syrup for sweetening instead of sugar. Tell me what you think of the result."

"How many children do you have?"

"Three. My oldest is at home running our Victory farm. Edward is away at training camp—he's the one I already told you about. My other son is coming back from school to help us prepare for Thanksgiving. It's been more than two months since I've seen him."

"I know about farms. I grew up on a rock farm in eastern Massachusetts."

"Rock farm?"

"That was all we could grow. When I was a kid, I dug for clams and sold them to help out. Clams and eggs and newspapers. I was the oldest. I had to help because my old man ran off and left my mother with five of us to raise."

"Must have been tough." John's background certainly is different from hers.

"It taught me how to work. I earned enough to buy a variety store in 1933, and with Prohibition ending, I could sell booze too. That's when I started making real money."

"Good for you." Eleanor is intrigued by John, and she admires his spunk, but she has trouble seeing how this story jibes with his love of poetry. "How did you happen upon Rupert Brooke?"

"I saw one of his poems in a magazine, and it really hit me. I read everything I can get my hands on."

"I love to read too." She continues out the rear door to retrieve plates, silverware, and a thermometer. Then she heads back to the front of the room.

Just then, a woman wearing a mink coat and hat breezes into the ward in a swirl of Chanel No. 5. She stops at Horace's bed.

"Darling," she cries as she removes her hat. "How *are* you?"

"Hello, Mater. As you can see, I'm confined to this bed." The coolness in the voice of this lovely young man surprises Eleanor.

Eleanor advances to meet Mrs. Peabody, who is pulling off long leather gloves. A large sapphire surrounded by diamonds sparkles from her left hand.

"My dear boy, I came as soon as I could." She places her hat and gloves on Horace's table.

"Mater, this is Nurse Sutton."

Mrs. Peabody barely glances at Eleanor as she murmurs, "Charmed." She doesn't seem to notice the hand Eleanor sticks out toward her after she sets the plates and silverware down on Horace's bed. Mrs. Peabody wriggles out of her fur coat while Eleanor lifts one of the pies from the hatbox and proceeds to cut it into slices.

"Darling Horace, tell me everything."

Eleanor slides a piece of pie onto two plates, adds forks, and takes them to the men in the beds closest to Horace. By the time she's finished bringing her treat to the last man in Horace's row, Mrs. Peabody has disappeared from sight.

"All right, Horace," Eleanor says, "I want to do an experiment. I'm going to take your temperature now, and then I want to take it after you've eaten some pie."

"Fine." Horace obediently opens his mouth for the thermometer.

She glances at her watch and then his bedside table. "I see you've got the radio today, and I must say I approve of your choice of station." Classical music plays quietly beside him. "It's smart to let each man have control of the radio for one day and then move it on to the next."

Horace nods up and down.

Eleanor looks at her watch again. Gently pulling the thermometer out, she reads his temperature. It is 103 degrees.

She keeps her voice calm as she asks, "May I pour you some more water, or would you like a glass of cold milk?"

"Water would be good," Horace replies.

When she returns with fresh water, she says, "What happened to your mother?"

"She's gone to find the doctor. She can't just sit—she has to push her weight around. She's always like that. I don't know why she even bothered to come."

"She's your mother, Horace. She cares about you."

"No, she doesn't. Not really."

Eleanor doesn't know how to respond. "Well, here's your dessert." She hands him the largest slice. "I'll be back in a few minutes to take your temperature again."

She distributes the pie to the men across the aisle from Horace. John is the last in that row of beds. She places a fork on the plate with his piece and carries it in both hands, aware of his eyes on her the whole way down the aisle between the beds. He receives the plate using both of his hands.

"Thank you, Eleanor. This looks delectable."

"I certainly hope so." She laughs. "I just realized—I haven't tasted it myself."

John extends the bit of apple on his fork to her. "Try some."

"No, but thanks anyway. I need to go see Nurse Downey."

She finds Nurse Downey leaning over the front desk checking a chart.

"I'm really worried about Horace," Eleanor tells her. "His temperature is one hundred and three degrees, and I don't like the look in his eyes. What are the doctors doing?"

Nurse Downey appears very serious. "Dr. Long had me start him on penicillin, this new miracle drug that fights infection, but I don't know. I'm worried too. Such a gentleman, even if he's not much older than I."

"What about his temperature? Is he getting aspirin?"

"Of course. We contacted Horace's family. We had a telegram that his mother is on her way."

"She's already here." Eleanor glances toward the ward, then back to her supervisor. "I don't think she's much comfort."

Eleanor returns to the ward. Horace has eaten only a little.

"Not hungry?" she asks.

"The bite I ate was wonderful. Can we leave the plate on my table for later?"

"Of course. Now, Horace, let's see about our little ex-periment." She pulls the thermometer out of her pocket, shakes it down, and places it in his mouth. While they wait, she says, "You have a beautiful mother."

Horace raises his eyebrows, as if to say, "So what?"

After another minute, she withdraws the thermometer. It still reads 103 degrees.

"Well, that's interesting. I thought the pie and water might bring your temperature down a bit, but they didn't. Let's see if it's time for more aspirin." She picks up his chart. "Not quite yet."

Mrs. Peabody's return is heralded by a burst of staccato taps as her high heels hurry across the linoleum floor. Horace turns toward his mother. "Look, Mater, Nurse Sutton has been taking wonderful care of me."

"Of course she has. That's her job," Mrs. Peabody tells Horace, not bothering to glance at Eleanor.

"Horace is a very special young man," Eleanor replies. "I enjoy our time together."

"Well, don't spoil him with too much attention," Mrs. Peabody declares as she sits down on Horace's bed. "It might go to his head."

Eleanor thinks Mrs. Peabody and George must have been cut from the same cloth. Putting her hands on her hips, she says, "Horace deserves all the attention we can give him. He's a fine young man, and he couldn't be spoiled even if you tried."

Horace smiles at Eleanor.

"Excuse me," Eleanor murmurs as she walks away.

The look on John's face stops her on her way down the room. She moves between his bed and the wall.

"Good job," he whispers. "I'm proud of you." He places his fingers lightly on her hand.

How long has it been since someone told her *that?*

Fourteen

NAT ARRIVES HOME late Friday night. When the taxi drops him off, George answers the front door.

"Welcome home, my boy," he says, taking Nat's suitcase.

Nat is shocked. Is his father mistaking him for Eddie?

"Well, thank you, sir. It's good to be home."

Harry comes running down the hall. "Is that you, Nattie?" She throws her arms around her brother.

Eleanor is close behind. "At last! I'm so glad you're home, Nat." She hugs him.

George starts down the hall with Nat's suitcase.

"Can I get you something to eat, Nat?" Eleanor asks.

"Would you have any cookies, Mother? I'd love some milk and cookies."

"Coming right up."

Nat turns to Harry. "What's going on?" he whispers. "Father has never greeted me like that."

"I don't know, Nat. Mother and Father have been acting very strangely with each other. It started this fall. I don't know what's going on with them. It could be that

Father's angry that Mother's working in a hospital all day. They certainly *seem* angry with each other."

Nat wonders if his mother has found out about the black-haired woman at the jazz club, but he won't say anything about that.

"How about you, Harry? Are you holding up under all the extra farmwork?"

"I'm fine, Nat. Mother is getting a lot of satisfaction from nursing. And I'm glad to help make that possible for her. What about you, Brother? Has the food gotten any better?"

"No. Everyone complains about it."

George returns from upstairs. "Your bag is in your room, Nat."

"Thank you, Father."

"See you in the morning." George heads for his study.

Eleanor returns with a plate of cookies and a glass of milk. "Why don't you take this to your room, Nat? It's awfully late. Harry says we'll need all hands on deck early tomorrow morning."

Eleanor, Nat, and Harry go to their rooms. While Eleanor changes into her nightclothes, she decides that if George comes in, she'll pretend to be asleep. She's been avoiding him. Has Harry noticed? It's much easier to think about John when George is absent. Eleanor recalls how warm John's hands are. His occasional touch makes her feel known and appreciated. She aches for more. What would it feel like if John were to put his arms around her and hold her close?

Saturday morning after Harry finishes milking the cows and Eleanor drops George off at the train station, Harry, Nat, Hamilton, Rosalee, and Eleanor gather in the dining room for breakfast.

Once they've passed the dishes of scrambled eggs and toast around the table and started eating, Harry says, "It's great to have you home, Nat."

"With the war on, Andover doesn't stop for Thanksgiving, so it's a treat to be here," Nat replies. "Thanks for getting me special permission to leave over Thanksgiving, Mother."

Eleanor says, "That was your father's doing, and it's only because we need all the hands we can get to dispatch the turkeys."

"Well, thanks anyway." After taking a bite, Nat looks up. "What do you hear from Eddie?"

"Not much," Eleanor says. "He must be very busy. After his basic training ended last week, they started him on a course of more specialized training."

"What kind of specialized training?"

"He didn't say."

"When will we see him?" Nat asks.

"I wish I knew," Eleanor replies sadly.

Nat shovels a forkful of eggs into his mouth, then looks up again. "Well, what's the news around here?"

Harry says, "Half the chickens stopped laying, so we had a guy come take them away. They aren't any good to us now."

"Can we eat them?"

"They were all scrawny and used up," Hamilton explains. "You wouldn't want to eat one of those birds."

"What about the hospital?" Nat asks Eleanor. "You haven't written in ages."

"I'm sorry, Nat. I've been so busy working, and it takes two hours each day to travel back and forth, so I'm pretty tired by the time I get home. Thank goodness Rosalee and Harry and Hamilton are taking such good care of things here."

"Do you like the patients?" Nat inquires.

"I enjoy a lot of them, but I have to be careful not to get too attached. We lose patients all the time."

"They go home to recuperate?"

Eleanor says, "Sometimes. Many die."

Harry says, "We should get cracking. We have one hundred and fifty turkeys to kill, eviscerate, pluck, chill, and deliver over the next four days. It's a big job."

"In your letter, Harry, you said that besides the hospitals, we need to take turkeys to Father's plant. Why is that?" Nat asked.

Harry explains, "Father wants to give them to his employees as a thank-you for working so hard all year. Some people are working double shifts, and others work all night."

"That's right," Eleanor says. "I think it's a good idea."

Rosalee looks around the table. "Everyone should wear their oldest work clothes," she says, "'cuz this is a messy, bloody business. And we'll need oilcloth aprons."

"They're already down at the barn," Harry says. "Rosalee, you and Hamilton will be in charge—you're the only ones who've done this before."

"That's fine, Miss Harriet."

Harry stands and starts clearing plates. "Your old tutor will be helping us today, Nat. I called Mark because we're short on hands."

"Oh no," Nat says, dropping his fork. "I haven't answered any of his letters."

"You can catch up in person," Harry replies.

Nat leaves the table and rushes upstairs. A few minutes later, he hurries down the driveway to intercept Mark on his way to the house.

Mark is walking up the hill.

Nat waits until he's a few feet away. "Hi, Mark. Your hair is longer."

"Yes, it is," he replies in a neutral tone of voice.

"Look, I'm sorry I didn't write you this fall," Nat says. "School is so hard, but I'm actually starting to get in the groove."

"That's good." Mark doesn't sound nearly as friendly as he did last summer.

"I thought you might like to hear that. Your tutoring really paid off." Nat hopes Mark will warm up at least a little.

Mark puts his hands in his pockets, and they stroll toward the barn.

Once the crew is assembled, Hamilton assigns roles. Rosalee catches the first turkey, and Nat grabs the feet while it flaps and squawks and struggles to get free. Mark holds the turkey's neck to the chopping block. Hamilton swiftly whacks the head off with an ax, then hands the carcass to Harry, who slits open the chest cavity to remove the innards. She scoops the guts out with her hands and drops them into a pail. Then Eleanor hangs the carcass upside down from a rafter so the blood can run out. The entire process takes about four minutes.

"Mother," Nat calls. "It stinks! I'm going to puke."

Mark looks over.

Eleanor says, "Try breathing through your mouth. You won't smell as much that way."

Nat's jaw drops open a little, and he breathes through his teeth. After inhaling a few times, he says, "You're right. That's better."

"I learned that on the battlefield," Eleanor says. "Now think about something else."

Mark starts to sing, "I am the Captain of the *Pinafore;* and a right good captain too!"

Does Mark forgive him? Smiling at Mark, Nat replies in song, "You're very, very good."

Mark responds, "And be it understood, I command a right good crew."

Between the two of them, they sing their way through the entire operetta. The louder the turkeys squawk, the louder the boys sing. Eleanor and Harry join in on the choruses, though Harry sings off-key. By the end of the morning, they have killed half the turkeys.

After lunch, Hamilton and Harry plunge the turkey carcasses into boiling water to loosen their feathers. Then Rosalee, Eleanor, Nat, and Mark pull all the feathers out of the tough skin. Once plucked, the turkeys are again hung from the rafters by their feet. At the end of the day, the floor is hosed down and covered with fresh straw.

Sunday night, Harry and Nat sprawl in chairs around a card table playing gin rummy. George is in his study. Sadie sleeps next to Nat's chair; he ruffles her fur. Eleanor sits nearby, knitting.

The soft music on the radio ends, and the news announcer comes on. Eleanor cranks up the volume.

"Earlier this week, the Poles tried, condemned, and executed Nazi leader Hugo Dietz in Warsaw. On Tuesday, large formations of US Eighth Air Force Flying Fortresses and Liberators surprised the Germans by blasting molybdenum mines and a power station in southern Norway, one of Hitler's northernmost outposts. And in the Mediterranean, the RAF is dropping Greek paratroopers on the island of Samos to reinforce endangered Dodecanese positions. In the Pacific theater, the Americans are pounding the Marshall and Gilbert Islands with persistent aerial attacks."

Lifting her head from scrutinizing her hand, Harry says, "Wow. We're really massacring them. Sort of like the turkeys."

Nat thinks Harry must be exhausted to make a joke like this.

Eleanor stops knitting. "These headlines translate into death and permanent injury for hundreds and thousands of young men. You have no idea how horrible bombing is . . . You're there on the ground seeing people get hit and wondering if you're next. Sometimes I think this war isn't real for either one of you."

"How can it be real for us?" Harry argues. "We've never been in a war. It seems like that's all you can think about. What about us, Mother? We're here!"

Nat exchanges glances with his sister.

"I thought we've been having some good times together, Harry," says Eleanor, taken aback.

"You're just so distracted!"

Eleanor sighs. Ever since learning about her real father, Harry has stuck unusually close to her mother. Eleanor can't imagine what more her daughter wants from her now.

"Many of the plans required to assemble the military organization necessary to bring the war to its grand conclusion in Europe are now complete. The American chief of staff, General George C. Marshall, will be made commander in London, and some military leaders believe that General Dwight D. Eisenhower will be brought back to Washington to take over Marshall's duties as soon as Rome is captured."

"Maybe Eddie will be home for Christmas," Harry says conciliatorily.

"I hope so," Eleanor says. "He thinks he'll get leave once he has completed this new round of training."

She gets up from her chair. Earlier that week, she'd read the poem "Attack" by Siegfried Sassoon to John. At the line "O Jesus, make it stop!" he put his hand on her arm, giving and seeking comfort at the same time. Recalling this moment, Eleanor feels a pressure deep inside, somewhere between an ache and an itch. She hasn't experienced a sensation like this in years. He's such an interesting combination of elements: a self-educated man from rough beginnings who's become more sophisticated than she would have expected. She doesn't know what to do with herself. Going into the central hallway, she paces its length back and forth. What is wrong with her?

Finally, she heads into the powder room.

On Wednesday, George goes into the city, and Eleanor and Rosalee start to prepare for Thanksgiving. They spend the day cleaning the house, polishing the silver, and ironing the tablecloths and napkins. Harry, Nat, and Hamilton catch up on the farmwork that had been pushed aside for the turkeys.

As Eleanor starts cooking the cranberry sauce, she thinks about John and her other patients—how will they be celebrating Thanksgiving?

Later that evening, George and his mother arrive in a cab from the train station. Abigail drinks a cocktail with George and Eleanor and then, saying she's tired, heads upstairs.

Eleanor follows her into the guest room and sits on one of the twin beds. "Do you have a minute, Abigail?"

Abigail takes the bench at the dressing table.

"I want to tell you about the plans for tomorrow. We'll be eating at noon, which I know is much earlier than you like. With Eddie away at training, there will be only five of us. I thought about asking Rosalee and Hamilton to share our meal, but I'm guessing you would not feel comfortable with that arrangement."

"Neither would they!" Abigail expostulates.

Her attitude infuriates Eleanor, who thinks her mother-in-law is the biggest bigot she knows. "You may be right about that. In any case, I decided we will eat early so Rosalee and Hamilton can have Thanksgiving dinner with some of their own family. Rosalee's parents live on a farm in Virginia, but she has a sister and brother-in-law who live nearby."

"That's awfully accommodating of you, Eleanor."

"They have performed yeoman service this week, working late into the night with us, processing all the turkeys we raised this year. They deserve the time off. So that's that." Eleanor sits up straighter. "And I want to ask you about George."

"What about George?" Abigail looks to the side, stalling.

Eleanor says, "I believe George is having an affair with Miriam Kaplan, and it appears to me that you are helping him in his deception."

"I don't know what you're talking about!" Abigail insists.

"Tell me the truth, Abigail."

"George comes and goes from my apartment as he pleases. He always has. He's a grown man. I'm not about to interrogate him."

"You're covering for him."

"If you have your suspicions, you must speak to George directly. This has nothing to do with me."

"Oh yes, it does. If George were to leave us, your grandchildren would be hurt—not just me. This is your family too."

"Not all of you."

"What?"

"I can count, Eleanor. You may have pulled the wool over my son's eyes, but not mine. If George is unfaithful to you, well, some would say you deserve it for lying to him." Eleanor feels punched in the gut. "That's a rotten thing to say! I never lied to George. I let him assume what he wanted."

All these years, Eleanor believed that neither George nor Abigail would question her because she was a respectable woman. How naive!

"That's what I thought," Abigail responds.

"I had to consider my child first and foremost. She needed a father."

Abigail's voice grows even louder as she exclaims, "You used my son!"

"Sh!" Eleanor hisses. "Someone might hear us."

"I hope they do," Abigail retorts. "Then the truth can come out."

Eleanor rises, her chin quivering. "None of this is Harry's fault. You've never treated her well."

"I don't blame Harry. I simply don't have much in the way of feelings for her."

"You're a mean woman with a small heart, Abigail. I hope none of my children takes after you."

"If you must know, Miriam has come to the apartment with George a few times. I've given her a drink because I'm a good hostess." Abigail looks sly and more than a little pleased with herself. "But that doesn't prove anything."

Before she can strangle Abigail—which is what she wants to do—Eleanor turns her back on her and walks away.

The following afternoon, as the family gathers for Thanksgiving dinner, Eleanor pours herself a glass full of sherry. She's dreading this meal.

As they take their chairs, she says, "I'd like to keep the chair on my right empty—for Eddie."

"Are you crazy?" George says. "An empty chair would signify that he's dead."

Abigail nods her agreement.

"I've never heard that," Eleanor says.

Seated on Eleanor's left side, Nat says, "Eddie wouldn't just show up without warning us, would he?"

Shaking her head, Harry says, "I can't imagine he would, Nat."

"I don't think so either," Eleanor responds, "but I want to save his place at the table anyway."

George is busily carving the turkey in front of him. After everyone's plate is full, Eleanor says, "I know we don't usually pronounce a blessing before we eat, but would someone like to say something today?"

Startled, George pauses.

Harry says, "I would." She bends her head and puts her hands together. "Dear Lord, almighty God, please keep Eddie safe and all the others we know and love who are busy defending our nation. Amen."

"That was nice, Harriet," Abigail says.

"Thank you, Harry," Eleanor replies. Then she raises her fork. "Doesn't this turkey look wonderful? And to think we raised and butchered it ourselves!"

George lifts his water glass to Harry, Nat, and Eleanor.

Harry says, "Next year, we could handle two hundred or two hundred and fifty turkeys. That is, assuming there's a need."

"It smells fabulous," Nat says.

Abigail leans over toward George and speaks quietly to him. Eleanor wonders what Abigail is saying. Is she warning George about Eleanor's suspicions? If so, will that provide George with some sort of perverse permission to move even closer to Miriam?

Nat notices his mother is glaring at his grandmother. What's going on between them? He overheard them shouting at each other last night, though he couldn't decipher the words. He doesn't like the feeling around this table at all.

Putting his hand on his mother's arm, Nat says, "Mummy, I've been writing a new song. This one is about my masters at Andover and how difficult their courses are."

"Excuse me a minute, Mother," George says. "I want to hear what Nat is talking about."

Eleanor can barely concentrate on Nat's words, but she's surprised that George is listening to his son.

Nat says, "It starts like this:

> *I am the Doc Marling: American history;*
> *And I am Bob Hayward: math, make no mistake;*
> *You will learn your English from me,*
> *Doctor Willoughby;*
> *Wake up with a bang: chemistry by Hake."*

"Very clever," George says. "Is Dr. Hake still there? I studied chemistry with him a million years ago."

"Eddie had him last year," Nat says, "and I've got him now."

George says, "I've met Dr. Marling. Randall says he's the toughest teacher they've ever had at Andover. But he teaches seniors, doesn't he, not lower middlers?"

"That's right, Father."

Eleanor is glad for Nat that George is finally showing some interest in him.

Abigail says, "George, didn't you tell me they've asked you to join the board at Andover?"

"Yes, I'm filling a sudden vacancy."

Nat says, "Does that mean you'll be coming up to school sometimes, Father?"

Eleanor hurts at the sound of hope in his voice.

"Probably not. Most of the meetings are held in New York."

"Can you do anything about the food?" Nat asks. "Eddie wrote me about how much he misses the meat loaf at Andover, but it's not the same this year."

"I can't do anything about the food, but I'll see to it that those nasty secret societies are shut down."

"Eddie told you what happened to him?"

George nods.

Abigail says, "I send Edward a postcard or a letter every week, though I must say he has only replied once."

"I hear from him pretty regularly," Eleanor says.

"Well, you *are* his mother," Abigail replies in a mean tone of voice.

Puzzled, Nat looks at Harry. She appears to be oblivious to the emotion swirling around.

"That's right," Eleanor tells Abigail. "Eddie only has time to write to those who really care about him. I guess he's figured out that you only care about yourself."

"Eleanor, that's uncalled for!" George cries.

Eleanor is astonished at herself for saying what she really thinks. She's embarrassed too. She should not behave like this in front of the children. Her heart is aching so much she hardly knows what she's doing.

"I'm sorry, Abigail," she says. "That remark was unkind. Please forgive me."

"It was cruel." Abigail sniffs.

Nat says, "Would you like some more gravy, Abba? I know you're a big fan of Rosalee's gravy."

"Thank you, Nathaniel, but I'm not hungry any longer."

"More sherry, Mother?" George asks.

"Thank you, dear. I'll have a little."

Eleanor scrutinizes her plate. *What is Eddie doing right now? Is he thinking of them? She can't stop thinking of him. It hurts so much that he isn't here . . .*

A few flakes of snow were flying sideways through the air when she boarded the train for Halloran the next day. But now as she descends the stairs, it has turned to sleet, which falls with small clicking sounds as it strikes the leaves remaining on the trees.

When Eleanor enters the hospital, everything seems normal, but up on the third floor, the nurses' station is empty. She hangs her coat in the nearby closet and hurries into her ward.

The sight of Horace's empty bed, made up with clean sheets that still show their creases, slams into her solar plexus. All his belongings are gone from his bedside table.

She can't breathe. Sitting abruptly on his cot, she stares at the brown linoleum floor while her hands stroke the rough sheet as though she were trying to comfort the bed. She presses her lips together so no sound can escape. She'll never ever see that sweet boy again.

Rising quickly, she whispers "I'm sorry" to her patients as she runs out of the room, down the hall, and into the supply closet. She grabs a pillow and covers her face so she can howl without being heard.

After several minutes, Eleanor regains control of herself. Once she's wiped her face and blown her nose into her handkerchief, she returns to her ward.

"I'm sorry, men," she tells them. "I wasn't ready for
the sight of Horace's empty bed. When did he die?"

John motions her over. Guido, Sergeant Jones, and
the other soldiers watch as she hurries down the aisle that
bisects the rows of beds.

John reaches for her hand and holds tight. "Horace
died Tuesday night. Blood poisoning."

"Was anyone with him?"

"Downey was here. She stayed all night."

Nurse Downey looks exhausted. "Eleanor. Welcome back.
We have an enormous backlog of ACE bandages needing
to be washed and dried. There are hardly any clean ones
left, so the men's baths will have to wait."

"I'll go down to the laundry room right away."

Washing hundreds of bandages in strong soap, bleach,
and hot water seems to be proper penance for not being
with Horace when he died. Eleanor's hands become red,
and they start to sting. As she rinses the soap and squeezes
the water out of a dozen bandages at a time, she realizes
the drying racks in the laundry room can accommodate
only five hundred. She'll have to come back and wash the
next batch later this afternoon, after the current batch
has dried.

When she returns to the ward through the swinging
doors, she sees that John is watching for her. The look he
gives her makes it seem as though he knows everything
she's thought about him during the past week.

Guido says, "John, your girl is back."

Eleanor blushes. Are her feelings that obvious to
the men?

Turning to Guido, she says, "It's been a while since
I've been called a girl. Thanks for the compliment."

"Anytime," Guido responds. "Do you have a few minutes?"

"Now?"

"I was hoping you'd write a letter to my mother for me."

"Of course."

An hour later, Eleanor returns to the basement to check on her bandages, which are still slightly damp. By midafternoon, she'll probably be able to spread out another five hundred more to dry overnight.

She delivers lunch trays to each of her patients, saving John's for last. She lays the tray gently on the bed next to his outstretched legs.

"What are you doing that keeps you popping in and out of the ward?" he asks. As he looks up at her, his eyes seem bluer than ever.

"I'm washing laundry. Hundreds of ACE bandages." She stops, wondering at herself for bragging to John. Is she trying to impress him? Actually, by focusing on her present task, she's trying to distract herself from Horace's death as well as the horrible Thanksgiving dinner she'd just endured.

"Hidden talents, Eleanor. I wonder what else you have hidden."

She feels a little squeamish at his tone. "Are you married, John?"

"In a manner of speaking."

"Hmm. I wonder what that means." Her heart begins to race.

"I'm sorry you learned about Horace in such a shocking way. I would have telephoned you if I'd known your number."

"It wouldn't be appropriate for me to give you my telephone number. I'm married too—'in a manner of speaking.'" She can't stop herself from flirting with him.

He laughs. "I wonder what that means."

"We can discuss that some other day. In the meantime, I don't want your lunch to get cold."

Sitting up straighter, John says, "I've been waiting to tell you: I started working with the physical therapist. He'll get some equipment installed around my bed so I can exercise and get stronger. I'm going to work and work so I can walk out of here someday. I can't stand the thought of having to depend on anyone."

"Really?"

John replies, "Dependency is the worst possible basis for a relationship. I'd much rather be with someone by choice." He looks intently at her, as if conveying a message with special significance.

Eleanor feels as awkward as a girl. And then she realizes how dependent she has become on George—her husband, the breadwinner, the father of their children. And in some ways, she's dependent on her children too; her role as their mother has defined her for the past twenty-four years. How independent does she really want to be? In taking on this job at Halloran, she's started to act more independently, but how far is she prepared to go?

Winter 1944

Just one look and then I knew,
That all I longed for long ago,
was you.

—Lyrics from "Long Ago and Far Away"
by Ira Gershwin, 1944

Fifteen

Dear Mother,

Thank you for the best Christmas of my life. It was so great to be home with you all. I'll never forget the time together playing games, singing around the piano, eating Rosalee's fabulous food.

And now I'm on my way to ███████████, *England, where I've been assigned to* ███████████. *The crossing has been rough, with heavy rains and lots of wind. I would not make a good captain of the Pinafore—I've been very, very sick at sea. After all those summer sailing lessons, I expected better from myself. I have learned that staying out on deck in the fresh air helps. Also eating nothing but tea and biscuits.*

I don't exactly know what to expect in ███████, *but I hope to make you and Father proud.*

Oops, back to the railing . . .

Love,

Eddie

✚

Sunday p.m.

Dear Nathaniel,

    It was good having Edward home over Christmas, and it made me glad to see you boys spending some time together in the playroom. I hope you were able to discern the maturity Edward has acquired with his army training. Think about emulating him.

    In fact, I expect you to behave like Edward. You must study hard and show your masters respect. Find friends and treat them well. Learn to enjoy playing sports. Be honest and honorable.

    It is critical that you succeed at Andover, Nathaniel. As you must be aware, fully one-third of the boys flunk out. That must not happen to you. You have brains enough to excel. It is not that I expect you to love studying. But I do expect you to acquire a love of learning and a strong appetite for work, so that when you discover something that interests you deeply, you can pursue it with passion, discipline, and thoroughness.

Now that I serve as a member of Andover's board of trustees, I will hear about everything you do. Be good, son.

Father

✚

"Mr. Sutton!"

Glancing around the room, Nat sees that all twelve of his classmates, slouched or sitting straight in old wooden chairs with arms that extend on the right, are watching him. Mr. Willoughby, his face redder than usual above his tight-buttoned shirt and bow tie, glares at Nat.

"Mr. Sutton, if you can tear yourself away from contemplating your navel," Mr. Willoughby drawls sarcastically, "I know we would all appreciate hearing your opinion about the text we are in the process of analyzing."

"Sir?" Nat sits up straighter and reflexively fingers his tie.

"As I was saying," Mr. Willoughby goes on, "Hardy's original title for this work was *Tess of the d'Ubervilles: A Pure Woman*. Tell me: Was Hardy's title ironic, or do you think he believed that Tess is essentially pure?"

The radiator clanks in the silence as Nat scrambles for the answer. Mr. Willoughby begins pacing across the front of the room.

"Tess wasn't pure for long," Nat replies, "so Hardy must have been ironic."

A couple of guys titter behind him.

Nat blushes, remembering what an erotic figure Tess seemed last night as he read in bed. Early in the novel, there is a line about young girls, "under whose bodices the life throbbed quick and warm." That image grabbed

Mr. Snake's attention and made him stand up. Fortunately Nat was reading the novel by flashlight under his bedcovers after Peter fell asleep, so he didn't have to hide his reaction from his roommate. Nat suspects Peter is attracted to him, so he avoids anything to do with sex when he's with Peter.

Anyway, Nat is sure that a woman who arouses him that much can't possibly be pure.

"But did Tess choose to lose her virtue?"

Nat thinks Mr. Willoughby's use of the word *but* might be a clue. "Not really," he says.

"In fact, wasn't it wrested from her?"

"Yes, but she allowed herself to be taken. She didn't put up a fight."

"She was sleeping soundly when d'Urberville had his way with her. How much of a fight could *you* put up if someone accosted you while you were sleeping?" Mr. Willoughby asks.

This is a fear Nat briefly entertained about Peter; he worried Peter might get into his bed with him when he was asleep, but that has never happened.

"So she really didn't have a chance to defend herself, did she, sir? That means she *was* pure," Nat concludes.

"In fact," Mr. Willoughby says, "Hardy shows Tess to be a victim not only of d'Urberville but of a social class system that bred injustice and hypocrisy. Mr. Morten," he says, turning to another student, "please give us another example of Hardy's critique of England's class system . . ."

Nat's attention wanders away from Mr. Willoughby to the latest letter he received from his father, who went on about how he should act more like Eddie—which is also ironic. Eddie puts on a good show, but Nat's pretty sure their father had no idea about Eddie's gambling.

Another hour and a half to wait until music. Maybe he should feign a stomachache and ask to go to the infirmary? Staring out the nearest window at the gray skies, Nat thinks winter will never end. Everything is gray, from the branches of trees to the light on Mr. Willoughby's face. The sun hasn't shone in days.

Ages later, Nat hurries down the steps of the classroom building. He starts across the dirty, crunchy snow, but the wind whipping across the quad is so strong that he can't advance very quickly. It takes his breath away. He's puffing by the time he gets to the chapel.

As he opens the door and steps inside, the sounds of a Bach fugue surround him. Across the sanctuary, he sees Dr. Honiger, whose huge torso dips and rises and slides from side to side as he moves his hands over the mighty Casavant hundred-stop organ. His hair is white, and it looks wilder than ever, sticking out every which way.

Nat sits in a back pew, stretches his legs out, and closes his eyes while the sonorous music washes over him. He doesn't want Dr. Honiger to stop playing. Studying music with him is the highlight of Nat's week. When Dr. Honiger lifts his hands from the organ and the last notes fade away, Nat begins to clap loudly.

Hearing Nat's applause, Dr. Honiger looks up and squints into the gloom. "Iss zat you, Mr. Sutton?" His accent is strong on sibilants, rich and guttural with the remnants of his native tongue.

Nat strides down the side aisle, his heels sounding loud on the stone floor. "That was fantastic, Dr. Honiger. Wow!"

The music master's round face turns pink with pleasure. "Zee music of Bach ist glorious." He rubs his hands down the legs of his black suit, unsuccessfully smoothing away the wrinkles.

"Come. Sit." He scoots over to make room for Nat. "I start at zee beginning. Tell me vat ist you hear." He plays more slowly this time.

After a number of measures, Nat says, "That was the subject."

Dr. Honiger nods agreement as he continues playing. "Now the subject is being imitated by a second voice," Nat adds. He is completely happy, his concentration on the Bach absolute. "And here comes the third voice." He inclines his head to the side as he listens closely. "And now the fourth."

Dr. Honiger plays to the end of the piece.

"It is almost as though the different voices are having a discussion, where they throw the subject back and forth, and then eventually they come to a conclusion."

Suddenly he remembers a very different discussion—the one at Thanksgiving—where the voices going back and forth were discordant and confusing. This is much more pleasant.

"Yesss!"

"How did Bach learn to write music like that?"

"He started to study at a very young age. His vater and bruder Johann Christoph taught him canons, but Bach progressed furder. You see zere ist structure to zee vay a fugue operates, and you might think zat structure vould mean music sounding like a machine." He demonstrates.

"That's like a player piano," Nat says.

"Now listen vhen I play like zis," Dr. Honiger invites him, playing the same notes. "Vhen you play vith your heart, not your head, zen you truly make music."

Nat isn't sure he hears much difference between the two versions, but he certainly believes in Dr. Honiger's philosophy about the importance of feeling in music.

"Shall I play the piece I've been practicing?" Nat asks.

"Try zis." He places the music for *Chorale: Christ lag in Todesbanden* on the music stand.

Nat takes a deep breath. He begins sight-reading the piece, and his hands are doing all right on the keyboard. But there are so many notes in the pedal line that his feet get tangled up and they throw off his hands. Nevertheless, he struggles through to the end.

"I'm sorry, Dr. Honiger. I butchered that."

"Not at all. Please, practice zis during zee veek so you get all the notes perfect. Zen ven you play it, you vill be brilliant."

No one else has ever suggested Nat could be brilliant—especially not his father.

After his music lesson, Nat heads up to the Beanery. Most of the seats are already taken. At the end of a row, he sees a table of seniors with two empty places. Eddie should be there, waving at him. Hesitantly, he pulls out a chair. Will they let a measly underclassman sit with them?

One of the smooth guys named Hazy Whitney, says, "Hey, Sutton, what do you think you're doing? This is a senior table."

"I know, but can't I join you just this time?"

"Sure, sit down. Tell us what you hear from your brother."

Nat seats himself. A platter of potatoes is sent his way. He says, "Edward's somewhere over in England now, preparing to make an assault on the Continent. I don't know a lot because the censors clip practically everything out. In his last letter, so much had been censored that I could hardly make sense of it."

Robby Woods, a tall guy with lots of acne scars, says, "Did you know the Germans are pounding London all over again? Last night, fighter-bombers dropped incendiaries that smashed a bunch of buildings, and they hit a gas main, causing a huge fire that took hours to extinguish."

Nat doesn't want to consider the possibility that Eddie's in London. Quietly he says, "I hope Edward's nowhere near there." He stabs a potato with his fork, puts it on his plate, and cuts it into smaller and smaller pieces.

Robby goes on. "The *New York Times* said it's as bad as the Blitz of 1940–41. Hundreds of civilians were crushed by buildings collapsing on top of them or by being burned in the fires."

"God. I read the *Boston Globe* this morning," Nat said. "I didn't see anything about this."

Remembering his mother's telling him and Harry that they don't see the war as real, he starts trying to imagine what it would be like to experience a blitz.

"Not much we can do about it here," Hazy says. "Meat, Sutton?" He slides the dish toward Nat.

Nat wants to put his anxiety aside. This is his chance to amuse some seniors.

"Ah, mystery meat," he croons. "I wonder what kind of animal this came from." He forks a piece, puts it on his plate, and makes a show of sawing at his meat with his table knife. "It's like shoe leather."

Hazy says, "I've never tried eating my shoes. Do you recommend it?"

"Only if the shoe's been marinated first," Nat retorts quickly.

Nat enters the library and takes up his favorite spot, a one-person table next to a window way off in a corner on the second floor. Although he's supposed to study, he pulls out the letter from his father, skips over the part about being like Eddie, and wonders what happens to the boys who flunk out of Andover. If they're old enough, do they enlist?

Other than music, there isn't any one subject he feels passionate about. But he knows his father would never allow him to become a musician. Yet he was surprised by his father's interest at Thanksgiving in his most recent song about Andover, and he's not sure what to make of that.

He arrives at his dorm just as Mr. Hayward, the housemaster at Adams, is locking the doors.

"Close call, Mr. Sutton!" Mr. Hayward remarks.

"Yes, sir," Nat agrees.

From the living room, Nat can hear the sounds of Tommy Dorsey's weekly radio broadcast. He sticks his head in to see what's going on, and there's Peter, his arms raised around an invisible partner, dancing to the tune "Well, Git It!"

"Hey, Nat, come on in. This is a great jump tune!"

"Jump tune?" Nat walks into the room.

"Yeah, because it makes you want to jump up and dance. I'm practicing for the dance this weekend. If you want, I'll show you the steps my sister taught me."

"You're a man of hidden talents, Peter. I didn't know you could dance."

"Come on—I'll be the boy." He opens his arms invitingly. "Don't you want to wow the girls on Friday?"

"I'd certainly like to meet a girl . . ."

"Here—put your hand on my shoulder. Now let me have your other hand."

Nat does as Peter instructs, but he feels strange for all sorts of reasons, not the least of which is that he towers over Peter.

"Let me be the boy, Peter. I'm taller."

"I only know how to do the boy's part," Peter says.

Nat thinks about closing the door so none of the other guys can see them. Then he thinks it doesn't matter—he'll show them all he's not a homosexual when he finds a girl to dance with on Friday.

Following Peter's lead, Nat is soon caught up by the speedy music. He throws his head back in a hyperdramatic pose, and in a high voice, he exclaims, "Oh, darling, you're so charming and debonair!" Then he places the back of his hand against his forehead and pretends he's about to faint.

The song changes to "All the Things You Are." Peter pulls Nat close for the slow, dreamy song.

Nat breaks Peter's hold and steps back. "What the—"

Just then Mr. Hayward sticks his head in. Giving them an admonitory look, he says, "Gentlemen, lights out in ten minutes!"

After he exits, Peter says, "Just kidding around, Nat."

"I hope so," Nat replies.

Once they're in their own room, Nat closes the door before he says, "I know *I'm* not interested in guys."

"How can you be sure?"

"There was a guy . . . my tutor . . . who made a pass at me."

"I had no idea," Peter says. "You never told me."

"I don't like to discuss private things." Nat sits to remove his trousers. While Peter pulls his pajama top over his head, Nat asks, "Have you ever tried anything with another boy?"

Once Peter's head is free, he says, "Not really."

"What does that mean?"

"I don't want to talk about this anymore," Peter says.

"What were you thinking back there when you pulled me close?"

"I . . . was just experimenting, to see what would happen."

"Peter, you're my best friend, but there'll never be anything like that with me."

"Are you sure?" Peter asks.

"Yes, I'm sure. I do not want to experiment."

Wednesday afternoon during free time, Nat takes some money from his desk and walks the six blocks into the village. The wind feels frigid, but the sun is shining and the birds twitter and zoom around the trees, so Nat believes spring might actually arrive someday.

Why can't his mother buy him new underwear and send it to him at school? He knows she's busy working at the hospital, but it's horrible having to shop for himself. He skulks through the aisles, passing by the briefs slowly enough that he can glance at them. Is medium the right size? He forgot to check his underwear that morning when he dressed.

Finally, he grabs six pairs of Arrow shorts and rushes up to the cash register with them. Fortunately, the clerk is a white-haired man who looks old enough to be his grandfather.

Nat asks, "What happens if they aren't the right size?"

The clerk squints at the cellophane package and then, looking Nat over, he says, "This should be just the ticket, young man. But if they don't work out for you, bring them back. That'll be five dollars."

Five dollars? With Eddie no longer around to give him extra spending money whenever he wants it, Nat has become much more aware of the cost of things.

While he stuffs the brown paper bag containing his purchase under his arm, the door opens. An attractive pink-cheeked girl with bouncy brown curls and green eyes pushes through.

"Hello," Nat says. Then he blushes to his ears as he thinks about the embarrassing transaction she came so close to witnessing.

The girl smiles at him, but she doesn't reply. He recalls that Abbot girls are not allowed to speak to Andover boys when they encounter each other downtown.

He turns to watch her walk down the first aisle. A small round hat is perched at an impossible angle on the back of her head. He can't understand why it doesn't fall off that shiny hair.

As he ambles along Main Street, he thinks how pretty the girl is. He wonders whether she'll be at the dance on Friday. He'd really like to talk to her. If the light in her eyes is any indication, this girl would be fun. Her hair is the color of a penny, isn't it? And her sassy curls remind him of Harry's.

If he could dance with her, he would show Peter that what he really wants is a girl.

Sixteen

February 7, 1944

Dear Nat,

I've been in England several weeks now. After training for the Signal Corps, I was assigned to work out of an RAF airstrip near ███████████. *The new* ███████████ *equipment we are using is remarkable, though I can't say anything more than that about it. Every morning I get up at 4:00 a.m., even earlier than the crew, to prepare our flight plan for the day. Each day seeing all those other guys climb into their planes, I wonder who won't be coming back. It's rough. I knew all the guys who didn't make it back. I drank beer with them the night before. I probably shouldn't be writing like this.*

Tell me all about life at school. Is Mr. Willoughby still there, teaching English literature? He really made

me think. He looked so old, though, that I'm wonder-
ing whether he might be retired now.

What's the musical this winter? Are you going to
help with the lights again?

Gotta go now. 4:00 a.m. will come all too soon.
Take care of yourself, buddy.

Eddie

✚

Nat has never attended a dance at Andover or Abbot. He
wishes Eddie were around to advise him, but he isn't, so
Nat seeks out Harvey Reid, one of the smoothest boys in
his class. Nat asks Harvey to meet him in front of the bell
tower after dinner because he doesn't want anyone over-
hearing his stupid questions.

He and Harvey stand facing each other. Nat's overcoat is buttoned, and he's wearing a wool cap. Harvey's
coat flaps in the wind.

"I only have a few minutes, Nat. Now what do you
want to know?" He sounds a little impatient.

"Well, you've been to lots of dances at Abbot, haven't
you, Harvey?"

"Sure."

"What time do they start?"

"It varies. Sometimes they're held in the late afternoon. This Friday, I think the dance starts right after
dinner."

"What are we supposed to wear?"

"Most guys wear a suit."

Hoping to make Harvey laugh, Nat jokes, "But not
their birthday suits, right?"

"Of course not. Anything else?"

"Where exactly do we go? I've never been on the Abbot campus."

"You'll see the lights. You can't miss the building—it's all lit up."

Thinking about how nervous he'll be Friday night, Nat says, "Um . . . you wouldn't happen to know where I could get some booze, would you?"

"No problem. Meet me here tomorrow at the same time, and bring some money."

"Thanks so much, Harvey. I know having a drink will help me relax, just as it does for my mother."

"Whatever you say, Nat. Tomorrow at seven."

Friday evening, Nat puts on his navy-blue suit and slicks his hair back. He pulls out the pint of bourbon he bought from Harvey. After forcing a little of the burning liquid down his throat, he brushes his teeth. He hides the bourbon in his suitcase up in the closet.

At 7:30, Nat and Peter leave their dorm and walk through town to the Abbot campus as snow falls on their bare heads. Nat is so nervous that he talks nonstop until they reach Abbot. They follow a stream of girls into a building ablaze with lights. Once they hang up their coats in the cloakroom inside the door, Nat and Peter hesitate, straightening their ties. Nat is so anxious he feels sick.

"Come on, pal. You can do this," Peter tells him.

"You don't look worried at all," Nat says. "Why not?"

"I'm just here to watch, Nat."

"But you're a good dancer, Peter."

"We'll see."

All the tables and chairs have been pushed against the walls to create a space for dancing. Along the back wall, a band of four elderly gentlemen in black are playing a

Strauss waltz. A good number of the masters from Andover are here, standing around the periphery talking with
each other and with women who must be Abbot faculty
members. Boys stand in groups on one side, girls in twos
and threes on the other side. Only a few brave couples are
actually dancing.

Nat looks for the girl with the penny-colored hair, but
when he thinks he sees her, he loses his nerve.

"Well? Is she here?" Peter asks after they've completed
a circuit around the room.

"I might have seen her, but I'm not sure—I only saw
the back of the girl's head."

"What are you waiting for? Let's go straight through
the middle."

He and Peter work their way through the clutch of
girls, and this time Nat sees that she is there. She notices
him too, and she smiles in recognition. She's talking with
two other girls, though. Nat moves over to the side, where
he can keep an eye on her.

After a few minutes, she leaves her friends and starts
toward him. Her shiny pink dress seems to cup her hips,
and it's tight around her thighs as she saunters up to him.
He can hardly breathe.

"I thought you must be an Andover student."

Nat notices that her eyes are even greener tonight. He
tells her, "I knew you were an Abbot girl."

"It's nice to see you again. My name is Emma—Emma
Briggs."

"I'm Nathaniel Sutton. Nat."

"Hello, Nat. What year are you?"

Nat knows she's really asking how old he is. "Lower
middler. You?"

She is *so* pretty!

"I'll be a senior next year."

Nat's hopes plummet at the thought that she's older than he.

"I skipped a year in grade school," Emma explains, "so I'm younger than most of the girls in my class."

"Good. I mean, congratulations for skipping. You must be very bright."

"Not really. Well . . .?" she says expectantly, opening her arms and the palms of her hands to the ceiling.

"You'd like to dance?" Nat says.

"Yes. I thought you'd never ask."

Emma turns and leads the way to the dance floor. Following her, Nat notices that her dress makes swishing sounds as she moves. He likes that.

Nat takes Emma's right hand in his left and lifts their hands to the height of her shoulder, then places his right hand gingerly on her waist, careful not to allow the bottom halves of their bodies to touch. He waits a moment to catch the beat, and then he steps out, leading her into a waltz.

Now for some scintillating conversation. *Come on, say something funny!* Desperate for a topic, Nat says, "Your dress . . . what is it made of?"

"I think It's taffeta."

"It whispers when you walk."

Turning her head to look into his face, Emma smiles warmly. "What a great image!"

Encouraged, Nat ventures further. "Do you like images generally? I mean, do you like poetry?" Somehow this seems like a terribly personal question.

"Oh yes! Elizabeth Barrett Browning and Shakespeare and John Donne are my favorites."

"What kind of music do you like?"

Emma misses a step. "Sorry!" She squeezes his hand as she moves a little closer.

Nat has to back up because Mr. Snake is wide awake now. Hazy Whitney waltzes by with a redhead in his arms. Hazy's eyes are on Emma.

"I don't really know much about music," she says. "How about you?" She lifts her left arm and does something to her hair, then drops her hand back to his shoulder.

"I listen to music of every kind. I like it all."

"Do you play an instrument?"

Although she has asked him a question, Nat senses that her attention has moved away. He replies, "I play piano and organ."

She misses another step, and then Nat stumbles too, but they keep moving.

"I guess I just don't have a very good sense of rhythm," she says as she turns her head to the side.

What is she looking at?

"That's all right," Nat replies. *You're agreeing that she's uncoordinated? Very suave, Nat!* "I mean, it's my fault," he goes on. "I must not be leading well." Tightening his hold on her, he stops moving. "Let me catch the beat again."

After a few measures, he launches them back into the crowd of whirling couples. They dance for a minute without speaking before Nat feels Emma relax a little.

"Sorry about that," Emma apologizes. "I guess I'm used to leading." She smiles ruefully. "I've only practiced with other girls, and because I'm tall, I always lead."

"I'll stop leading if you want to take over."

Emma's eyes twinkle at his response. *Such green eyes!*

"Oh no, that's your role. I have to learn to follow, though I must say it's more natural for me to take charge. I'm the oldest of four, don't you know."

"I'm the youngest, so I'm used to being bossed."

Emma continues, "I'm so glad my mother shipped me

off to boarding school this year. With Dad away in the war, she's been a nervous wreck trying to manage everything on her own. She wanted me to help her all the time, and ... I don't know ... sometimes it seemed like she was asking me to be the other parent. But then she'd treat me like a child too. It was impossible to please her."

Nat is touched by Emma's disclosing such personal information about herself.

"That's about the opposite of my parents. Where's your father?"

"We don't really know because his letters have these huge sections the censors have cut out."

"My brother's letters are like that too. Is your father an officer?"

"He's some kind of commander in the army. He has a lot of other guys under him, and he's had a promotion, but I don't know exactly what his rank is now."

"Is he in Europe or in the Pacific theater?"

"Mother thinks he's on the Continent."

They dance in silence for a minute or two. Then the waltz ends.

Emma steps away. "Well, this has been nice, Nat. Thank you."

"Wouldn't you like to dance again?"

"Maybe later. Thanks." She turns and walks away.

Nat feels terribly deflated, especially after such a promising beginning. He makes a beeline for the punch table; he wants to look as though he were terribly busy. Once he's had some punch, he wanders around the edges of the crowd. Off to one side, he spots Emma speaking intently to two other girls, and then all three break into laughter. Are they laughing about him?

Nat wishes Eddie were here. Things would be so much easier; he'd have somebody to talk to about Emma's behavior and what's going on at home. He wouldn't feel so alone.

As Hazy walks by, Nat grabs his sleeve. "Who was that redhead I saw you dancing with?"

"That was Gee Steiner. How about the knockout you were with?"

In an effort to protect Emma from Hazy, Nat lies. "I don't know her name."

"Never mind. I'll find out," Hazy tells Nat. He heads off in Emma's direction.

Was Hazy the reason she'd been distracted?

Nat watches Hazy approach Emma, and then when they start to dance, he leaves. Picking up his overcoat, he pulls it on. As he hurries back to his dorm through the rising wind and swirling snow, he feels humiliated.

Wow, Nat, you sure were smooth. A real charmer. So articulate and intelligent. No wonder she laughed at you with her friends.

In his room, he goes directly over to the mirror. There's a big juicy pimple in the middle of his forehead. He squeezes it savagely, splattering the mirror in the process. Then there's another pimple and another. Splat. Splat. He feels a perverse pleasure in putting his mark on the mirror.

Or maybe Emma wasn't laughing at you?

He puts on his pajamas. Then he takes his desk chair into the closet and stands on the chair to reach his suitcase. He carries it down, removes the pint of bourbon, and takes a big swallow of the booze. It makes him cough, but soon he feels much warmer inside. He moves to his bed and sits with his back against the headrest. As he sips the bourbon, it goes down more easily.

Emma seemed to be attracted to you at first. Maybe you aren't a total loss.

Nat pulls a silk stocking out from inside his pillowcase. He'd filched it from Harry's wastebasket a long time
ago; fortunately she didn't miss it. He places the stocking
across his thigh and starts to stroke it with his left hand,
imagining he's stroking Emma's leg. He remembers the
way Emma's dress embraced her hips and how it felt to
have her in his arms . . .

Peter stands next to Nat's bed holding the stocking between two fingers as if it were a dead rat he gripped by
the tail.

"What in the world is this, Nat? Did you smuggle a girl
into our room?"

Nat stares at him stupidly. How can he explain having
an intimate item of his sister's? And what time is it, anyway?

"I wish!" is all he can reply.

"They'd boot you out of school if you ever pulled
something like that."

Peter hides the stocking behind his back. Nat lunges
for it, loses his balance, and falls across the bed. He rolls
over and looks up at his roommate.

"Come on, Peter. Give me that. It's none of your
business."

Peter dangles the stocking over Nat's head, then finally lets it fall onto his chest.

"What happened at the dance? I saw you with this bru-
nette in a gorgeous dress, and the next thing I knew, you
disappeared."

"I needed a drink."

Nat feels dizzy. He stuffs the stocking back inside his
pillowcase, then pulls the sheet and blankets up to cover
himself. He closes his eyes, but the room keeps swirling,
so he opens them again. Now he feels awful. Is he going to
throw up? He moves into a sitting position.

"Where's the bourbon?" Peter says.

Nat extracts the bottle from between his sheets and offers it to Peter. "Did you have a good time?"

Peter takes a sip before answering. "Not really. It's not as much fun to watch as it is to dance."

Nat stands, finds he's still dizzy, and sits back down on his bed. Now everything about his life seems sickening.

"There's something I haven't told you about that's really been bothering me."

Peter hands the bottle back to Nat. "I'm all ears," he says.

"Last summer at a jazz club in New York, I saw my father with a beautiful woman I didn't recognize. They were all caught up in each other, so he didn't notice me. Later I sort of hinted that I'd seen him, but he didn't explain—and he would have if it'd been an innocent meeting, right?" Nat lifts the bottle for a small swallow.

Peter winces. "I would think so," he says.

"Then at Thanksgiving when I went home to kill the turkeys, there was all this anger in the air. And at Christmas, I don't think my parents said a single word to each other. I don't know what to do."

"There probably isn't much you can do, Nat. Hopefully they'll figure it out. They are grownups, after all."

"I guess. I'm sorry I didn't come find you when I was ready to leave the dance tonight. I was pretty upset."

"That's all right, Nat. I forgive you."

"Thank you, Peter. You're a true friend."

When the alarm clock rings the next morning, Peter gets up right away, takes his towel and toilet kit, and heads out the door.

Cautiously Nat opens his eyes, slowly sits up, and then shifts his legs over so he can place his feet on the floor. Not bad. He stands up. No more dizziness, just a slightly queasy sensation in his stomach. He can hold his liquor after all.

Quickly, Nat strips the sheets off his bed and takes them down to the hamper in the laundry room, where he buries them at the bottom. Then he gets clean sheets to take back upstairs. Nat is glad no one messes with his bed. That's one good thing about the war: maids used to make the beds at Andover, but now the boys take care of their own.

You should throw Harry's stocking away, he tells himself. *Remove the temptation before you become totally depraved.*

"It tempts you into immoral behavior. You should try to develop some redeeming qualities."

Peter appears at Nat's elbow. "Talking to yourself again?"

"Am I? Well, of course. I'm the most fascinating conversationalist imaginable."

He's not really embarrassed that Peter overheard him. Peter knows him.

Peter starts snapping his towel at Nat. "Come on— we're going to be late."

Over breakfast, Nat complains, "Does winter last forever in Massachusetts? The sky has been gray for months now. I can't believe we'll ever see blue skies again."

His mouth full of viscous oatmeal, Peter says, "Of course we will. Spring's right around the corner."

Jonas—a small, studious-looking boy with steel-rimmed glasses—says, "You guys see the paper this morning? They're asking for one hundred thousand new recruits. The armed services are short of men. They already have ten million guys ages eighteen to thirty-eight, but apparently they need one hundred thousand more every month as replacements."

"Does that mean one hundred thousand American soldiers are being wounded or killed every month?" Nat asks. "That's staggering!" He swallows hard. "I hope to God my brother's okay."

"I'm sorry, Nat. I forgot your brother's in the military," Jonas says.

"Mr. Sutton?"

Nat looks up. Dr. Honiger stands across the table from him, looking flustered.

"Pleaz to come to my office. Ten minutes?"

"I'll be there."

Dr. Honiger bustles off.

Nat's tablemates are subdued as they finish their meals. Nat eats quickly, grabs his coat, and dashes out of Commons. As he hurries across the filthy snow covering the quad, he worries. Has something happened to Eddie? But why would Dr. Honiger be the one to give him news? Unless Headmaster Randall knows Nat feels close to Dr. Honiger? What else could it be?

When Nat arrives at the music building, he finds Dr. Honiger pacing the floor outside his office, running his hands through his hair.

"We haf a tremendiz problem, Nathaniel. Josh Brewster had to leave schul. Now we haf no accompaniment for *Pirates of Penzance*. I could play, but zen I vould not be able to conduct zee chorus and soloists too."

"Josh Brewster left?"

Any departure from the school is cause for concern, but Nat is enormously relieved that nothing has happened to his brother.

"Wait a minute—you want me? You want *me* to be the accompanist? I would *love* to be the accompanist!" Nat bursts out.

"You vould?"

"But isn't there some senior who could do it? Guys usually don't get chances like this 'til senior year."

"No one vould do as vell as you."

Nat flushes with pride. Finally someone besides his mother really believes in him. Then suddenly he feels daunted by the task ahead of him as he thinks about all the masters and students—and the Abbot girls—who would see the performance.

"Now zee show goes on. You muss practice night and day to learn zee music. Zhere ist no time to lose. Mr. Randall gives special permission for you to use practice room in zee music building vhen you haf time, even during zee nighttime study hours. I haf key for you."

As his sense of the responsibility Dr. Honiger is handing him blooms, Nat feels honored. He must not let his music teacher down.

"Zis veek and next I vill accompany rehearsals vile you vork on learning. But zen you muss be ready to play zee last week vhen zee young ladies join us. Now I muss get copy of zee complete score for you."

Which young ladies?

"When should I start?"

"I vill give zee score to you at lunch, and you muss start playing through in zee activity period. After dinner, ve vill go to zee music building and vork together."

Nat sails off to his first class of the day, his mind churning. As the bell rings and he opens his French textbook, Nat realizes he'll have to concentrate on his studies more than he ever has before. In fact, he'll need to become extremely efficient with his time so his grades won't slip while he's involved in *Pirates*.

Four hours later, on the way into lunch, Nat's eyes are arrested by a headline in a newspaper lying on a table in the lounge outside Commons: "Henry Ford Says War Will End in Two Months!"
Thank God, Nat thinks. Soon Eddie will be safe.

✚

Thursday night

Dear Jessica,

There is nothing quite like the comfort of other women. They understand you in a way your husband and children cannot. Since I started working at Halloran, I haven't been able to participate in our daytime knitting circle, and I really missed the fellowship of those women. Finally I asked whether they would mind meeting in the evening from time to time so I can be part of the group again. They agreed. Thank goodness!

It doesn't matter that our backgrounds are different or that some of us went to college and others did not. We are united in the desire to help our soldiers. Besides knitting stockings and sweaters and caps and mittens for our fighting men, now we are organizing a scrap drive for the children to collect waste paper, old rags, and rubber as well as scrap metal that can be reused as bullets.

I'm sorry Harry doesn't care to join us. I thought she could benefit from being part of this group, so I invited her to come with me. But she said she doesn't

have the time—and besides, she said she has no inter-
est in clothing or makeup or gossip. I assured her we
never discuss those sorts of things. Harry is so serious
and practical, I suspect she's actually more comfort-
able dealing with men, but of course, there are very
few men her age around here anymore. Now that I
think of it, I'm not sure Harry's all that comfortable
with emotion, or at least she's uncomfortable with any
effusive expression of emotion. In any case, she seems
to be busy, for she disappears after dinner most eve-
nings these days.

Nat sounds very happy in his latest letter. Even
though he's just a lower middler, his music teacher
has him playing the accompaniment for the spring
musical the students are preparing. I hope he doesn't
neglect his studies during this period of rehearsals.

You are a saint, Jessica, to get Mother to move in
with you and Drew for the duration. I'm sure it's a
great relief for her to be there with you, and I hope she
can help with the children. Thank you for taking her
in! I wondered whether I should have offered, but I'm
gone so much of the time now.

Letters from Eddie are few and far between, but
he seems to be keeping his head up. Thank you for
thinking of him.

Your grateful sister,

Ellie

Seventeen

Thursday evening

Dear Nathaniel,

Last week your mother informed me about the role you will be playing in the musical "Pirates of Penzance," and then Randall wrote me to the same effect. I trust Dr. Honiger knows what he is doing by giving this job to such a young man. All I can say is that you must not let this extraneous activity distract you from your studies. You know how important it is that you do well at Andover. Your mother is rarely home these days—she works some nights as well as days at the hospital—but I know that she too would admonish you to keep up your studying.

Harry's gone a lot of evenings too. She seems to have a newly acquired interest in the movies. I'll wa-

ger you've seen some good movies yourself, unless rehearsals extend to Saturday nights.

Yours,

Father

✚

Pirates of Penzance is the most amusing operetta Nat has ever encountered, and the next several weeks blur by. The silliness of Gilbert and Sullivan suits Nat's sense of humor perfectly.

And things are going better for the Allies on several fronts: the Russians are rolling over the Nazi army in the Ukraine, the RAF hammered Frankfurt in the heart of Germany, and American troops are landing on the island of New Guinea.

Nat is blissful, consumed by the process of putting on a musical production. However, he keeps thinking that Eddie would have played the role of Frederic if he hadn't enlisted. The senior who's been cast in that role is a decent tenor, but he's much shorter and less commanding than Eddie.

At one point in the operetta, Frederic sings:

> *Oh, is there not one maiden breast*
> *Which does not feel the moral beauty*
> *Of making worldly interest*
> *Subordinate to sense of duty?*

The first time Nat hears this, the concept of "moral beauty" captures his imagination. He starts to look at everything through the lens of moral beauty. Before long,

Peter tells Nat he is sick of hearing that brushing one's teeth before breakfast is a matter of moral beauty or that spitting phlegm on the sidewalk is not morally beautiful.

During the weeks of rehearsal, Nat zips through his homework so he can get back to practicing. Surprisingly, his grades improve. He works hard for Dr. Honiger, who treats him with affection and respect. And it's exciting to get to know the upperclassmen in the cast. When he passes them in the hallways or the dining room, he greets them by name. It usually takes the older students a moment to recognize Nat, but then they respond with some sort of acknowledgment. Nat has something unique to contribute to the school now, and for the first time since he arrived on campus, he feels he belongs.

The only missive from his mother during this period is a postcard indicating she will try to get up to Andover for the performance; in contrast, he receives letters from his father frequently.

During the last week of rehearsals, the girls from Abbot join in, and—mirabile dictu!—Emma is there, in charge of stage lighting. She is wearing her Abbot uniform with stockings that look thick and brown . . . the wartime rayon hose his sister complains about. They don't look nearly as smooth and attractive as the silk stocking of Harry's that he still keeps hidden. Emma's stockings sag around her knees. The shape of her legs, on the other hand, is perfect.

Nat doesn't say anything to her beyond hello, but he is very much aware of her moving around backstage. At the end of rehearsal, she comes up to him.

"I had no idea you were such a good pianist," she says, smiling at him as he runs through drills.

"Thanks," Nat says, then he asks, "Have you heard from your father lately?"

"No. Any news from your brother?"

She remembered!

"Not much, though my father reports on the letters Eddie writes home."

"Oh, his name is Eddie. I'll keep him in my thoughts." The fact that she remembers causes a sensation of warmth in his chest. All he can say is "Thank you." Then he adds, "And I'll think about your father. What is his name?"

"Aren't you nice! His name is Roger Briggs."

"I'll remember."

Nat feels so encouraged by Emma's friendliness that he tells her, "You have real moral beauty." By this he means that she thinks of others. His mother has moral beauty too, but he doesn't think his father does.

"Moral beauty?" Emma leans in, putting her elbow on the top of the piano. She seems to catch the reference, for her eyes twinkle with amusement. Then she steps away from the piano. "I should go. See you."

Later that night, Nat receives an unprecedented telephone call from his mother. She and his father will both be attending the Saturday night performance of *Pirates of Penzance*. He hopes this means they're getting along better now.

Nat feels surprisingly calm going into the G. W. H. Auditorium for the final performance of *Pirates*. He wonders how many of the seven hundred seats will be occupied. As he walks down a side aisle and ascends the steps at stage right, he sees that quite a few parents have already found places, but not his yet.

Tonight Nat is wearing his best navy-blue suit, a clean white shirt, and a red-striped tie. He has wet his hair and combed it carefully; he thinks he looks as good as he can. He sits on the piano bench and rubs his sweaty palms on his trousers. Then he starts to warm up. A few minutes later, Emma appears, and she winks at him as she hurries backstage. Over the last week, they have become quite friendly, chatting during breaks, so he feels quite comfortable with her now. After playing a little longer, he goes back to wait with the cast while the auditorium fills up.

Finally at 8:00 p.m., Dr. Honiger crosses in front of the curtains with Nat right behind him. Dr. Honiger descends the steps at the side and moves onto the floor of the auditorium, where his music stand is positioned, facing the stage.

As Nat takes his place at the piano bench adjacent to Dr. Honiger, he spots his parents in the front row of the huge audience. His hands begin to tremble. His mother's legs are crossed, one over the other, and she bounces her top leg rapidly. Is she nervous too?

When Dr. Honiger raises his arms, the noisy crowd of parents, students, and teachers from Andover and Abbot starts to quiet down. Dr. Honiger keeps his arms raised until the hall falls silent. Then he gestures for Nat to begin.

The show flows smoothly until the Abbot girl playing Mabel starts making up lyrics when she can't remember the right ones. No one sings along to help her remember, though. Another snafu occurs when Frederic trips and crushes a fake rock, but he catches himself and continues on as if nothing happened.

Before Nat knows it, the performance is over. The audience claps and hoots and bravoes for a long time while the cast take their bows. Then Dr. Honiger takes his bows, and then it's Nat's turn. People clap long and hard for him too, and he actually hears a few bravos, which is much more than he expects. There were no bravos after the previous performances.

Once the audience starts getting up from their seats, his mother hurries to Nat, her coat over her arm. It looks as though she has tears in her eyes.

"You were great, Nattie!"

As he wipes his hand across his brow, Nat becomes aware that his shirt is wet with sweat. "My playing wasn't perfect."

His father is right behind Eleanor, trailing a large white handkerchief. Nat realizes he must have shed some tears too.

George says, "Well done, Nathaniel," and shakes Nat's hand. Then George snorts. "That's got to be Gilbert and Sullivan's most ridiculous operetta of all. I loved it!"

"I thought you didn't like Gilbert and Sullivan. You said their music isn't serious."

"It's not serious in the context of classical music, but their operettas are terribly entertaining."

Dr. Honiger extracts himself from a nearby group and comes over to Nat with both arms outstretched. Beaming, he grabs each of Nat's hands. "Bravissimo!" Dr. Honiger keeps hold of one of Nat's hands as he turns to George. "Herr Sutton, your son ist very talented. Never have I taught such exceptional student. He muss study at New England Conservatory or Juilliard after graduation from Andover."

"That's fabulous news, Dr. Honiger!" Eleanor says.

"Be careful what you say in front of an impressionable boy," George replies. "I heard much the same thing from my piano teacher many years ago. But my father expected me to take over the company, and that was the end of that."

George sounds so bitter; Nat realizes his father had dreams like his own long ago.

"Ist not zee same for Nathaniel. He ist too young for anysing but school."

"That's right," Eleanor puts in. "We should encourage Nat to follow his dreams."

Dr. Honiger nods assent.

Putting his long hands into the deep pockets of his suit pants, George says, "We'll talk about that later."

"Thank you, Dr. Honiger," Eleanor says. "Nat has told us how much he enjoys working with you. Your Sunday evening performances of Bach are the high point of his week."

The senior who played the Pirate King, with rouge on his cheeks and dark penciled eyebrows, races across to the edge of the stage.

Nat sings, "For you are a Pirate King!"

Spreading his arms out wide as though he were still in the center of the stage, the boy replies, "And it is, it is a glorious thing, To be a Pirate King!" Then he jumps off the stage and runs down the aisle into the crowd.

"I don't know what you're thinking, Honiger—putting crazy ideas like this in the boy's head," George says. "He must be sensible. Only a handful of musicians are good enough to make a career of it."

"But George," Eleanor says, "you're the one who gave Nat his first piano lessons when he was five. Dr. Honiger is right. Going to a conservatory would be the best thing in the world for Nat. Wouldn't you have him pursue his passion?"

She doesn't voice her other reason for encouraging Nat to stay in school; that way, he wouldn't be enlisting any time soon.

Nat has never heard his mother argue with his father like this in front of other people—it is shocking. He looks more closely at her. Her jaw is fixed and her gaze is unwavering as she stares down his father. She seems much more defiant than usual.

"It's my life you're talking about," Nat says. "I should get to choose what school I go to."

George says, "You don't seem to realize how difficult it would be if you didn't succeed, because then it would be too late to do anything else professionally. Music is no way to make a living."

Eleanor says, "If Nat's as talented as Dr. Honiger says, he would make a living as a musician."

"And feed a wife and family?"

Shaking his head, Dr. Honiger bows. "You muss excuse me."

Eleanor says, "We can continue this discussion in private. We needn't air our disagreements here."

"I want to be part of the discussion," Nat says. "It's my life—you have to include me. Otherwise you won't have any moral beauty at all."

"What are you talking about?" his father asks.

"Frederic sings about moral beauty. It means doing what's best for someone else, rather than acting in your own selfish interest."

Eleanor grins, clearly amused by Nat's remark. She says, "We can finish this conversation at the inn. What time do you need to be back in your dorm, Nat?"

"Not 'til midnight, so long as I'm with you."

His mother checks her watch. "It's ten thirty now. Let's go."

She turns and starts up the aisle, inserting her arms into her coat as she goes. Nat tries to help her, but he's too slow. He notices, though, a little bounce in her step. His father lags behind.

Outside, Nat scans the sky. "So many stars out to-night," he says, hoping to break the tension between his parents. Eleanor and George make no reply.

Once they get to the Andover Inn, Nat looks up the brick walkway to the large wooden door with the shiny brass handle. "I've never actually been inside," he remarks.

Eleanor opens the door and enters the foyer, with George close behind. Nat closes the door behind him. They can hear people talking and laughing around the corner, but the front room is deserted.

"Let's sit here. Would you get us drinks, George? I'll have a manhattan. Orange soda for you, Nat?" Eleanor removes her coat and sits in a stuffed wingback chair covered in huge pink and red flowers.

Intending to draw their fire, Nat says, "I'd rather have a real drink." He sits next to his mother but keeps his coat on, for his damp, sweaty shirt makes him feel cold now.

George replies, "A 'real drink' it is. Nathaniel earned it." He leaves the room.

Eleanor says, "George is right." Stretching her legs out in front of her, she asks, "How has your winter gone, Nat? We haven't had many letters from you."

"I haven't heard from you much this winter either."

"Well, you know I work all day every day now, and by the time I get home, I'm pretty beat."

"Father's been writing to me."

"Really? I didn't know that."

Nat can see that his mother is quite surprised and possibly pleased by this news about George, but then she looks a little sad.

Appearing in the doorway with three drinks on a tray, George says, "Didn't know what?"

"I didn't know you've been writing to Nat."

"There are all sorts of things you don't know, Eleanor, the more time you spend at that hospital."

Nat flinches. That wasn't a nice thing to say.

George hands a tall glass to his son. "I got you a rum and ginger ale, Nathaniel. Let me know what you think."

"Thanks, Father." He takes a cautious sip. The drink tastes pretty good.

George passes Eleanor's glass to her. She says, "I was under the impression that the more hours I work at Halloran, the better I am discharging my patriotic duty."

"Within reason," George says. "You usually get home later than I do now. I don't know how you can spend that much time changing bedpans."

"George, that's not all I do!"

Nat has to change the subject. "I read that Henry Ford thinks we'll win the war in a month or two. Do you think he's right, Father?"

"No. Henry Ford is overly optimistic."

Eleanor says, "You sound so pessimistic, George. Is that why you were rude to Dr. Honiger?"

"Rude? I'm simply trying to save Nathaniel from disappointment. It nearly destroyed me when my own father wouldn't let me pursue music. I also know it's devilishly difficult to succeed as a professional musician."

"But George, you're doing the same thing to Nat that your father did to you."

George is silent a moment. Then he says, "I see your point."

Eleanor continues, "I have a patient who wasn't supposed to walk ever again, according to the doctors, but he has started taking a few steps. It's remarkable to see the difference that willpower and self-discipline can make." Her cheeks are flushed. "John got the physical therapist to construct a sort of jungle gym around his bed so he could strengthen his arms and legs. He practices his exercises six hours a day."

"Who's John?" Nat asks. Why is she going on about him like this? Is his mother sweet on this guy named John?

"He's the patient I've been talking about. It's amazing how hard he works and how much progress he has achieved."

"I'm sure that's interesting to those who care for him, but not to me," George says.

Nat has had enough. He's worn out from performing *Pirates*, and it's exhausting to be around his parents when they're acting this way. He excuses himself.

On the way back to his dormitory, Nat acknowledges to himself that he's never seen his parents so openly angry with each other. He doesn't want to think about what it might mean, though. He'd much rather think about Emma.

He'll write a song about Emma's hose. *Baggy, tattered rayon hose.* That could be one line. His step quickens.

In their room, Peter sits in bed with a volume of Byron's poetry. Putting his book down, Peter says, "Fabulous performance, Nat. You must be very proud."

"I had a great time," Nat replies. "But there's something I need to write down before I forget."

He sits at his desk, grabs a pencil and piece of paper, and writes, "Baggy tattered rayon hose." And "The worst of wartime clothes" . . . that rhymes, so he writes it down too. How can he explain the way they bag around Emma's knees? It's almost as though the impression of her knees lingers in her stockings. How about this: "Leave your chair, find your stockings still have knees." Nat starts chuckling at the ridiculous image he has conjured up.

Peter says, "What's so funny?"

Nat explains, "I'm writing a song about rayon hose. 'Leave your chair, find your stockings still have knees.' What do you think?"

"What is it about stockings, Sutton? You're positively obsessed."

"I'm a leg man. What more can I say?"

Before long, Nat has written:

> *Abbot, like most boarding schools,*
> *Has a rigid set of rules*
> *Some seem almost sensible*
> *Others indefensible*
> *Possibly the worst of these*
> *Covers our extremities*
> *Downtown one end wears a hat*
> *Other fares much worse than that*
> *Once more we must swathe each limb*
> *As for dinner, hymn, and gym*
> *In the worst of wartime clothes,*
> *Tattered, baggy rayon hose,*
> *Tattered, baggy rayon hose.*

Once he's done with that, Nat writes a letter to Harry asking for her thoughts on how they can get their parents to stop fighting.

✛

March 30, 1944

Dear Father and Mother,

> *You'll be glad to know, Father, that I've learned to do things the army way, with no guff, no discussion, no talking back. You didn't raise me quite like this!*

I know I have to take orders and follow them or I'll be punished. I'm really not used to punishment, but that's the army.

Although I've been stationed on the west coast of England near ▮▮▮▮▮▮▮*, the guys are saying we'll be moved closer to* ▮▮▮▮▮▮ *sometime in the coming weeks, and then I should be* ▮▮▮▮▮▮*, so you can relax, Mother.* ▮▮▮▮▮▮▮▮▮▮

With rumors flying every which way, the suspense is growing as we wait here, not knowing what is to come. Along with most of my buddies, I smoke cigarettes to soothe my nerves. I'm up to a package every day, which gives some evidence of the tension we're all feeling.

How's your job at the hospital going, Mother? Please keep those letters coming! It's great to hear the news from home.

I miss you more than I can say—I think of you all the time.

Love,

Your son Edward

Spring 1944

Is you is or is you ain't my baby
Maybe baby's found somebody new
Or is my baby still my baby true

—Lyrics from "Is You Is Or Is You Ain't My Baby?"
by Louis Jordan and Billy Austin, 1944

Eighteen

April

ELEANOR DIDN'T LIE to George when she told him she needed to go to Boston to help Jessica assess the winter storm damage to the family's summer place. But she neglected to mention she'd be traveling with John. John can walk with the aid of a cane now, and today he is being discharged from Halloran to complete his recuperation at home in Ipswich.

As Eleanor mounts the steps of her usual train to Halloran, carrying her suitcase and a picnic basket, the conductor smiles and nods.

"Going on a trip?" His long white hair makes him seem ancient.

Eleanor feels as though he can read her thoughts. Her face gets hot, but she shakes her head no.

"I'm off to visit my sister."

"Good for you, ma'am."

After she places her suitcase in the rack overhead, she takes a seat. There is no question of adultery here; she and John are simply having an affair of the heart. She's not immoral. They haven't done anything. Nevertheless, he's so quick and bright and insightful, and he makes her feel so alive . . . it's probably just as well that there are no private compartments on the train to Boston.

She's brought the controversial new book *Strange Fruit* by Lillian Smith to discuss on the train with John, and she's packed a picnic lunch: deviled ham sandwiches, a tin of salted almonds, dried apricots, a bottle of red wine, and small juice glasses, which are more innocuous (in case Jessica spots them) than actual wineglasses.

It feels strange to approach the hospital wearing civilian clothes. She hopes she won't have to go all the way up to her ward.

Fortunately, John is waiting for her near the front desk, wearing a uniform that is much too large for him. A khaki-colored canvas duffel is by his feet. In one hand he holds a wooden cane. His eyes seem bluer than usual, and his smile is wider than ever.

"Today's the day!" he says.

Eleanor puts her luggage down. "This is so exciting, John!"

"The army has given me leave for one month." He stares at her mouth. "Then I need to report back for duty."

Is he going to kiss her? Here?

Anxiously, Eleanor looks around. "Where's our ride? I thought someone was driving us to Grand Central."

Consulting a watch she's never seen, he replies, "The driver should be here in a few minutes. Let's go outside. I've been counting the hours 'til I could walk out of this hospital with you, Eleanor." He pushes the door open for her.

She's a little disconcerted by his directness. Outside the hospital, she says, "Are you going to miss Guido and the other men on the ward?"

"I'll see Guido again. We exchanged addresses. There's some business we might do together once this war is won."

She looks down at her scuffed black pumps. His reference to his address reminds Eleanor that John has a wife and a life she knows very little about.

"Why hasn't your wife come to visit? Boston isn't that far away."

John's frown extends to his forehead. "She has to stay home to take care of our business. We own a store on Route 133."

Over the months of getting to know each other in the hospital, they usually discussed the present, not the past.

"What do you sell?"

"Food, tobacco and booze, magazines and comic books, tools, fabric, fishing tackle, bait . . . pretty much anything you can think of."

"Couldn't your wife get someone to cover the store for a day or two?"

John stands a little straighter. "I wrote my wife a few months ago to tell her I want a divorce. She talked about splitting up before the war came along, but then someone had to run the business, so she's staying put for the duration."

"Oh!" Eleanor doesn't know anyone who's had a divorce.

Placing his hand under her chin, John lifts it so they can gaze directly into each other's eyes. "You look beautiful, Eleanor. I haven't been able to tell you that before, but it's true. Especially today, with your hair all shiny and that dress, which emphasizes all the right places."

Her pulse jumps.

"There was a lot we couldn't say in the hospital," he continues.

"That's true."

She knows she's been testing herself and teasing them both for months now. Discovering George's infidelity has made her feel a little freer to experiment with this relationship.

"I'm . . . going to miss you so much," she says.

An official army car approaches the entrance to Halloran. Eleanor steps back from John and turns to look at the driver, a uniformed soldier wearing thick glasses. The driver stops the car, jumps out, and salutes.

"Major Peterson?"

John replies, "Yes, Corporal, I'm Major Peterson."

The young man opens the back door of the sedan for John and Eleanor. John slides across the backseat, motioning Eleanor to follow him. She grabs the picnic basket and places it on the floor. The driver closes the door behind them. After a moment she hears the trunk shut on their luggage.

Once the car is moving, John says, "Are you picking anyone else up?"

"No, sir. You're it."

John reaches across the seat to take Eleanor's hand. Eleanor looks at the rearview mirror to see whether the driver is watching, but his eyes seem to be on the road. She squeezes John's fingers. His hand is so warm; she revels in the feel of it. His pulse seems to reverberate through her body.

Looking out his window, John says, "The forsythia is in bloom. I'd forgotten there'd be forsythia this time of year. It's so bright, it almost hurts my eyes."

"Isn't it lovely?" Eleanor replies.

John turns toward her. He whispers, "So are you." He moves his hand over to rest on her leg. Now his hand feels hot.

She closes her eyes a moment. What are they doing, indulging in this foolish infatuation? It can't possibly go anywhere. But she doesn't want him to take his hand away.

Opening her eyes, she turns to look at him. She wants him to know more about her life. Where should she start?

He puts his hand back in his own lap. "When we get there, the first thing I want is a drink. It's been months since I've had a drop."

"I brought wine for lunch."

"A shot of whiskey is what I had in mind, but we can open the wine now."

"It isn't even noon yet!"

"So what? I want a drink."

Silently Eleanor chides herself for being a prude as she lifts the lid of the picnic basket at her feet and pulls out a bottle of well-aged Bordeaux. After rooting around for the corkscrew, she tries opening the bottle.

"Here, let me do it." Using the sharp end of the corkscrew, John tears the seal off and handily removes the cork.

She passes him the glasses. After he pours some wine for each of them, he lifts his glass and swallows, then looks beyond her.

The driver says, "What about those Yankees, Major? Hank Borowy blanked the Red Sox something fierce yesterday."

"Bet the Sox will level the Yanks today. They have the better team by far."

"I take it you're a Red Sox fan, Major?"

"Born and bred near Boston. Seen any action, soldier?"

The driver keeps his eyes on the road while he replies, "No, sir. My eyesight has me sidelined."

Eleanor says, "I bet your mother's happy about that."

"Ma'am?"

"Glad you aren't serving on the front lines. You're safer here."

"Ma hasn't said nothing except I'm to follow orders and do my duty."

"That's right, Corporal," John says. "We all have orders to follow." He turns toward Eleanor and grins. "How about one of those sandwiches, Eleanor? I'm dying for some real food."

Eleanor brings out a sandwich and hands it to him along with a napkin.

"My, aren't we fancy?"

"I thought linen napkins would be nice. Of course, I imagined we'd eat on the train." Now she sounds stuffy to herself.

"We can always buy more food. Mm, this is delicious." Smooshed bread and deviled ham show between his teeth.

"Would you like another? You may have mine." She's too scared and excited to eat.

"I'll take as many as you've got."

"You're so skinny—I didn't realize you had such a big appetite."

"There wasn't anything decent at the hospital. I've got a lot of catching up to do." He bites into her sandwich. "The traffic is remarkable. I've never seen so many trucks in one place."

"Lots of matériel getting shipped out, sir," the driver replies.

Taking a sip of wine, Eleanor asks, "Is that because of the invasion?"

"Ma'am, we're not allowed to talk about it. Loose lips sink ships."

"But it's all over the newspapers. Everyone knows there'll be an invasion by the Allies. We just don't know where or when."

Everyone is quiet for a few minutes while John finishes his sandwiches.

"Cigarette, Eleanor?"

Eleanor hasn't smoked since the Great War. "Sure," she tells John.

His mouth reminds her so much of Henri's. Drinking wine before noon reminds her of working near the front lines, falling in love.

He hands her a cigarette and extends a lit Zippo toward her.

"Here we are, sir."

They stand on the sidewalk in front of Grand Central Station with their luggage at their feet. John looks across the street at the Biltmore Hotel.

"That's where I'm going to get a drink."

As they enter the grand lobby of the hotel, John says, "Let's see if they have a room. I'd rather drink alone with you, not with a bunch of strangers." He pauses, waiting for her response.

Eleanor's heart thunders in her ears. This is what all these months have been leading up to. *Can I be brave and follow my heart, or do I duck the chance to love again?*

"We have time before our train," John prompts.

"All right."

As she waits with their luggage while John goes to the desk, Eleanor feels shy and embarrassed—unnerving sensations at her age. *It would probably be better if the hotel were full.*

Then the clerk passes John something to fill out, and he removes his wallet to pay.

John returns to her. "They're sending up a bottle of whiskey. We can leave our luggage with the bellhop."

When they enter the elevator, a uniformed black man asks for their floor. Standing behind the operator, John grasps Eleanor's hand. She reminds herself she can still say no.

As they walk down the hall together, John sings, "Blue skies, nothing but blue skies, nothing but blue skies, when you're in love." His voice sounds surprisingly good.

Pleased to hear him use the word *love*, she teases, "That's not exactly how the song goes."

"I don't care."

In the room, John closes and locks the door. As he approaches her, she sees such heat in his eyes that she feels weak. He wraps his arms around her waist and pulls her tight. His erection presses against her stomach as he places his mouth on hers.

He turns his head to the side. "God, it's been so long!"

He begins to fumble through her silk dress for the clasp on her brassiere.

"Wait!" she says. "Kiss me again." She wants to savor every moment.

There's a knock. They pull apart, and John answers the door. Once the uniformed waiter puts down the tray with the bottle of Jack Daniel's, a bucket of ice, and glasses, John pays him. From the waiter's reaction, Eleanor can tell he hasn't been tipped very generously.

After John locks the door, he pours them each a glass. "Ice?"

"I'll take it neat."

She drinks a little of the whiskey for courage.

"Now, where were we?" John says, putting his glass down.

He's so attractive with that thick wavy brown hair and craggy face that Eleanor can hardly stand it. She walks into his arms.

Raising her mouth to his, she says flirtatiously, "Right here."

Their kiss goes on and on. He feels so good; she presses her breasts against his chest. She wants to sink all the way into him, to be surrounded by him. She loves feeling so juicy. As she rocks her hips back and forth against him, John groans, lifting up her skirt.

Eleanor pulls back. "Let's not rush." She reaches for her glass. "Little more?"

John pours another inch of Jack Daniel's into both of their glasses.

"Tasty," Eleanor comments.

"So are you." John takes her hand and leads her to the bed.

Eleanor steps out of her shoes, and then she peels back the covers. She lies down. John climbs on top of her. Leaning on his elbows, he cups her face with his hands.

"You're everything I ever dreamed of." He kisses her fervently. "I want to feel your skin against mine."

"Yes."

"Take off your clothes." John stands up to undo his belt and remove his trousers.

Eleanor doesn't want John to see her saggy breasts and belly in the light of day. She goes into the bathroom to remove her clothing. Then she wraps a towel around herself and returns to bed. John smiles, then tugs her towel off.

"You're beautiful, Eleanor."

She knows that isn't true, but she's glad he said so. She looks at his bare flesh; he is much hairier than George. He grabs her breasts and kneads them hard, then shoves his knee between her legs.

"You're too rough. Let me show you."

Eleanor rolls on top of John and kisses him all over. Closing her eyes, she pretends he is Henri. As she rubs herself on him, she feels like a cat in heat. Soon, she raises herself up to take him inside her. He slides in easily. He rolls so he is on top. After three thrusts, she feels him spasm.

"God, oh God," he says, collapsing on top of her.

Eleanor nearly cries.

What the hell was I thinking?

"I know that was a little quick, but I was awfully horny. We'll go slower next time."

Eleanor is absolutely furious with herself. She's been lying to herself about John, convincing herself that he's like Henri. He isn't anything like Henri!

She wants to get away from John as quickly as possible. She pulls herself out from under him and hurries into the bathroom. As she washes John off her body, she asks herself, *Now what?* Need she worry about getting pregnant? Probably not. Putting her clothes back on, she returns to the bedroom.

John still lies naked on the bed. He looks scrawny and pale.

"There won't be any 'next time,'" Eleanor says.

"What do you mean? I love you."

"We've got to hurry, or we'll miss our train."

While Eleanor leads the way down the aisle of car number 7 in search of their reserved seats, she wonders how she'll bear sitting next to John for the long trip to Boston.

Once they're settled, John takes her hands in his. "Eleanor, I want to marry you."

"I *am* married, John. I have children and a home and people who depend on me."

"Then what were you doing in that hotel with me?"

Good question.

For months, she felt attracted to him. She told herself there was nothing wrong with what she was doing. It wasn't as though she were having an affair the way George was. She felt superior to George because she hadn't acted on her passion in an explicitly sexual way. Until this morning, she held the moral high ground over George. But that is a pathetic comparison to make.

She says, "I was there because I thought I'd fallen in love with you."

John squeezes her hands.

"And my husband is having an affair."

"So . . . you wanted to get back at him? What's good for the goose is good for the gander, or however that goes?" Dropping her hands, John stands up. "I'm going to the club car," he says coldly and leaves.

Eleanor stares out the window unseeing as the train rattles over the tracks. She feels so bad she can't even cry. She considers changing seats. She never wants to see him again; he reminds her that she can no longer consider herself virtuous or honest. Moving to another car would be cowardly, though. She leans back and closes her eyes.

A while later, John returns. "So what happened at the hotel? You went from loving me to refusing me. I thought you were going to help me be better than I am." His eyes water.

"I'm sorry, John. I'm worse than I thought I was."

"Would you have ever married me?"

"No."

"So you used me."

"That wasn't my intention, but you're right." She bows her head.

"Now what?"

"We go home to our separate lives."

"I can't sit next to you for the rest of this trip." He picks up his luggage and moves away.

Eleanor's sense of relief is powerful. Over the next hour, she thinks about John and Henri. How could she have deluded herself about John so completely? She has lied to herself. She's never known anyone as passionate and loving as Henri, and they were cheated. They only had two months together. What if Henri hadn't died? How different would her life have been?

She would have stayed in France.

But he did die. And she hurried back to the States, never allowing herself to think about the what-ifs because of the baby in her belly. The truth was that her honeymoon with Henri had never ended. Until now. Deep in her heart, she has never been completely committed to George.

This insight makes Eleanor cry hard.

As she is climbing down the steps in South Station, she spots John on the platform. She has to touch his arm to get his attention.

"I'm sorry, John. I never meant to hurt you. If there's ever anything I can do for you, please let me know."

Stepping out of her reach, he says, "I can't imagine coming to you for anything. Ever."

He hates her, and she can understand why.

"Goodbye," she says.

John bobs his head and moves on.

Eleanor has a lot of thinking to do. She should bury

those boots spattered with Henri's blood, along with the plain gold ring he'd given her. She'll invite Harry to help. Though maybe Harry will prefer to keep the ring for herself? That would be fitting. Eleanor will offer that ring to Harry, but the boots should definitely go into the ground, where they will finally become dirt.

She hurries toward the exit. Her sister awaits her.

Nineteen

Early May

Dear Nat,

    To answer your questions, I'm doing fine, and no, I haven't had to kill anyone yet. As the ███████████, *I don't kill anyone directly, but I'm glad they taught us how to kill the enemy during basic training so I'll be prepared if I find myself on the ground in enemy territory. I know how to throw a man down and where to kick him with the most damaging effect. I know how to use weapons.*

    There's so much I can't tell you. What I can say is that I'm still in England. It's beautiful around here, though the weather has been awfully rainy and cold. We sleep in barracks and make practice runs and clean our equipment over and over again. The conditions are most uncomfortable, but I've gotten used to it. Everyone has a strong feeling of rising tension as the weather improves. I'm not scared so much as I'm anxious to see how it will all turn out.

Aside from that, I feel pretty damn homesick at times, which is a surprise. I never felt homesick at Andover. You can't imagine how much I miss home, especially things like real eggs and butter, ice cream, hamburgers, music. God, I miss hearing classical music! I wish I could have been there for your "Pirates of Penzance" performance. Father wrote that you played "creditably." Doesn't that sound just like him?

Now don't let this scare you, Nat, but if I don't make it home, I want you to promise me you won't let that affect what you do with your life. Whether I get back or not, don't work at the factory for Father unless that's truly what you desire for yourself. Do not be led by your sense of duty. Your life is yours to live as you see fit. But don't worry about me. I have a feeling I'm going to come through.

Take care, old chap.

Love,

Edward

✚

This is the most terrifying letter Nat has ever received. In all his letters to Nat, Eddie has never signed "love" before. How can Nat possibly put this letter aside and go to the tea dance at Abbot?

He stands next to his mailbox, staring into space. Eddie really could get killed. Everyone knows a big invasion of the Continent is coming soon, and it sounds as if Eddie will be part of this assault. The passageways in Nat's lungs and throat begin to constrict. He sits down on the floor and makes a tent with his fingers to capture his damp exhalations. He breathes as slowly as he can.

Then Nat folds Eddie's letter carefully and pushes it into his pocket. *Please, please, please, keep Eddie safe. Let him return in one piece. I miss him.*

As he starts to calm down, Nat realizes how much he has counted on Eddie to come home and play the role of dutiful older son, pleasing their father and letting Nat off the hook. He can't see himself volunteering for the armed forces. After he graduates from Andover, Nat wants to pursue his music and Emma, not Nazis or Japs.

Emma. He hasn't seen her since the last performance of *Pirates*. But he has polished the song about "tattered, baggy rayon hose," and he's dying to play it for her. Tonight is his only chance to see her before the school year ends.

If he goes to the dance, will he be betraying his brother? He pulls Eddie's letter out again. *It's your life for you to live as you see fit.*

He rushes across the quad to his dorm room to change into a suit.

"Why are you wearing a necktie for a belt?"

"I'll explain if you dance with me."

"You've got a deal," Emma responds.

Her hair is lifted up, and it curves toward the top of her head. She's wearing a blue dress that moves as she lifts her arms to him. She's gorgeous.

Nat glances at Dean Rightly, who leans against a pillar by the entrance. Will the dean insist that Nat remove the necktie at his waist? It *is* a violation of the dress code, but the rules have gotten a little looser this final week of classes, with papers and exams looming over everyone.

He places his left hand in the middle of Emma's back and grasps her right hand in his. Catching the beat, he grips Emma a little tighter while he moves his right foot forward.

"How do you make your hair swoop like that?"

"Have you heard of hairpins?"

"Of course. I have a sister and a mother, so I know about some stuff."

"Well, I used every hairpin I own and a few of my roommate's. I hope you can't see them."

"Not at all."

"Tell me about the tie."

"My roommate, Peter, created a cartoon character called Sammy Phillips, named after the founder of Phillips Academy Andover."

"Really?" She sounds as if she will laugh at whatever he says next.

"Sammy is the typical student at Andover, although he wears a necktie for a belt. Peter says Sammy gives him a way to comment on our pretensions and the absurdities of this place."

Suddenly Emma's foot is beneath his.

"I'm sorry."

"You've only crushed my toes slightly."

"Oh no, I'm so sorry." Nat stops moving. "Shall I get you some ice?"

"I'm only teasing. Let's keep dancing."

She really seems to like him. He says, "May I ask you a question?"

"Of course."

"When we danced together last time, after we stopped dancing you went off with some girls, and then you were all laughing, and it seemed like you were laughing at me."

"No. I'd never laugh at you. Not unless you've told a joke."

Her eyes are so clear and guileless that Nat believes her. He's starting to think he and Emma might really have something special. His chest expands with a huge sensation of longing. He doesn't know what he's hoping for, exactly.

He really wants to tell her about the song he's written, but what if she doesn't think it's great? Should he take the risk? He wants to impress her so she won't forget him over the summer.

"There's something I'd really like to play for you."

"We can sneak down to the piano practice room in the basement," Emma says. "Though you realize we could get in trouble for leaving the dance." She sounds excited.

Nat dances them over to a side door. Without a word, they exit as unobtrusively as they can.

Emma grabs Nat's hand. As he follows her down a set of stairs, he says, "You were the inspiration for this song."

Emma stops and turns around to look at him in the dim light. "Really?"

What if she doesn't like the song? What if she isn't amused? Maybe she'll feel offended by his writing about her hose . . .

Emma leads the way into a small room and turns on the light. Nat moves to the upright against the wall and plays a few notes. The piano is in tune. After pulling out the bench, he sits and plays the song through without words. Then he begins to sing.

Abbot, like most boarding schools,
Has a rigid set of rules
Some seem almost sensible
Others indefensible

Standing behind him, Emma hasn't made a sound. Then he gets to the refrain:

Tattered, baggy rayon hose,
Tattered, baggy rayon hose

She chuckles. He goes on.

We are dressed by the numbers toe to head,
So obsessed, even wear our hats to bed.
Leave your chair, find your stockings
still have knees;
Everywhere, rampant runs will cause
your legs to freeze.

Now she's laughing out loud.

When he finishes, Emma says, "I *love* the part about 'your stockings still have knees.' Play it again."

After he completes a second run-though, Emma says, "You're really talented!"

Nat ducks his head. "Thanks."

He steps close and places his hands tentatively at her waist. Then he presses his lips on hers, which are so warm and soft he feels as if he were sinking into a thick down pillow. Then he pulls back.

"Wow! That was nice."

I really do like girls.

"Yes," Emma agrees.

"We should probably go back upstairs before we get in trouble."

As he follows Emma up the chipped linoleum steps, Nat admires the curve of her bottom. When they reach the top, he says, "I'm so glad you enjoyed my song."

"I'm honored to be the inspiration."

"I know that 'tattered, baggy rayon hose' isn't exactly flattering."

"It's a great description. What are you going to do with the song?"

"I have no idea." He pauses, then says, "Emma, could I write you over the summer? Would you mind?"

"That would be super. I've never had a letter from a boy before."

They continue down the hall to the dance without speaking further. At the entrance to the assembly hall, they see the musicians are taking a break and all the boys and girls have returned to their separate sides of the room. Everyone's eyes seem to be on them. Dean Rightly takes a step in their direction, but then, seeming to change his mind, he turns away. A few moments later, the musicians return to their stands. The music starts up again.

Outside Boston's South Station, Eleanor catches a cab. On the way to North Station, she inspects her face in her compact. Her eyes are still a little red and puffy, so she pinches her cheeks and applies lipstick in the hope that Jessica won't notice she's been crying. Jessica, who lives nearby in Newton, has arrived at the station first. She's waiting near the ticket counter.

"Ellie!"

"Jessie!"

The women embrace warmly and then, still in each other's arms, lean back to look each other over. "You've lost a lot of weight since I saw you last." As the older sister, Eleanor is in the habit of looking out for Jessica.

"I'm fine, Ellie. With rationing and all, I've been eating less than I used to."

"It's so good to see you! Have you already bought your ticket?"

Once Eleanor purchases her own ticket, they head for the gate. After settling into their seats, Eleanor asks, "How bad *was* the storm damage?"

"Earl wrote that the boathouse was smashed. I don't know what other damage there was. He just went on and on about the boathouse. We'll have to see for ourselves what we have to deal with." Jessica smiles. "I'd rather spend our time together now catching up. How are you, really?"

Eleanor glances out the window, where narrow clapboard houses blur by. "Oh, Jessie." Eleanor's lips begin to tremble, and she ducks her head as she tries to contain her tears. "You know George has been having an affair—I wrote you all about that. Well, I had an affair of sorts too."

"What?" Jessica sounds incredulous. "You never mentioned anything like this in your letters."

"It was a mistake . . ."

Eleanor is so ashamed of her behavior that she really doesn't want to think about John any longer, and she certainly doesn't intend to tell Jessica the tawdry details. What really matters is what she learned from her experience with John.

"I haven't been fair to George all these years. As soon as I knew I was pregnant, I had to find my baby a father. I got him to fall in love with me. But I never loved George the way I loved Henri."

"Every love is different."

"I enshrined Henri in my heart. That's really how I cheated George. No wonder he looked elsewhere."

"Ellie, you don't need to justify George's bad behavior to me."

"I behaved just as badly."

"What I can't believe is how little you and George talk about the important things. George makes you act as if Henri never existed, as if you'd never driven an ambulance, as if you'd never had an 'early' baby. Secrets carry a price."

"George wanted to believe he was the first man I'd ever known—"

"That's too bad." Her sister's vehemence surprises Eleanor. "The fact is that George was *not* the first man you loved and married. Eleanor, you and George *have* to discuss all the things that are keeping you apart. If you don't, you'll grow lonelier and lonelier."

"Maybe George and I can start afresh." Eleanor begins to feel a glimmer of hope. "Except that Miriam's in the way. If we could just start fresh, perhaps we'd have a chance."

"You two have got to talk, Ellie. That's all there is to it. You won't know where you are with George until you have an honest conversation."

They ride in silence for a long time while Eleanor considers Jessica's advice. As the train slows to stop at the Gloucester station, Eleanor eventually says, "I worry about Eddie."

"Of course you do."

When the two women step down from the train, they spot Earl, the caretaker for their summer house, standing next to an ancient Ford. The burly man is much grayer than the last time Eleanor saw him, but he seems just as anxious to please as ever. A local man, he has helped the family for decades.

Eleanor says, "How are you, Earl? It's been nearly three years since I've seen you. Except for wartimes, I've come here with Mother every year since I was born."

"You'll find a few changes around the place, but not too many," Earl replies, opening the rear door of the car.

Eleanor climbs into the backseat. Jessica joins Earl in front.

While Earl tells them about the nor'easter that caused so much damage in January, Eleanor looks all around, eagerly reviewing the familiar landmarks. The houses look shabbier than she remembers, but of course paint is in short supply. The air still smells the same, though—that wonderful saltwater scent seems fresher than anything.

Soon Earl turns onto a driveway that winds through the woods. As shrubs covered with oriental bittersweet scrape against the sides of the Ford, Eleanor thinks they badly need to be cut back, but that's a task for another day, or another year.

Finally Earl pulls to a stop in the parking circle, and Eleanor jumps out of the car. The expanse of space and light envelope her. *This is home.* Sky and sea, only a shade of color separating them, reflect each other all the way to the horizon. She breathes in deeply, recalling sleepy afternoon naps and long nights of deep rest in this place. She loves being here—she knows herself here.

She wanders past clumps of *Rosa rugosa* toward the bluff above the ocean.

Surprised to find that the sea is filled with all sorts of vessels, Eleanor turns back to Earl. "What's going on here? It's so busy."

He says, "This is part of the Coast Guard's regular beat now. They patrol the coast along here round the clock, looking for Nazi subs. At night the sky is full of search-lights. It's quite a sight."

"Of course. That makes sense. I hadn't thought."

The boathouse *is* a mess. One side was bashed in by the waves, everything inside was jumbled together, and the whole structure leans in such a way that it looks as though a big wind would push it into the house.

"I think it needs to come down," Earl says.

The women agree. While Earl and Jessica discuss de-tails, Eleanor's attention wanders. Jessica is right. She has to talk with George. She has to ask him about Miriam. And she must tell him about John.

The night Eleanor arrives home from Boston, she puts her suitcase and the picnic basket down in the hall, takes off her raincoat, and marches right into George's study before she can lose her nerve. He's sitting at his desk, a mass of papers spread all over the surface. He lifts his head at her entrance.

"Welcome back," he says. "I didn't expect you until tomorrow."

"We have got to talk, George. This can't wait."

"Shall I get us drinks?" he replies. She thinks he's stalling.

"No. Come sit over here with me." She takes one of the chairs facing the fire, which has burned down to coals.

George lifts a couple of logs from the holder and plac-es them on top of the coals. Then he picks up the bellows.

"Sit down, George!"

"All right, Eleanor—here I am," he says, pulling his chair into position so they can face each other.

She stares at him. "Don't you have something to tell me?"

"No."

"Come on, George. We've got to talk about Miriam."

George groans.

"I know you're in love with her. You've been having an affair with her for months, maybe longer."

George puts his face in his hands. His words are muffled as he says, "How long have you known?"

"Since the gala at the Plaza last fall. I had my suspicions before then, but I knew for certain when I saw you together." Her heart still hurts at his betrayal. "How could you, George? How could you do that to me? To our family? You've jeopardized everything we've built together over all these years." Tears start leaking down her face.

He lifts his head. "It was insane, I know. I felt so guilty, but I couldn't stop myself." He drops his eyes.

Eleanor nods, and her tears stop. She knows what he's talking about.

George looks up. "Falling for Miriam was all mixed up with the war and saving refugees and I don't know what else . . . A million times I promised myself I'd give her up, but it was like some kind of addiction. I kept coming back." As he shakes his head, Eleanor sees from his face that he's mystified.

"Do you want to marry her?" She holds her breath.

"She ended it three months ago."

Eleanor feels an enormous sense of relief, but she still needs to know. "Would you have married her if she hadn't ended it?"

"No. I never thought of marrying Miriam."

Now Eleanor relaxes a little.

George keeps shaking his head. "I still can't believe what I did." He pounds his fist against his thigh. "There is no honest way to justify an affair!" He stands and starts pacing while he adds, more softly, "I've always considered myself an honorable man. My behavior didn't fit with my morality or who I thought I was."

"I know what you mean," Eleanor replies.

"You do?" Abruptly, George sits down again.

"I had an affair of sorts myself."

"When?" He straightens his back.

"It was more an affair of the heart," Eleanor says, hoping she won't have to say more.

"I had no idea you were unfaithful." His voice is cool and matter-of-fact.

"We only acted on it once."

"Who is he?" Now George sounds angry.

"He was one of the wounded soldiers at Halloran. But it doesn't matter who. He's gone home now. I'll never see him again."

"It's over, then?"

"Yes."

"So we both had affairs." George starts to get up, but then he sits back in his chair. "Where does this leave us?"

"I'm not sure," Eleanor says. "I thought you didn't love me anymore."

He says, "I guess I was lonesome. You were so preoccupied with the children."

"How do people heal from these kinds of wounds?" Eleanor asks, understanding it's probably a rhetorical question.

"I don't know."

"I have to tell you, George, something really important came out of my affair."

"What could that possibly be?" he replies skeptically.

"I realized I never really gave you my whole heart. I always held a part of it back. The part that still loved Henri." This will make all the difference going forward.

From the sound George emits, it's as if she'd just kicked him in the gut. Then he feels in his pocket for a cigarette. "I guess I knew that down deep. I always envied Henri." He lights up. "He got you first." Exhaling, he asks, "Do you still love Henri?"

"I'll always love him, but he's part of my past, not my present or future. I never had a family or made a life with him, the way I have with you."

George looks wary. "What are you saying?" He takes a deep drag on his cigarette. "Are you saying you are ready to commit to me completely now?"

Eleanor sees the longing in his eyes. "I believe so."

She puts her hand out to him. Eventually he takes it and squeezes.

"We've been holding on to too many secrets," she says. "If I hadn't kept my experiences on the battlefield a secret from the children, would Eddie have been so quick to enlist? I wonder."

Dropping her hand, George looks away, then back at Eleanor. "Nat might have seen me with Miriam last summer, at a jazz club in the city."

"Oh no."

"He hinted as much, but I never answered him. Do I need to talk with him about that?"

"I don't know, George."

"If you really want us to air all our secrets, Eleanor, let's talk about Harriet." He extinguishes his cigarette by screwing it into the ashtray. "Tell me: When was Harry actually conceived? In France, as I suspect—or here with me?" George squints in such a way that he could be flinching.

Eleanor shuts her eyes. "Harry was conceived in France. I tried to make you believe she was yours, born prematurely, but that wasn't true."

"Why didn't you tell me you were pregnant when we were courting, Eleanor?"

"I couldn't risk it." Her voice quivers. "I was afraid you wouldn't marry me."

"You never gave me a chance."

"That's true. I'm sorry."

George jumps up. He nearly shouts as he tells her, "I would have married you anyway. Don't you know that?"

Eleanor begins to cry.

Taking both of her hands, he pulls her out of her chair and holds her at arm's length, looking deeply into her eyes. "I loved you, Eleanor. I wanted you for my wife."

Eleanor cries harder.

"And I've loved Harriet from the first moment I saw her."

Finally Eleanor steps into his embrace. "It's all my fault," she murmurs. "I should have told you everything from the start."

He rocks her back and forth. "We've both made mistakes, El."

After a while, Eleanor reaches for the handkerchief in her pocket and wipes her face.

George says, "Feeling better?"

"I am, actually. Much better."

Twenty

Saturday afternoon

Dear Jessica,

You were right. George and I had a long talk when I got back from Boston. Finally we spoke the truth to each other about Miriam and John and Henri and Harry. While we're both feeling bruised by each other's betrayals and a little precarious about the future, I know I feel much closer to George now, and he's warmer to me than he's been in years. Now that Nat's home from school, I hope our family can get back to normal. As close to normal, that is, as we can with Eddie overseas.

I can't tell you what a relief it is for me to be completely honest, for a change. I had no idea how good it would feel to speak my whole truth, no matter how embarrassing and unsavory. Finally I feel like I can be true to myself.

Before Nat returned from Andover, George and I agreed that we shouldn't tell the boys about Harry's father—it's up to Harry to share that secret with them if she chooses. Does this make sense? My habit of secrecy is so strong that I'm not sure anymore.

Most days before dinner now, George and Harry have a drink together, just the two of them, which they call "the farm report meeting." Harry is thrilled by George's interest and attention. Then after dinner, she's usually off somewhere.

I can never thank you enough, Jessie, for your wise counsel. You may have saved our marriage.

All my love,

Ellie

✚

George, Eleanor, Harry, and Nat are sitting on the porch. Harry has just set up the pegs on the cribbage board for a game with Nat when the radio announcer breaks in on the music. Eleanor quickly leans forward to turn up the volume.

"The Supreme Commander General Dwight D. Eisenhower has just announced that the Allied forces began 'landing this morning on the northern coast of France.'"

Nat says, "At last! Now Eddie and his buddies can chase the Nazis all the way back to Germany. I bet it'll be over by the end of the summer."

"Sh!" says Harry. "I want to hear what they say."

After some hissing sounds and then dead air, music resumes on the radio.

"I wonder where Eddie is right now," Eleanor says.

George says, "It won't be easy to push the Nazis back, Nathaniel." His father looks old, with gaunt cheeks, dark smudges beneath his eyes. His hair seems grayer, but maybe that's the light. "And don't forget about the Pacific."

Nat sees the veins in his mother's neck protrude as she frowns at George. "Do you have to be pessimistic?"

"I hope I'm simply realistic," George replies.

Without saying a word, Harry gestures at Nat to start their game.

"It's so hot," Eleanor says.

Nat has a hard time concentrating on the game. Maybe that's true for everyone because no one talks as music continues to play on the radio.

"Father?" Nat speaks hesitantly; he is afraid to ask, but he has to. "Do you think Eddie will be all right?"

George looks up from his newspaper. "I don't know, Nathaniel."

"Eddie will be fine," Eleanor says. The indentation between her eyebrows is deeper than ever. Her face is so flushed that Nat's afraid she'll have a heart attack.

"I have no idea what will happen to him," George says. "If Edward's killed, I don't think I could bear it."

Eleanor takes a deep breath and exhales noisily. The radio still plays music.

She bursts out, "This waiting drives me crazy!"

Just then the radio announcer says, "We have General Eisenhower—he is about to speak." The radio crackles.

"Peoples of western Europe," says the voice on the radio, sounding as if it came from far away, "a landing was made this morning on the coast of France by troops of the Allied expeditionary forces. This landing is part of the

United Nations plan for the liberation of Europe, made in conjunction with our great Russian allies."

Eisenhower tells them that RAF bombers swept the English Channel for days, providing aerial assaults on enemy vessels and planes to prepare the way, while boats brought thousands of men over to storm the beaches.

Nat grows more excited as he visualizes the action General Eisenhower describes. But at the same time, he wonders why General Eisenhower is giving out so much information about what is transpiring right now—shouldn't that stay secret?

Eisenhower continues. "The hour is approaching. Resistance groups and patriots, follow the instructions you have received but don't needlessly endanger lives until I give the signal to rise and strike the enemy. Be patient! Prepare!"

Nat is curious to hear this. Will everyone emerge from their hiding places and start shooting Nazis at a certain signal? What kind of signal would that be?

"It'll be another year or more before it's all over," George says.

Eleanor moans.

Nat's sense of anticipation collapses under the weight of his father's remark.

"But getting into France is a major step forward," Harry insists.

"That's right, Harry," Nat says, trying to shore up his own hopes. "This is really progress."

Eleanor stands. Clenching her fists, she says, "I am more than ready for this war to end."

Ten days later, Harry surprises everyone by bringing a date, a boy named Frank, to Sunday dinner. When he arrives just before they are about to sit down, Eleanor tells Nat to set another place quickly. Once everyone is seated in the dining room, Eleanor brings the casserole in and places it in front of George. Then she sits at her own end of the table.

Nat can see that Frank likes Harry very much. Nat stares at Frank. How did he get his hair to look so smooth and perfect? Frank has an awful lot of hair, and it's blond enough to appear white.

George leans forward to inspect the dish, which is filled with poached eggs surrounded by noodles and topped with cheese. "What is this?"

"It's called Eggs in Noodle Nests," replies Eleanor. "I have to do something to make these endless egg dishes seem like something new. Aren't they cute?"

"*Cute* is not a word I would ever think to employ under any circumstance whatsoever," George answers, a smile lurking in his eyes.

Eleanor chuckles. "You're right, George!"

Nat can't think of the last time he's seen his parents act playful with each other. It's a pleasant change.

"What's your last name, young man?" George inquires as he dishes the casserole onto plates that Harry hands him.

"It's Hallowell, Mr. Sutton."

"Are your people British?" George replies.

"Yes, sir. My family emigrated from England in 1900." The salad bowl is passed around.

Eleanor says, "You must forgive our informality, Frank. Dig in. We don't usually say grace at meals."

"Thank you for including me, Mrs. Sutton." Frank looks around at them, and everyone starts to eat. "I suppose you all want to take a good look at me if I'm going out with your daughter." He turns his attention to George. "Right, Mr. Sutton?"

George presses his lips together. He snorts all of a sudden, then he begins to guffaw. Nat is astounded.

"You're absolutely right, young man," George says. "Good for you to call a spade a spade."

Eleanor says, "How did you and Harriet meet?"

"At the Palisades Movie Theater last winter. We happened to sit near each other, and we both laughed at the same things, so after the movie we started talking."

Harry is looking at Frank so fondly that Nat wants to puke. "What exactly are your intentions toward my sister?" he asks outright.

George snorts again.

Frank says, "I can assure you my intentions are honorable. I respect your sister, and I admire her. Even though Harriet is a little bossy." He nods at Harry as though this were some sort of joke between them.

Nat is appalled. How dare Frank make fun of Harry?

George asks Frank, "What sort of work do you do?"

"I'm an administrator at the Essex County Hospital in Newark. I like the job a lot. I've been there a couple of years."

"What's wrong with you?" Nat asks. "Why aren't you fighting in the war?"

Harry says, "Come on, Nat. Be nice."

"More salad, Frank?" Eleanor asks.

He shakes his head no as he replies, "It's a natural enough question, Nat. My draft board exempted me from military service because I'm the breadwinner for my family—my mother and sister. My father died when I was ten, and my mother isn't well, so they need me at home. But I wouldn't have gone to war in any case. I'm a Quaker—a pacifist. I don't believe in killing."

Eleanor raises her drink and salutes him. Then she says quietly, "You make me think of my first husband."

Nat waits for his father to choke. Frank looks inquiringly at Harry.

Harry says softly, "Mummy lost her first husband in the Great War. He was a doctor."

"Ah," Frank says.

George asks, "What if someone attacked your mother or your sister or Harriet here? Wouldn't you defend them with everything you have?"

"Father, that's not fair," Harry says.

"I'd talk to him," Frank answers. "I'd do everything I could to find a peaceful resolution."

Shaking his head, George says, "You're an idealist."

"Call me what you like," Frank says, raising his open hands. While polite, he sounds completely assured that his position is absolutely correct. He is immovable.

Nat is struck by the strength of Frank's conviction, especially given that he is a relatively young man trying to impress their parents. Nat is beginning to respect Frank for standing up to his father, but he can't state that directly. Instead, he says, "You have moral beauty, just like my mother, because you work at a hospital."

George and Eleanor exchange a glance.

"Thank you," Frank replies.

George says, "Nathaniel, enough with this business about moral beauty."

Changing the subject, Nat says, "Did anyone read the article in *Life* on General Montgomery? He's the Irishman whose army chased the Nazis out of North Africa, and then he fought in Sicily and Italy. Apparently Monty treats his troops as men of intelligence who have a right to know what their job is and what they are getting into. I hope Eddie has a commander like that."

Eleanor says, "Frank, are you the reason we've seen so little of Harry lately?"

"Yes, ma'am. We've been together whenever we can."

George says, "How are you getting on with that saxophone, Nat?"

"Saxophone?" Harry asks.

"I borrowed one for the summer from a classmate. Father makes me practice in the barn because I don't sound very good." He adds, "These nests are delicious!"

"Thank you, Nat. Everyone, leave some room for dessert," Eleanor says. "We have ice cream."

"That will be a treat, Mrs. Sutton," Frank says.

Nat spots a figure in the distance slowly bicycling up the long driveway. It's a man in a brown Western Union uniform riding toward their house. His heart begins to squeeze shut.

"I've been saving cream for a few days, and there are lots of ripe strawberries in the patch," says Eleanor.

Black dots begin to crowd Nat's field of vision; the conversation recedes.

The doorbell rings loudly.

"Who could that be on a Sunday night?" Eleanor says. She stands.

George says, "I'll get it."

Nat feels woozy as he rises. He, Harry, and Frank follow Eleanor and George down the hall. Once they round the corner, they can all see the Western Union man standing beyond the screened door.

"Oh!" Eleanor cries.

George opens the door. Eleanor, her face white, grabs George's arm as though she would stop him.

"Telegram," the Western Union man says.

George reaches out, tears the telegram open, skims it, and hands it to Eleanor. After glancing at it, Eleanor drops it to the floor as she covers her head with her hands, wailing, "*NO!*"

Nat swoops down to pick up the piece of paper: *Regret that your son Private Second Class Edward S. Sutton killed in action. The Adjutant General.*

Not moving, George stares out the door.

Frank places his hand gingerly on Harry's shoulder. "I'm so sorry, Harriet."

Nat wants to kick Frank in the shins. What is he doing here in the midst of their family?

"Is there anything I can do to help?" Frank asks. When no one responds, he says, "In that case, I'll get out of your way." He turns and quietly lets himself out the front door.

Harry steps around to face George. "Father? Daddy?"

George shakes his head back and forth.

Nat reaches for his mother, but she shrieks, "*My baby!* This is your fault, George!" She rocks back on her heels. "I knew it would come to this!"

George hurries down the hall toward his study. Eleanor runs after him.

"I know all about death. You should have listened to me! You thought Edward would come back a hero and then you could brag about him. You gambled with my son's *life!* This was all to prove *your* goddamned manhood!" Eleanor follows George into the room, crying, "Your manhood has cost us everything!"

The door to the study slams shut.

Although a solid wooden door separates them, Nat hears his father roar with such rage and pain it sounds as if he were being gored.

Harry runs up the stairs.

Nat can't bear it; he moves over to the phonograph. What should he put on: Brahms's Third Symphony? Gershwin's *Rhapsody in Blue?* He doesn't really want to listen to any recording he can think of. He doesn't know what to do. His chest feels so tight he starts to groan.

He should try whistling like Eddie—maybe that will ease this pain. But he can't produce any sound except the exhalation of his breath. No good.

Eddie!

He races up the stairs, into Eddie's room. Heaving with breathlessness, he stands in the space that was his brother's. Football trophies adorn the top of Eddie's bookshelf, along with his leather helmet.

Nat climbs onto Eddie's bed. Lying facedown, he squeezes his eyes shut, trying for the relief of tears. He can't cry. This is so much worse than anything he's ever imagined.

He knows his father didn't kill his brother—but whose fault is it? It has to be *someone's* fault he's lost his only brother. Anxiously his brain skitters around, seeking some sort of lesson he can take away so he can make sure nothing like this ever happens again.

But there is no lesson. This can never happen again because he has only one brother.

Had one brother.

Nat begins to rock back and forth. His heart is cracking apart. Maybe if he tries to write a song—maybe that will help. He reaches for a word, an image, a note. Nothing comes to him. He will never get over this.

None of them will.

It's your life for you to live as you see fit.

Somehow Eddie's words provide a wisp of comfort.

After a while, Nat wanders back downstairs to the living room, where he sits at the piano, idly moving his fingers over the keys. He can hear a heated exchange between his parents in the next room, but he's unable to discern what they're saying.

The door to the study opens. Standing up from the piano bench, Nat moves closer to the room where his parents have been closeted.

George's voice is muffled.

Eleanor replies, "I'll never recover from losing Eddie, George—but I know our war must end."

Nat closes his eyes and bows his head. *Amen.*

Acknowledgments

Many people have helped me over the fifteen years and multiple drafts it took to complete this manuscript. Five of those named below are no longer living—but I still feel gratitude to each of them.

I owe Benjy Stevens, Phebe Miner, Peter Stevens, Jack Sheldon, and Amos Sheldon thanks for the information and perspectives they provided me in the early stages of conceiving this novel. Thanks to Susan Eilertsen, Pamela McClanahan, Sally Power, Maggie Gluek, Beatriz Garcia-Arteaga Sheldon, Peter Brown, Sue Zumberge, and Patricia McDonald for providing helpful comments on drafts. Throughout the years, timely inspiration and crucial support have come from Marylee Hardenbergh, Louise Miner, Sallie Sheldon, Ann Hutchins, and Judy Healey.

I wish to thank Ruth Quattlebaum, archivist at Phillips Academy Andover, for her dogged pursuit of answers to my many questions about the minutiae of student life at Andover during the early 1940s; Wheelock Whitney for the loan of his copy of the 1944 *Pot Pourri;* and Jim Wall for letting me walk away with his copy of *Asimov's Annotated Gilbert & Sullivan* for months at a time.

Thanks to Terry Sheldon and Bonnie Andersen Sweeney for answers to my medical questions and to Chalmers Hardenbergh for information about train routes in the

Northeast during WWII. Thanks to Lukie Wells for in-sights into living in a boarding school and to Tom Crosby for his description of making the transition from Blake School to Andover. Thanks to Polly Grose and Mary Lee Dayton for stories about the home front during WWII. Any errors of fact or interpretation are mine alone.

I am indebted to Ian Leask and the members of his writing seminar—especially Jerry Bour, Jina Penn-Tra-cy, Charlie Locks, Cynthia Kraack, Brandon Bailey, Dan Hauser, Sandra Mahaniah, and Carolyn Crane—for their kind and helpful criticism.

I am grateful to Tom Kerber, Lily Cole, Alicia Ester, and the rest of the wonderful team at Beaver's Pond Press; I am especially grateful to the incomparable copyeditor Angie Wiechmann and to designer Laura Drew, who cre-ated a great cover for this novel. Thanks as well to Allison McCabe, a brilliant developmental editor who guided me through three rewrites, and to Sharon Bowers, who saw promise in an early draft.

Most of all I give thanks to my daughter, Wave, for her generosity, patience, enthusiastic support, and love, and to my husband, Andy, who listened to me read the entire manuscript more than once, who asked questions, suggested the title for the novel, and made me laugh ev-ery single day.

AMES SHELDON is an author and editor of the ground-breaking *Women's History Sources: a Guide to Archives and Manuscript Collections in the United States* (1979), which helped launch the field of women's history. *Eleanor's Wars* is her first novel. Like many fiction writers, she learned about human nature through a variety of real world jobs ranging from work in an auto salvage yard to the Minnesota Historical Society. A native of Minneapolis, she lives with her husband in the nearby suburb of Eden Prairie.

Ames Sheldon would be delighted to visit your book club. For contact information and news about readings, please check her website amessheldon.com or her Facebook page AmesSheldonAuthor.

If you enjoyed this novel, please post a review on Amazon or Goodreads.